SPOTLIGHT ON MURDER

"As we worship the success of the show business idol, we also watch with fascinated interest their missteps and failures. The greater the scandal, the deeper our fascination—and the most violent reversal a show business personality can suffer is to be guilty of a crime, especially the quintessential crime of murder! Murder brings not only the frisson of violent death to our senses, but the horrified thrill of knowing that a lofty career will at once be ruined, and that a god or goddess will fall from heaven.

"In real life it would not be kind of us to feel like this, but in fiction we can indulge our wicked impulse, and yet do no one harm. Here in this anthology, then, we bring you a score of tales that combine show business and murder, and we can enjoy ourselves freely."

—From the Introduction by Isaac Asimov

Other Avon Books Edited by

**Carol-Lynn Rössell Waugh,
Martin Harry Greenberg and
Isaac Asimov**

THE BIG APPLE MYSTERIES
THE TWELVE CRIMES OF CHRISTMAS

SHOW BUSINESS IS MURDER

EDITED BY CAROL-LYNN RÖSSEL WAUGH,
MARTIN HARRY GREENBERG AND ISAAC ASIMOV

AVON
PUBLISHERS OF BARD, CAMELOT, DISCUS AND FLARE BOOKS

PS
648
.D4
.S5

SHOW BUSINESS IS MURDER is an original publication of Avon Books. This work has never before appeared in book form.

AVON BOOKS
A division of
The Hearst Corporation
959 Eighth Avenue
New York, New York 10019

First Avon Printing, March, 1983

WFH 10 9 8 7 6 5 4 3 2 1

ACKNOWLEDGMENTS

"Mystery Tune," by Isaac Asimov. Copyright © 1981 by Montcalm Publishing Corporation. First published in *Gallery* as "Death Song." Reprinted by permission of the author.

"The Confrontation Scene," by William Bankier. Copyright © 1981 by William Bankier. All rights reserved. First published in *Alfred Hitchcock's Mystery Magazine*. Reprinted by permission of Curtis Brown, Ltd.

"What'sisname," by George Baxt. Copyright © 1981 by George Baxt. First published in *Ellery Queen's Mystery Magazine*. Reprinted by permission of the author.

"Sock Finish," by Robert Bloch. Copyright © 1957 by Mercury Publications, Inc. First published in *Ellery Queen's Mystery Magazine*. Reprinted by permission of Kirby McCauley, Ltd.

"The Acting of a Dreadful Thing," by Lionel Booker. Copyright © 1981 by Lionel Booker. First published in *Ellery Queen's Mystery Magazine*. Reprinted by permission of Bertha Klausner International Literary Agency, Inc.

"Bad Actor," by Gary Brandner. Copyright © 1973 by ASD Publications. First published by *Alfred Hitchcock's Mystery Magazine*. Reprinted by permission of the author.

"The Lithuanian Eraser Mystery," by Jon L. Breen. Copyright © 1969 by Jon L. Breen. First published in *Ellery Queen's Mystery Magazine*. Reprinted by permission of the author.

"On Different Tracks," by Michael Scott Cain. Copyright © 1981 by Michael Scott Cain. First published in *Alfred Hitchcock's Mystery Magazine*. Reprinted by permission of the author.

For Frank D. McSherry, Jr., with thanks for all of his detective work.

CONTENTS

INTRODUCTION: SHOW BUSINESS   1
   Isaac Asimov

MYSTERY TUNE   5
   Isaac Asimov

THE CONFRONTATION SCENE   12
   William Bankier

WHAT'SISNAME   27
   George Baxt

SOCK FINISH   36
   Robert Bloch

THE ACTING OF A DREADFUL THING   57
   Lionel Booker

BAD ACTOR   73
   Gary Brandner

THE LITHUANIAN ERASER MYSTERY   86
   Jon L. Breen

ON DIFFERENT TRACKS   95
   Michael Scott Cain

MURDER IN THE MOVIES   105
   Karl Detzer

CLIFFHANGER   124
   Georgiana Eidukas

THE DECLINE AND FALL OF   131
    NORBERT TUFFY
    Ron Goulart

JUST A GAG   144
    Tex Hill

THE SPY WHO STAYED UP ALL NIGHT   155
    Edward D. Hoch

THE KUMQUATS AFFAIR   171
    Francis M. Nevins, Jr.

THE ADVENTURE OF THE   189
    HANGING ACROBAT
    Ellery Queen

TEN PERCENT OF MURDER   214
    Henry Slesar

CREDIT TO SHAKESPEARE   223
    Julian Symons

DEATH AT THE OPERA   230
    Michael Underwood

Introduction: SHOW BUSINESS

by Isaac Asimov

There is a story about an unfortunate who was sitting at a table in a bar, huddled over a beer and wearing a look of intense misery on his face. A newcomer, observing this, and feeling his soft heart ache at the sight of unhappiness so obvious, took his drink to the table and said, "My friend, you seem unhappy. Would it help to talk about it?"

The unfortunate heaved a sigh and said, "It is just that I have no friends. Even here in this bar I am avoided. It is kind of you to come here, but I'm sure you will leave soon."

"Why should I?"

"Well, by profession I am one of the elephant-tenders at the circus. It is my job to sweep up after the elephants and, as you can well imagine, the odor of elephant dung clings to me."

"Yes," said the other, uneasily. "I am aware of a certain effluvium."

"There you are. No matter how I wash or how often I change my clothes, there is this distressing odor which drives everyone from me and condemns me to a life of loneliness and despair."

Said the other, consolingly, "But, sir, why do you not find a different job?"

The unfortunate's eyes widened and he sprang to his feet. "What," he thundered, *"and leave show business?"*

We laugh at the joke, but we must see that there is a germ of truth to it.

There are not many professions which are, in and of themselves, glamorous, but surely of the few which are, show business in all its many manifestations ranks at the top. Consider the reasons:

1. Show business is a thing of tinsel and pretense. Butchers are only butchers and clerks are only clerks. An actor, however, can be a king or an angel or a mur-

1

derer or a businessman or—anything at all. And he
can switch from one to another from one night to the
next. Naturally, we all know that these are imaginary
identifications; that underneath the costume, inside the
paint there is just a human being who is, perhaps, in
some ways, far less impressive than the local butcher,
both physically and morally. It doesn't matter; the ap-
purtenances cling, and we envy the excitement and
glamor of the surface life we perceive, caring nothing
for the dull anticlimax it may hide.

2. Show business lures the practitioner as well as
the observer. To be in show business is to be in one of
the few professions (if not the only one) in which one's
service produces an instant reward. A butcher may possibly be thanked—eventually; a writer may even be
adulated for a best-selling book he has written—eventually; but someone on the stage, delivering a clan-
gourous line, or performing an unusual feat, or perhaps
merely making his entrance, is greeted at once by the
thunder of applause, and he knows it is meant for *him*,
and for him only. He takes his bow in pleased acknowl-
edgment and, at that moment, he is content with his
role in life. Even though he may be underpaid, even
though his dressing room and everything else with which
he must work are mean and poor, even though his
profession through most of time and to many super-
respectables today seems to be the next thing to vag-
abondage, that applause and that bow is, for the while,
all he wants of life.

3. Show business can be profitable. Someone in show
business can become supremely wealthy; sometimes as
a result of a single success. This should not hide the
fact that the large majority of people in show business
make only moderate livings, or even very poor ones—
but it does. It is the wild successes that attract attention. This is, to some extent, true in every profession.
The very occasional billionaire executive obscures the
thousands who achieve no more than middle-class sub-
urbia. The great best-selling writer overshadows the
many thousands of writers who are acquainted chiefly
with rejection slips and whose novels are doomed to
obscurity even after being published. In no profession
but show business, however, are the anomalies of suc-

cess so clearly in view, so sharply in focus. In no other profession do they so completely and sensationally wipe out all that is mediocre or poor—or even merely modestly proficient.

4. In other professions where success can be noted and admired, we usually are simply admiring money or power. We can note the great oil billionaires and envy them their wealth, but nothing else about them. We can observe the President of the United States and envy him his ability to command the headlines, but not wish to be in his place. In show business, however, the great successes are very often those whose faces and bodies are what we conceive to be virtual symbols of beauty and of sexual attractiveness. We, the admiring public, want not only the wealth and power of the stars, we want to *be* them or, at the very least, *look* like them. We may envy a billionaire or a president, but we *adulate* a movie star. We form fan clubs, scream for them, follow them, fight for an autograph, and dream of them. We can never have enough of them.

From all this, it follows that as we worship the success of show business idols, we also watch with fascinated interest their missteps and failures. In some cases, this does them no harm, for their position seems to put them above the requirements of ordinary morality. Their extramarital affairs, their repeated divorces and remarriages are the very food of our own fantasies. Oh, if we could only defy conventions as they do!

More malevolently, there is keen interest on our part in less happy violations of social mores. We follow tales and whispers of alcoholism and of drug addiction with a readiness to believe. We quickly accept accounts of professional jealousies and hatreds, of tantrums on the set, of decay of talents—almost as though, having given up any dreams we might have had of matching the place in the sun of these idols of ours, we are only too delighted to see them descend to our own level or below, thus punishing them for having dared to be famous and rich and happy.

The death of a star reassures us, even while we grieve, that our idols are mortal. And, of course, the greater the scandal, the deeper our fascination. The most violent reversal that a show business personality can suffer is to be guilty of a crime, especially the quintessential crime of murder! Most things can be forgiven when someone is famous enough and is sufficiently adulated—but not murder. Murder brings not only the frisson of violent death to our senses, but the horrified thrill of knowing that a lofty career will at once be ruined, and that a god or goddess will fall from heaven.

In real life it would not be kind of us to feel like this, but in fiction we can indulge our wicked impulse, and yet do no one harm. Here in this anthology, then, we bring you a score of tales that combine show business and murder, and we can enjoy ourselves freely.

What's more, we have tried to bring you a variety of aspects of show business. The characters in these stories are by no means all leading men and women. There are also show business has-beens, screenwriters, agents, stuntmen, vaudevillians, even (in the case of my own story) a piano player in a saloon.

Show business, after all, especially these days, takes in a very broad spectrum of activity, and may well include even those industrious gentlemen who sweep up after the elephants at the circus.

MYSTERY TUNE

by Isaac Asimov

Isaac Asimov has probably written books, articles, and short stories in more diverse areas than anyone alive. He is perhaps best known for his scientific fact and science fiction work. His best-known mystery creation is "The Black Widowers," a group of hungry New Yorkers who digest crime with their meals. They have appeared in three volumes: Tales of the Black Widowers *(1974),* More Tales of the Black Widowers *(1976), and* Casebook of the Black Widowers *(1980).*

Baranov rustled his paper with definite annoyance as we sat within the august confines of the Union Club that evening. He said, "There's been another gang-killing in Brooklyn."

"What else is new?" I asked, unimpressed.

"Well, damn it," said Baranov, "now they'll put in who knows how many police man-hours on the case while valuable police work languishes. Who cares if one gangster kills another? Let them."

"It sets a bad precedent," said Jennings, sententiously. "Murder is murder, and you can't let it go. Besides, you don't really know it's a gang-killing till you investigate."

"Then again," I added, "hardly any of them are ever solved, so maybe the police don't waste too much time."

"Yes, they do," responded Baranov hotly. "There's plenty of waste, however little time they spend on it. No one involved will talk, and the police aren't allowed to beat it out of them. Even close relatives of the victim won't talk, the damn fools. You'd think they'd want to see the murderer caught."

It was at this time that Griswold stirred. His soft snore ended in a brief period of near-strangulation and, recovering, he smoothed his white mustache with the hand that wasn't holding his Scotch-and-soda.

He said, "Of course they want to see the murderer

get his, but not by police procedure. They want it by
gang vengeance, which is more sure in any case. The
criminal ethic depends on the closed mouth. Without
that, the forces of society learn too much, and they all
suffer. There was the case once—"

For a moment, it looked as though he might drop off
again, but Jennings, who was seated closest, kicked his
ankle, and Griswold's eyes opened wide. With a soft
"ouch" he continued....

There was the case once [said Griswold] of Eighty-
Eight Jinks. He was christened Christopher, I believe,
but he was a pianist by talent, and the way he stroked
the eighty-eight keys rechristened him. At least, no one
ever called him anything else but Eighty-Eight to my
knowledge.

He might have become a great pianist, too, many
people thought. He could play anything he had ever
heard, in any style, and could improvise chords that
would tear your heart out. He had a good voice, too.
Something was missing, though. The drive wasn't there.
And he drank quite expertly, and that ruined what
chance remained.

By the time he was thirty-five, he was making a
precarious living by tinkling the keys in various bar-
rooms and second-rate nightspots, and running errands
for the gangs. He was a gentle guy even when he was
the worse for drink—which was most of the time, though
that never seemed to get in the way of his fingers on
the keyboard.

The police knew him well and laid off him generally.
He never made a nuisance of himself so there was never
occasion to lodge a drunk and disorderly charge against
him. He did not use drugs or push them; he had no part
in the operations of the ladies of the evening who infest
the establishments for which he played; and the errands
he ran for the boys were innocuous enough as such
things go.

Sometimes the police did try to pump him for something, but he would never talk.

One time he said, "Look, fellows, it don't do me any
good to be seen with you. It ain't just me. I got a sister
who works hard, and she's married and got a little kid.

I ain't no credit to her, and just my being alive does her enough harm. I don't want to bring her anything worse. I don't want her hassled, and she'll *be* hassled if anyone thinks I'm with the cops too much."

And that, of course, is one reason why people are so closemouthed even when you would think that it would be to their interest to talk. It never is. Talking is the unforgiveable sin, and the strikeback is not only at the talker but at those near to him.

So the police let him alone, because they saw his point and knew he wouldn't talk and that he didn't have anything to talk about anyway.

Which made it sad when he was knocked off.

He was found with a knife in his back in an alley. When the police got there he was still alive, because for once the knifing was reported. At least someone called in to say there were cries of help from the alley. Whoever called didn't leave his name, of course, and hung up quickly, but we don't usually get even that much in that neighborhood. Generally, the corpse is found only well after the fact, after which everyone in the neighborhood gets glassy-eyed when questions are asked and a surprising number of them turn out not even to speak English.

The police never found out why Eighty-Eight was knifed. Anyone would have thought he was harmless enough. On the other hand, there are internal politics in gangs, as anywhere else, and some errand that Eighty-Eight had run might well have discomfited a gang member in some way.

The policeman who was on the scene knew Eighty-Eight well, and once he found the poor fellow alive, sent out the call for an ambulance at once. Eighty-Eight stared at the policeman peacefully, with no look of concern in his eyes.

The policeman said, "We'll get you out of here, Eighty-Eight. You'll be all right."

Eighty-Eight smiled. "What are you talking about, cop? I'm dying. I'll be all right? When I die, I'll be all right. I'll be down in hell with my friends and my hopes, and if they've got a red-hot piano down there, I'll manage."

"Who did this to you, Eighty-Eight?"

"What's it to you, or to anyone?"

"Don't you want to get the rat who did this to you?"

"Why? If you get him, does that mean I heal up? I die anyway. Maybe he did me a favor. If I had guts I'd of done this to me myself years ago."

"We've got to get him, Eighty-Eight. Help us out. If you're dying, it won't hurt you. What can he do to you? Dance on your grave?"

Eighty-Eight smiled more weakly. "Probably won't find no grave. I'll just be dumped on the garbage heap—with the other garbage. They won't dance there; they'll dance on my sister. Can't have that. I'd appreciate it if you'd just let it be known I didn't say *nothing*."

"We'll say that, Eighty-Eight, don't worry. But make it a lie. Just give us a name, or a hint, or a sign with your head. Anything. Look, Eighty-Eight, it could help me out on my job, and I won't let on you did anything."

Eighty-Eight seemed faintly amused. "You want help? All right, how's this?" His fingers moved as though they were tapping on invisible piano keys, and he hummed a few notes of music.

"What's that?" asked the policeman.

"Your hint, cop. I can't talk no more."

Eighty-Eight closed his eyes and died en route to the hospital.

They called me in the next day. It was getting to be a habit with them, and I didn't like it. I had work of my own to do and helping them brought me thanks, but nothing tangible. I couldn't even get a traffic ticket fixed out of it.

I said, "A gangland killing? Who cares? What's the difference if you solve it or not?" The natural reaction, in other words.

I was talking to Carmody, a lieutenant in the homicide division.

He said, with a growl, "Do I have to get that from you? Isn't it enough we get it from idiots in general. For one thing, the guy who got it was a poor bastard who harmed no one but himself and who deserved better of life—but let's not be sentimental. Look at it this way—If we can pin this on someone, we shake up the organization he belongs to. That might amount to nothing. We might not get a conviction, or, if we do, the gang carries on without him. But there's a chance—just a chance—that the shake-up will work cracks in the organization. We might be able to take advantage of those cracks and bust them wide open and pick up the pieces as far as Newark. We've got to play for that, Griswold, and you've got to try to help us."

"But how?" I asked.

"We've got a lead to the killer. I want you to talk to Officer Rodney, who was with Eighty-Eight Jinks—he's the dead man—before he died."

Officer Rodney did not look happy. Having a lead he could neither understand nor communicate was no road to advancement.

Painstakingly, he told us of the conversation with Eighty-Eight, the same conversation I myself have just described. I don't know how accurate his account was, but, of course, it was the tune that counted.

I said to him, "What kind of tune?"

"I don't know, sir. Just a few notes."

"Did you recognize it? Ever hear it before? Can you name it?"

"No, sir. I never heard it before. It didn't sound like it was part of a popular song or anything like that. Just a few notes that didn't sound like anything."

"Can you remember it? Can you hum it or sing it?"

Rodney looked at me rather horrified. "I'm not much of a singer."

"We're not holding auditions. Just do your best."

He tried several times, and then gave up in complete misery. "I'm sorry, sir. He only sang it once, and it was like nothing I ever heard. I can't come up with anything."

So we let him go, and he looked relieved at the chance of getting away from questioning that made him seem helpless.

Carmody looked at me anxiously. "What do we do? Do you suppose we could have him put under hypnotism? He might remember then."

I said, "Suppose we did, and he remembered the tune and we recognized it and saw the relationship to a suspect. Could we introduce it all as evidence? Would Rodney survive cross-examination? Would it be convincing to a jury?"

"No, to all three. But if we were satisfied we knew who it was, we could try to break him down—find motive, means and opportunity."

"Do you have any suspects at all?"

"There's a neighborhood gang, of course, and they include three men we have good reason to think have been involved in past killings."

"Get after all three, then."

"Not convincing. If you're after all three, none are scared, since we're clearly in the dark. And it might be someone else altogether, too. If we know one man and zero in on *him* and him alone—"

"Well," I said, "what are the names of the three suspects you just mentioned."

He said, "Moose Matty, Ace Begad, and Gent Diamond."

"In that case," I said, "we may not have a problem. Get Officer Rodney and get us both to the nearest piano."

We located a piano in the studio across the street, and I said to Rodney, "Listen to this, officer, and tell me if this is what Eighty-Eight hummed." I tapped out several notes.

Rodney looked surprised. "It does sound like it, sir! Could you do it again?"

I did it again. "Just this one more time, officer," I said, "Or you'll start believing it to be the tune no matter what I play. Now is this it?"

"Yes it is," he said in excitement. "That's it exactly."

"Thank you, officer. Good job and I'm sure you'll get a commendation for it. Lieutenant, we know who the murderer is, or at least we know who Eighty-Eight said it was."

Well, I don't know whether there were repercussions as far as Newark, because I didn't follow the case thereafter, but I understand they got the murderer and even put him in prison, which is a happy ending. Officer Rodney got a commendation; Lieutenant Carmody got the credit; I got back to my own work; and all of you, of course, see what happened.

*   *   *   *   *

"No, we don't," roared Jennings, "and don't go to

sleep on us. This time, Griswold, you have gone too far and you're simply putting us on. How could you reconstruct the notes and how could you use them to spot the murderer?"

Griswold snorted. "Where's the need for explanation. There are only seven notes and then the eighth starts the series over again—*do, re, mi, fa, sol, la, ti,* and then *do* starts it over. Well, they are also expressed as letters: *C, D, E, F, G, A, B,* and then *C* again. You've heard of 'middle *C*' and the 'key of *G*' or '*D* minor' and so on.

"Very well. It is possible, though not usual, for a name to consist only of the note-letters of *A* through *G*. Ace Begad is an example, and as soon as I heard it, I felt sure he was the murderer. I spelled the name in musical notes: *la, do, mi, ti, mi, sol, ti, re* or *A, C, E, B, E, G, A, D,* with a short pause between the third and fourth notes, and Rodney recognized the combination when I played it—and that's all there was to it."

THE CONFRONTATION SCENE

by William Bankier

*A native of Belleville, Ontario, William Bankier worked
as a bellhop, as a desk clerk, and as an announcer on a
local radio station before winning an announcing contest on a Canadian Broadcasting Corporation network
show in Montreal. This led to an announcing job at
station CMB in that city. He later moved into advertising
and also spent thirteen weeks as a gag writer and radio
comedian on a CBC summer replacement show. He has
published numerous stories in* Ellery Queen's Mystery
Magazine *and* Alfred Hitchcock's Mystery Magazine.

Julian Carsfield clapped his hands. The actors came
to order, turned, and looked across the stage apron to
where he was standing on a chair. They were like his
school children; they wanted to be led.

"That was the worst dress rehearsal I've ever seen,"
he said cheerfully. "It should mean a fine opening night."

Betty Dolan stood splay-footed, her hands resting on
her generous abdomen. This wasn't costuming, she
really was pregnant.

"It's only three-thirty," she said. "Can't we do Act
One again?"

The others hesitated. On a Sunday afternoon, am-
ateur-dramatic-society members like to be finished early
and off home. Danny Dolan spoke for them all when he
said, "I don't want you overdoing it, my dear."

She dismissed him with a thrust of her chin. "I'm
sorry I married you."

"Good thing you did though." He patted her tummy
with a paternal hand and everybody laughed.

Carsfield's broad freckled face remained aimed at
the stage like a radar dish until order was restored. He
was a remote, unbuttoned man, reticent, absent-minded.
After evening rehearsals he had to be dragged away
from the hall or he would ramble on indefinitely. His
pupils at the school in south London were amused by

his foggy manner, but they liked the way he was always organizing things for them to do. They sensed that Carsfield lived for them. The dramatic society felt the same thing.

"No more rehearsal today," he proclaimed. When he took charge, Carsfield's shy murmur became a stentorian boom. "We open in four days—I may arrange a run-through before then. But today I have organized a little celebration."

Griffith Mooney snatched the dead pipe from between his teeth. "Gone to practically no expense, I can assure you." The pipe went back with a click.

There was a stir of anticipation onstage. Free wine at somebody's house, a spontaneous booze-up—not the least of the reasons why they belonged to the society.

"So if you'll get out of your costumes quickly," Carsfield said, "you'll discover that transport has been laid on."

In the interval of anarchy that followed, Meredith Hay had time to wonder if she'd done the right thing in granting Carsfield the use of her summer house on the island. It was only an hour's drive to the coast and the launch had been set up by telephone. The novelty of the adventure would please everybody, but there was something desperate about the director's secrecy.

Meredith was closer to Carsfield than any of the others. It was she who dragged him away at the end of rehearsals and drove him home in her car. Sometimes they parked and talked about his life now that his parents were dead or about her existence with a husband whose business success provided all the satisfaction he needed. Twice they had made love. On the other nights they'd exchanged one innocent kiss on parting.

"Ready to go?" Carsfield drifted up behind Meredith, barely audible again, the apologetic intruder.

"I put two baskets of food and drink in the minibus," she said. "And here's the key to the summer house."

He took the key from her, pocketed it, and led the way to the stage door. It was the first time she had seen him in a hurry to proceed anywhere.

It had been clear to Meredith for some weeks that once again Julian Carsfield was losing touch with reality. You couldn't call it going mad, an expression which suggested foaming at the mouth. Carsfield remained calm in these phases he went through, but he tended to say things that made no sense in the context of the conversation.

Once, at a society dinner, he got up from the table without warning, pale-faced and tight-lipped, and stalked from the dining room, not to return that evening. Meredith, his unofficial apologist, dispelled the shock on that occasion by saying, "Well, we are a *dramatic* society, aren't we?"

The minibus raced along open highway to the south coast, crowded and twittering like an aviary. The cast had been persuaded to leave their cars in the parking lot at the hall. Ahead lay a chance to expand, to drink and eat, to touch and be touched in ways they could only dream of through the week.

"They'll be missing me at home," Echo Templeton said plaintively. Her Liverpool accent with its Irish overtone never failed to arouse merriment in the south of England. It could not be trusted on stage, so she filled the role of prompter.

"Don't fret," Griffith Mooney said. "They'll read about you in the papers tomorrow. 'Ravished beauty washed up on beach.'"

This prediction opened the gates to a flood of talk about sudden violent death and the cast chattered on happily all the way to the boathouse and private pier where a villager who knew the Hay family and looked after their boats was standing by.

"Here's the key," he said. "She's running well and there's petrol to spare for the return trip. Quiet water between here and the island. Have a good time."

Carsfield slipped into the role of captain, took charge of the key, saw his people aboard the luxurious craft, and soon had the engine rumbling confidently. The island could just be seen, a gray dot on the southern horizon. With the throttle two-thirds open, Carsfield covered the distance in a little over an hour. Somebody managed to open a bottle of Italian red wine on the way. They were singing as they tied up at a wooden pier and straggled up the steep path to Summerheath.

"I feel as if I've died and gone to heaven," Danny Dolan said when a satisfying meal of cold cuts and cheese had failed to diminish his wine-inspired glow.

"That happens later," his wife said, "when Julian makes us swim home."

"You'd be all right," Mooney said. His pipe was actually lit and emitting the smell of a burned-out warehouse. "You've got all that extra buoyancy."

"I'll thank you to speak well of my wife," Dolan said.

"Well of your wife."

"Thank you."

As the sun went down, but with plenty of light left in the summer sky, they drifted outside onto the lawn in front of the house. It was a rambling one-story structure, soundly built, with a huge circular roof of tile on brick pillars.

"'In Xanadu,'" Mooney orated, "'did Kubla Khan a stately pleasure-dome decree...'"

Dolan took up the quotation. "'Where Alph, the sacred river, ran...'"

"Alf is the name of my landlord," Echo Templeton mused. "He'll be wondering where I am."

"Give her a drink," Betty Dolan said through the groans.

"I don't want to be a bad hostess," Meredith said, "but it's going to be dark soon. We should start back."

That was when Carsfield astounded them all. As calmly as if he had been announcing an extra rehearsal, he said, "We aren't going back. We're staying here."

The discussion that followed began as good-humored disbelief. Then, when Carsfield explained himself and convinced them he wasn't joking, it turned into a serious argument with philosophical overtones. Actors enjoy probing motivation. Primed with free wine, they can sustain the dialogue for a long time.

They all saw Carsfield's point and sympathized with him. As director, he took possession of a play from the outset. By casting them in the various roles, he gave the production its appearance and sound, he dictated the way it would move on stage. While rehearsals went on, the play remained his. He guided its development, changed it slightly from one week to the next, saw it evolve into a creation of which he could be proud.

"I'm not joking," he said. "The production is my baby. I nurture it. I think about it last thing at night and first thing in the morning."

"We understand," Danny Dolan said, holding the hand of his pregnant wife. "It's like your own living thing."

Meredith Hay shivered and folded her arms. It was not just the night chill; Julian was slipping into his raving phase. Last time she'd heard him as wide-eyed and articulate as this, he'd ended up not teaching school for a month while he calmed down at home on a program of medication.

"Until dress rehearsal," Carsfield went on, "the production is still mine. Then suddenly it's taken away from me—it belongs to you, the actors, and partly I suppose to the audience. The curtain goes up and you take it and do what you will. I can only watch what once was mine slipping away from me." He stood on the porch steps like an ambassador, addressing them with one hand in the pocket of his tweed jacket, the other raising a goblet of wine to his lips more frequently than was customary.

"We're with you," Meredith said. It was time to nip this fantasy in the bud. "But can't we talk about it another time? Who's for the launch?"

Before the others could respond and as Meredith moved onto the sloping path, Carsfield stopped her in her tracks. "I have the keys and I'm keeping them. The launch goes nowhere."

Griffith Mooney gave his stagey Australian laugh. "Come on, mate, we all have places to go. Let's not play games."

"It's no game. I intend to keep hold of this production as long as I can. It won't be stolen like all the others."

"That's enough, Julian." Danny Dolan left his wife and moved toward the director. "Give me the keys."

The gun came out of Carsfield's pocket in a fluid, practiced way. "Don't come one step closer." The penetrating voice confirmed what they had always known—that Julian could be a better actor than any of them had he not preferred to direct. "Please understand that

I am serious about this. We stay on this island as long as I say and we rehearse the play until I am ready to let it go."

After a pause, Mooney laughed again and said, "What a performance! He's bluffing, of course."

Dolan took a step forward, then froze as the gun fired and a bullet smashed into the trunk of an elm at the edge of the lawn.

"Damn it, I'm not bluffing." Expertly, Carsfield altered his tone from anger to patience. "This can be an interesting experience for all of us. Please don't turn it into a tragedy."

Later, with rooms assigned in the house, the cast gathered in the kitchen. Echo Templeton was in tears. "Can't we telephone somebody?"

"There's no telephone," Meredith said. "We keep this place isolated."

"We'll get pretty bloody hungry if it goes on too long," Mooney grumbled. "We should have conserved the food we brought."

Meredith went to a freezer cabinet and lifted the lid. "There's enough for a few days. Julian asked me if there was food here. Now I know why." She smiled ruefully. "But besides instant coffee, all there is to drink is wine."

"Let zem dreenk wine," Mooney proclaimed in a cartoon French accent.

"This is madness," Dolan said, his voice falsetto with frustration. "He *can't* just kidnap the lot of us."

"He's keeping us from kidnapping his production," Meredith said gloomily. She had seen the logic of Julian's argument and the fact that it was indeed madness did not weaken his position.

"There isn't much we can do while he's got that gun," Betty Dolan said. She yawned—the placid, pregnant wife. "Can we go to bed?"

"We'll overpower him when he's sleeping," Mooney suggested. "I need two volunteers. You and me, Dolan."

"He's sleeping in the master bedroom with the door locked," Meredith informed them. "It's solid oak. Ten strokes with an axe, minimum."

"Then we'll just have to surprise him and get the

gun from him in the morning," Echo Templeton said. "The poor man should be in hospital."

"You'll have your chance at ten o'clock," Meredith said. "He's called a rehearsal then in the main salon."

After breakfast, they straggled from the kitchen into the large room at the front of the house where Carsfield was seated behind a table at one end of the room. The gun was on the table in front of him and his eyes had a glossy, alert look. Meredith decided he was on some kind of uppers.

He had moved the furniture around into the positions required for the stage setting. When the cast trooped in, he took the gun in his right hand, cradling it in his left. "Good morning," he said in his most authoritarian voice. "I hope you slept well. I expect you to give me a good rehearsal."

Mooney tried a German accent this time. "Discipline at Fort Summerheath," he snarled, "will be harsh."

"Don't be a silly ass, Major," Carsfield said. He had stopped using their real names, addressing them most of the time as the characters they played. "Your role is weaker than anybody's. Can we begin with Act One, Scene One, please? Watch your pacing, pick up the cues. I want to take a timing."

Meredith felt that she, as the person closest to the director, was obliged to make an effort. "Julian, there's no point. The play opens in three days in south London and we're all here."

"Let me worry about that."

"What about the people who are worried about us? I'm only one, but I *have* got a husband—"

"That's news to Julian," Mooney said in a waspish tone. He had taken a bottle of wine to bed with him. Now he was in a manic mood.

"People have gone missing before now," Carsfield said. "The fact that several of you have disappeared at once doesn't change things much. I doubt if anybody will make the connection for a couple of days. The police certainly won't get involved before then."

They had no choice but to rehearse. The men, after consultation over breakfast, remained alert for any opportunity of jumping their captor. But Carsfield didn't move onto the stage area. He stayed at his table. When anyone approached him, he backed off, gun in hand, and put his back to a wall.

They rehearsed all morning and then the girls prepared lunch while the men drank in the lounge. Carsfield sat by himself on the lawn under the elm tree the bullet had gone into last night. Meredith brought him a tray, having been told he would not eat with the others.

With her, he seemed more himself. He put the gun at his side and helped himself to a chicken sandwich. She squatted on the ground a yard away and watched him eat. If she picked her moment and moved quickly enough, she might get the gun. But betraying Julian in this way seemed out of the question. There had to be another way of persuading him to let the play—and the players—go. "How are you feeling?" she asked.

"Still a little troubled. The Major keeps masking Uncle Ben during his main speech in Act Two."

"I mean yourself. You've seemed tense recently."

"I was holding my breath over this affair. Now that it's working, I'm fine."

Meredith took a wedge of tomato from the tray and let the time that passed while she ate it draw them closer together. "But, Julian, they aren't characters in a play, they're real people. They aren't the Major and Uncle Ben. They happen to be Griffith Mooney and Danny Dolan."

His smile was one of mild exasperation. "I know that."

"Do you know how you're disturbing them? Upsetting their lives? You have no right to take them over."

"How about people upsetting *my* life?"

"When you agree to direct a play, that's part of the bargain. You put yourself into it and in the end the actors run away with it. You have to accept that."

"It isn't only the plays. It's the same thing at the school." Carsfield's face hardened; only his pale-blue eyes were vulnerable. It was as if the freckled face was a copper mask and behind it a soft, defenseless thing peered out furtively through two oval apertures.

"Year after year I start with a new crop of boys. They're a grotty bunch, most of them, with their scabby knees and the way their hair smells when I stand over them. One or two are slightly civilized. Then, as the months go by, I begin to know them." Carsfield had finished eating but he swallowed now with difficulty. "They're all unique, you see—different little characters. By Christmas they've become Simon with his jokes and Clive with half an apple in his pocket. Silly brute, he eats half and tucks the rest away inside that filthy pocket. I find I'm counting the days during the holiday, anxious to get back to them."

"Julian—"

"Then, before I know it, the year is over. They're so anxious to get away they don't look back. I watch them go and realize I'll never see them again. Because even when I do run into them and they call out 'Hello, sir!' they aren't the same. They've grown and changed."

Meredith moved next to him, took his hand in both of hers. The gun lay closer to her than to him. "I never realized—you're lonely."

Carsfield said nothing, but he looked at Meredith and smiled and his eyelids lowered gently and rose again. She knew it as his expression of assent for situations when words would be uncomfortable. She had seen him use it to grant permission for an actor to refuse a part. The boys in his class probably took it as evidence that "sir" was letting them go to the playing field.

Later, in the house, Danny Dolan was hopping with frustration. "You had him! We were watching you! Why didn't you grab the gun?"

"He's in trouble," Meredith said quietly.

"He's in trouble?" Griffith Mooney snatched his glass from the mantelpiece and turned away. "I'm an accountant. I have clients expecting me to audit their books."

"This is important for him. And we aren't really being hurt. I can't say more." Meredith looked for support. "I think we should show tolerance."

"It's bloody against the law!" Mooney barked as he stormed out of the room.

When he reappeared, his entrance was startling. The others were on stage preparing to run through a scene and Carsfield was at his table when Mooney strode across the room dressed only in his shorts.

"Anyone for tennis?" Dolan said, raising a laugh.

Mooney paused in the doorway to the front porch. "I don't know about the rest of you, but Australians are good swimmers. I can see the mainland from the pier, and anything I can see I can reach."

Carsfield stood up. As Mooney opened the door, the director shouted in a voice that rattled the windows, "Major!"

Mooney looked back.

"You cannot leave the island. I won't permit it."

"Get stuffed, Julian. I'm sending back the police—and one psychiatrist."

Mooney swung open the door. Carsfield raised the gun, aimed carefully, and fired. The noise was deafening in the enclosed space. Mooney cried out and fell to the floor.

This ended rehearsals for the time being and established two things: Carsfield would not hesitate to use the gun on anyone attempting to flee, and his aim was good—the bullet had passed through the calf of Mooney's leg.

Later that day, with the wounded man bandaged and in bed, the others sat in the kitchen, which had become their unofficial meeting place. "We have to do something," Echo said, "before he kills us all."

"He *avoided* killing Mooney," Meredith pointed out.

"If we started a fire," Dolan suggested, "they'd see it from the mainland and send a boat across to put it out."

"Arriving in time to hose down the ashes of my property. Thank you very much."

The group went to bed for the second night in captivity feeling relatively stable. It was true that Julian had carefully inflicted only a flesh wound on Mooney. That was sane behavior. If they went along with him for a few more days, they would probably come away unharmed with stories they could dine out on for years. The publicity might even boost their audiences. In the meantime, there was no real emergency, no cause for alarm.

* * *

The situation changed in the morning. Danny Dolan and his wife were not among those present in the rehearsal room. Carsfield was about to send Echo to roust them out when Dolan came in at a run.

"No more fun and games, Julian," he said. "Betty had contractions this morning."

"Is she in bed?"

"And there she stays. I'm not taking any chances with her welfare or the baby's."

"Quite right. We'll do scenes she doesn't appear in."

"Damn it, I want her off the island and within reach of a hospital. If it starts again she could miscarry."

"We both know that isn't liable to happen."

"What do you mean by that?"

"You're trying it on. The two of you made this up so I'd let you go."

"You arrogant—" Dolan moved toward the table but stopped when the gun came up quickly.

"Don't force my hand," Carsfield said. "Meredith, go up and have a word with her. See how she is."

When Meredith returned, she looked sober. "It's no hoax, Julian. I've seen enough women in labor at the hospital where I do my volunteer work. She ought to be taken home."

"Is she experiencing anything now?"

"Not at the moment, but—"

"Then we're all right. Act Two, please. Take it from Uncle Ben's entrance. Echo, will you read in the part of the expectant mother?"

Dolan was outraged. "You mean we're going on as if—"

"That's why we're here. This is my production, Danny. I made it, and I mean to see it through to the end."

Dolan's idea occurred to him over lunch. He outlined it to the others. "It might work," he said, "especially since Carsfield is determined to let nothing stop rehearsals."

"I'm not sure I could do it," Meredith said.

"You'll only have to wound him," Dolan said. "He wounded Mooney. Anyway, hospital is the best place for him. He'll get treatment—an enforced rest."

"I suppose you're right."

"I know I'm right." Dolan turned to Echo. "Nip on stage and get rid of the prop gun I use at the end of the play. Hide it somewhere."

She hurried away and the cast went on eating lunch in silence. At last Meredith said, "You're asking a lot of me."

"You saw Betty," Dolan reminded her. "We have to get her home."

The afternoon rehearsal went well. Carsfield checked his stopwatch from time to time. "Great pacing," he called to them. "For the first time it feels right."

"Julian," Dolan said from the stage, "can we do the end of the play? It's never gone properly for me."

"Yes, the confrontation between you and Meredith. Fine. Places, everybody."

There was tension in the air as the players ran through the final scene leading up to the climax. When that point arrived, Dolan and Meredith were in the heat of an argument. Her affair with the Major had been uncovered. Dolan cursed her out, then, his jealousy fueled by several drinks, he stumbled to the desk, opened a drawer, and—stopped.

"Come on," he said, dropping out of character, "the gun isn't here."

"Props!" Carsfield bellowed.

"I haven't seen it!" Echo wailed from the wings.

"Carry on," Carsfield droned.

"What am I supposed to do? Point my finger and say bang?"

"Don't lose the momentum!" The director's voice was rising.

"I aim at Meredith, we struggle, she manages to turn the gun on me, it goes off, and I fall down dead." Dolan wheeled away. "I can't do all that without a gun."

"Ladies and gentlemen, this is the climax of the play." Carsfield was on his feet. He sounded pedantic, the schoolmaster on an afternoon when the class is troublesome. "The rehearsal has been going well. Let's not lose it."

Meredith said tentatively, "Julian—if you don't mind, you've got a gun."

"That's an idea," Dolan said in an offhand way.

"I'm sure you'd like to get your hands on this gun."

"You can take the bullets out of it."

For the first time on the island, Carsfield laughed. "You must think I'm mad. Without bullets in the gun I'd have no control over you."

Dolan pretended to think. Then he said, "The problem for me is the moves in the struggle with Meredith. You keep the gun, but do my part. Show me how it's supposed to go."

They all stood frozen, watching Carsfield, wondering which way the coin would drop. At last he made up his mind. "Very well. Come down here, everybody except Meredith. I'll go up there." He did. "We'll do the confrontation. And pay attention, Danny. This is the way it's meant to end."

Carsfield took his place at the desk. Meredith stood by the settee. Echo held her script ready to prompt, but it was unnecessary—the director knew the lines. There was a brief stage wait and then Carsfield turned with the gun in his hand.

"There's only one way to deal with you and the Major," he said. "I see that now."

"Don't be a fool." Meredith approached him. "You'd never get away with it."

"I don't care any more."

"Don't you?" She was close enough to grapple with him. She did, seizing the gun hand.

"This is the way it goes," Carsfield called to Dolan. "It's like choreography. My arm around her shoulder, hers around my waist. Her hand on the gun. The hands move so that the gun is concealed between us. Nobody knows who has it."

The figures on stage were locked together. There was silence from the room until Dolan called, "Shoot, Meredith! Shoot him!"

Their faces were inches apart. Only on those occasions in the car when they said goodnight had they been this close. His pressure on the gun was firm, but now Meredith felt herself gaining control. She was supposed to wound him—but how? There was no time and with the weapon where it was no way she could take aim.

Their eyes met and she realized that he understood everything. He was smiling at her and his eyelids lowered gently and rose again in that familiar sign of acquiescence. The gun went off and instantly he became a dead weight in her arms. As the others ran toward them, she lowered Julian onto the settee.

The launch was halfway between the island and the mainland. Nobody had said anything for ten minutes. They were not looking at each other. Griffith Mooney had brought a bottle of wine with him and was drinking from it, his bandaged leg propped on a seat. He turned now to look back at Julian Carsfield's body, wrapped in a blanket.

"Tell you what I'd like to do," he slurred. "I'd like to bury the bastard at sea."

There was no response until Meredith spoke almost a minute later. "Maybe you'll understand when and if you sober up," she said. "He loved us a lot more than we loved him."

Carsfield's legacy troubled Meredith more than anything that had happened while he was still alive. The letter to the police was found in his jacket pocket when he was being processed at the morgue. It explained in concise, academic language that he had been kidnapped by the players. Their motive, he said, was personal acrimony; they intended to sabotage his current production and did not want him around to oppose them.

He had tried once to escape. There was a struggle and one of the actors was shot in the leg. Anything might happen next time. He even anticipated the question of the villager who saw him boarding the launch in good spirits. At that time there was no indication he was to be held prisoner.

At the hearing, the combined stories of the cast outweighed Carsfield's accusation. The case against them could not be proven and was dismissed. But notoriety hung in the air like the acrid stench that follows a pistol shot. The dramatic society could not live it down; they disbanded soon after.

Griffith Mooney began accepting parts with a rival group. Meredith went to see one of the productions and had a drink with the Australian afterward. They talked about Carsfield.

"He had his way in the end," she said. "He stopped us from stealing any more plays."

"Still think he loved us?"

"You should know, Griffith, that it's possible to love and hate at the same time."

As they left the bar, Meredith said, "Your limp looks artistic on stage. Is the leg troubling you much?"

"No, it's completely healed. The limp is a cheat for dramatic purposes," Mooney said. "If life plays a trick on you, turn it to your advantage." He gave her a wink. "I learned that from Carsfield."

WHAT'SISNAME

by George Baxt

George Baxt is best known to mystery readers as the author of seven outstanding novels, five of which feature some of the most memorable series characters in the history of the genre. A Parade of Cockeyed Creatures; or, Did Someone Murder Our Wandering Boy? (1967) and "I!" Said the Demon (1969) star the team of Sylvia Plotkin and Max Van Larsen, while three others, A Queer Kind of Death (1966), Swing Low, Sweet Harriet (1967) and Topsy and Evil (1968), tell of the adventures of police detective Pharoah Love, and constitute a trio of the best books of their kind.

This is the story I didn't include in my autobiography, the one so darkly alluded to by one of our leading gossip columnists a few weeks ago. Of course those who read her regularly (and I hereby confess my addiction) recognize all her allusions as dark ones, otherwise how else tease and titillate her readers? This is the item she printed verbatim: "Who threatened Andy Newlin into deleting from his autobiography the true story behind Michael Camba's murder?"

I, Andrew Newlin, can give you the answer to that one in one word: nobody. Michael's killer had neither family nor crime connections, and there wasn't even a lover in mourning. Michael's killer left behind nothing but the memory of his infamous deed. Michael Camba was a genius, his killer was merely talented, and therein lies the clue. I'm printing the story now only to set the record straight.

Only a true crime buff will recognize this name—Sami Brzniwyrzi. You can also find it indexed in a few theatrical histories, but most of those are out of print. Sami hadn't designed a show on or off Broadway for almost decades before the murder. Michael, in the year of his murder, won both the Pulitzer Prize and the Tony Award.

Sami and Michael grew up together in the Canarsie section of Brooklyn. They were companions in grade school, high school, and college, each nurturing his ambition—Sami to be a great architect, Michael to be a great writer. The Second World War interrupted Michael's ambition for over two years. Sami had suffered as a child with a rheumatic heart, and so he spent the war years apprenticing with an architectural firm on Wall Street.

Michael emerged from the war with the material for his first novel, *Dog Face*. He wrote it while sharing an apartment with Sami on Manhattan's West Side, in the Seventies just off Riverside Drive. Sami was the successful one, or so Sami told you. Michael took on odd jobs to support himself, not that Sami wasn't generous in covering the monthly rent, whenever Michael was running short.

It's a cliché, of course, to say they were just like brothers, though on the other hand I know lots of brothers who despise each other. Take my word for it, they loved each other and respected each other. They shared their ambitions and they shared their friends. A mutual friend introduced me to them at the time Michael submitted *Dog Face* to an agent. I handled the legal problems for Michael when the book was placed with Thalia House. I had just come to Klauds & Bergnoff as a junior clerk, and bringing in Michael proved quite a feather in my cap, especially when the reviews on publication a year later were mostly laudatory.

I should have sensed danger then. But who thinks of danger when you're in your twenties and a mutual friend has published his first novel and there are parties and new friends to be found. But when Sami made more of Michael's sudden celebrity than Michael did, I should have recognized the dark side of Sami.

Then all of a sudden Sami was out of a job. Michael was now the breadwinner. The positions were reversed and where Michael thrived, Sami brooded, and brooding breeds. Michael sold three short stories, one of which I thought was quite good, but the other two I felt traded on his celebrity.

Sami loathed the three of them.

"Keep grinding out this junk and you'll soon write

yourself dry!" I remember Sami warning Michael. Sami's warning must have taken subliminal effect because Michael abandoned short stories to write a play, I realize now much to Sami's regret. In the meantime friends in the theater urged Sami to try his hand at stage design. He did and he was quite good. He passed the test to join the Set Designer's Union and in no time he was hired to do the sets for Lillian Jaekel's farce, *Three on a Mismatch*. It flopped, but Sami's ingenious depiction of a triplex led to a second commission.

Meantime, Michael rewrote and rewrote his play and there were some of us who thought he'd never finish it. Sami confided to me he thought Michael didn't want to finish it because he couldn't face adverse criticism. I told him I thought he was being disloyal and he told me to do something that is physically impossible. I laughed it off at the time, my mind then dwelling heavily on my romance with my first wife and an opportunity to join a new law firm as a partner.

Of course, Michael eventually finished *September Mourn*. His agent recognized the work as something special and warned him she didn't think it would be an easy job placing it for Broadway production; but the lady was loyal and a fighter and was determined to see it mounted. Sami in the meantime was in the heat of his short-lived success. In all, he saw five of his designs make it to Broadway. But he rarely discussed the dozen or so that producers discarded. It was perfectly clear to almost everyone except Sami that his was a nice but slight talent. The fact that he tossed off his designs with the prolificity of a tired hack soon became common talk in theatrical circles.

The devastating blow came when *September Mourn* was finally optioned by a brave young man obsessed with becoming a success in the theater (and he did succeed). The brave young man was brave enough to stand up to Michael when Michael wanted Sami to design the set.

"Never!" shouted the young neophyte producer. "Your play deserves the best! Bel Geddes, Jo Mielziner, somebody like that. But your friend what'sisname? No way!"

I think that's when it began. What'sisname. Of course no one could pronounce Sami's last name. Go ahead, try it. Brzniwyrzi. He refused to change it, even though the father from whom he inherited it died a drunkard's death and was buried in Potter's Field. (I unearthed this information only recently. Sami concocted a fantasy that he was descended from Balkan royalty. His mother didn't deny it either and she embroidered the fantasy by throwing in some early Moorish ties and stood fast by the claim right up to her death.)

Brzniwyrzi. Hopeless.

Michael Camba's was an easy name to remember. *September Mourn* was a *succès d'estime*. It was a satire set in hell just as it was about to freeze over, and even the presence of three tired Hollywood "names" above the title did little to lure an audience. Today, of course, it is frequently revived by universities and regional theaters, and as I write this, a new production is being mounted by the Spiegelgasse Players of East Germany. It was Michael's second play, as you remember, that put him over the top. *Living with Lola* was a magnificent travesty based on the bawdy life of Lola Montez and it sold to the movies for half a million dollars and Michael Camba from that moment on could seemingly do no wrong.

Sami did not share in his best friend's success. He could have, because much against my advice Michael invited Sami to continue living with him when he bought his townhouse off Gramercy Park. But Sami was fed up living in reflected glory. Everywhere he went it was Michael-Camba-this and Michael-Camba-that, but never Sami-anything unless it was Sami What'sisname.

So Sami chose to remain in the old apartment while Michael moved on in affluence. Strangely enough, it was Michael who kept his head. He remained steady, sober, and industrious. His wit grew wrier and his talent continued to develop. He was still on the threshold of his greatest acclaim.

Sami, through the help of a charming woman who was madly in love with him, embarked on a new career as a freelance department-store window designer. It was at this period in his life he became a name dropper. The charming woman was a fringe personality in the entertainment world and her Sunday salons for a while were a "must." Michael came to many as did the oc-

casional brilliant actor, author, politician, and poet. And
Sami began detonating "names" like the mad bomber
who was terrorizing New York at the same time Sami
was terrorizing café society.

For example, Sami would enter a cocktail party declaiming, "Sorry I'm late!"—nobody having noticed—
"I was having tea with Kit and Guthrie and Alfred and
Lynn were there and Tallu dropped by with Cecil and..."
so on ad infant item. After a while it got to be terribly
funny and Sami's name dropping became an "in" joke
that spread from coast to coast and over three conti-
nents. But it was Michael's devastating comment when
Sami broke his leg that I think started the wheels of
hatred turning in Sami's head: "Whose name did he
drop on it?" The remark found its way into Earl Wil-
son's column and was later appropriated by Bennett
Cerf for one of his humor anthologies. It made Sami's
long-sought-after reputation, but it was not the reputation Sami had wanted.

The leg mended but the breach that now existed
between Michael and Sami seemed irreparable. Michael was unhappy about this. He loved Sami. Sami
would always be his best friend. Oh, they continued to
phone each other and meet for an occasional drink, but
Sami confided to me at the time, "I no longer know how
to deal with Michael." Of course I stupidly told that to
Michael whose face briefly became a study. Then he
said, "It's jealousy." I agreed. "Why is he so jealous of
me? He's not a writer. He never wanted to be a writer!"

"He wants fame," I told Michael. "He wants the
equivalent of your success and your celebrity. Everyone
knows the name Michael Camba. But who the hell knows
Sami Brzn—ch—ch—" And I still don't know why, but
we both broke into hysterical laughter. Michael accepted that he and Sami were no longer close friends.
There were new people in Michael's life—some were
really enjoyable and Michael was friendly with my third
wife. (The second came and went too quickly, and I can
barely remember what she looks like.)

We'd occasionally run into Sami at the theater and
in restaurants, and it was Michael who began to recognize the tragic signs. Sami was becoming an alco-
holic. We saw his face fall into a plate of soup at Sardi's.

At one opening night he fell out of his seat into the aisle in the middle of Ethel Merman's big number, and after that incident he never dared drop her name again, although she certainly dropped his.

At about this time Michael fell in love with an English actress and went to live and work in London to be with her while she appeared with the Old Vic. He fell in love with the city too and the British took to him and soon he traveled less and less to New York. He bought a house in posh Chester Square, and my fourth wife and I spent our honeymoon with him. I reported on Sami.

"He's been dried out twice but he's on his third binge. He's tried to write a novel and short stories and I heard he was collaborating on a play with some woman who I suspect is paying his bills."

"Should I send him some money?" asked Michael gravely and sincerely.

My fourth wife said, "If you did and I was Sami, I'd hate you even more."

"Even *more?*" Michael was almost in shock. "You mean he *hates* me?"

"I'm sure he does," she said with what I thought was unbecoming relish and may explain why three years later she was to speak unbecomingly of my fifth wife. "You've got what he wants—fame, money, celebrated friends, and a magnificent gift. He's fifth-rate. There are fifth-raters who know how to make a secondary talent work"—and she rattled off a roll call of movie stars and writers most of whom have since disappeared—"but Sami is too busy being bitter to be successful. I'd be careful, Michael."

"Of what?"

"Sami What'sisname. I suspect for years now he's built up in his mind a series of grievances against you. Now let me finish!" Michael had begun to remonstrate and I could see he was perplexed and upset. She began to tick off everything Michael had achieved that would forever elude Sami. Concluding, she said, "You've left him in the back stretch of an abandoned racetrack. It's too late for him. The parade's passed by. You're the parade."

"I'm going to New York. I'm going to find him and help him."

There was no arguing with Michael. We preceded him to New York and got the townhouse ready for his return. He wrapped up the revisions of his new play, *Sidney and Lewis,* which of course was based on Sami and himself when they were living in the apartment near Riverside Drive. Meantime, I began tracking down Sami and located the woman with whom he had been collaborating on the play.

Her name was Freda Quintain and she owned a bookstore on Third Avenue below Fourteenth Street.

"He walked out on me a couple of months ago." I'll spare you the details of their briefly sordid romance. It was obvious she wanted him back in any condition and she knew she had my sympathy. I almost blanched when she told me the play they had been working on was about life with Michael before Michael's success, but instead I choked on the brandy I was sipping. I almost burst into tears when she said softly and with great dignity, "If you run into Sami, tell him I want him to come back. He needs me to look after him. He's practically got no liver left."

I had a private detective on Sami's trail, but no Sami. Michael returned to Gramercy Park, and *Sidney and Lewis* went into production. On opening night I could have sworn I saw Sami lurking in the shadows of a building across the street from the theater. That opening night, as you theater buffs know, was a complete triumph for Michael. *Sidney and Lewis* was funny and sad and warm and ridiculous and to quote a famous critic, "It is almost too brilliant and that's just fine by me."

Yet when Michael emerged from Sardi's after the opening night party, a tomato smacked him in the chest. "My God," gasped the doorman, "that could have been a bullet!" My fiancée (soon to be my fifth wife) and I were with Michael and hurried him into his chauffeur-driven Rolls-Royce, and we sped away to Michael's townhouse.

Later over drinks I urged Michael to report the tomato incident to the police. "What's the use? Did any of us see who threw it?"

"You know who threw it."

Michael stared into his glass. "I didn't see Sami. Did you?" I shook my head "No." He asked my fiancée. But she'd never met Sami—she wouldn't know what he looked like.

I felt there was an invisible cloud of doom hanging over the room, but I said nothing. On this night of his glorious triumph Michael Camba was the saddest man in the world. He was going to win the Pulitzer Prize and the Tony Award and I still have a vision of Sami sitting in some dingy bar somewhere watching the Tony Awards on television, and when Michael Camba's name was announced, hurling his glass with hatred and envy at the television screen.

It turns out that's exactly what happened. Sami told me this in his jail cell. He told me how he planned to finally make the name Sami Brzniwyrzi (I have double-checked this spelling) famous. He would assassinate a celebrity. The celebrity he chose, of course, was Michael Camba. It was all too easy. I don't think Michael fell into a trap. I think he knew that his fate was inevitable and decided not to prolong it.

As Sami related it to me, when he phoned Michael and pleaded to see him, Michael told him to come at once. Half an hour later Sami plunged the steak knife into Michael's heart. Death was instantaneous. Sami phoned the police and when they arrived, he confessed with alacrity, carefully spelling out his surname.

When I arrived, I was surrounded by the press. I was now a celebrity lawyer and my soon-to-be fifth wife was the daughter of a famous Washington family, and what with my being Michael's close friend, lawyer, and adviser, the press was having a field day.

But poor Sami. I did him in again. Talk about the best laid plans of mice and men, Sami's certainly went awry. You see, I had no idea who had murdered Michael when I arrived at the house. I had only been told on the phone that Michael had been killed, but not the name of the culprit. So when a reporter told me who had murdered Michael, I blurted out, "What'sisname? You mean he was murdered by What'sisname?"

The windows of the living room where Michael's body lay covered by a sheet, and where Sami sat in a straight-back chair guarded by three policemen, were open. One of the policemen later told me that when Sami heard me refer to him not once but twice as What'sisname, he burst into tears. Poor Sami.

Poor Michael.

The memorial service was held at Radio City Music Hall and the overflow reached into the Avenue of the Americas. When Sami read about this in his jail cell, I'm told he beat his head mercilessly against the cement wall. I hoped his lawyers would enter a plea of insanity, and I am told they wanted to do just that, but Sami refused to acquiesce. He wanted the death penalty. Unfortunately, there is no death penalty in New York State. Sami drew thirty years to life. By the time he was sentenced, Michael's murder was old hat. There had been juicier celebrity killings since.

So Sami made one last effort to achieve fame. And this too was doomed to failure, my dear gossip columnist, which is why I chose out of kindness to ignore the incident in my autobiography (though my sixth wife argued I was wrong to do this). Sami committed suicide in his jail cell. He hanged himself with a bedsheet. And the irony is, only one tabloid made note of his self-destruction and this was the tiny heading of the one-paragraph obituary:

What'sisname a Suicide.

SOCK FINISH

by Robert Bloch

*Robert Bloch has been writing and selling his work since
he graduated from high school. His over four hundred
short stories and novels, and his scripts for movie, television, and radio dramas are hard to pigeonhole. Perhaps his best-known work is* Psycho *(1959), which was
made into the famous Hitchcock film. It exemplifies his
style, combining crime, mystery, and horror.*

The name of the victim was Artie Ames. I doubt if
you remember him. I didn't, and when he walked into
my Beverly Hills office that afternoon and announced
himself to my girl, I couldn't have cared less.

Of course, I didn't know he was a victim then.

Let's get one thing straight: I try to see the people
who come into the office, but I'm an agent. When I'm
on the job, my first duty is to my clients. And an agent's
office is Mecca for every Arab in Hollywood. Hollywood
is full of Arabs without camels, Arabs with three-
humped camels, Arabs with caravans of millions of
imaginary camels, all looking for agents.

So I let Artie Ames sit on the mourner's bench in
my outer reception room while I spent the afternoon
slaving over a hot telephone. I was working out a deal
with Dick Melvin at Metromount. He wanted to sign
one of my properties, Tommy Nolan, as juvenile lead
for a big Cinemascope turkey they were cooking up for
the Thanksgiving trade. He'd already tested Nolan and
liked what he saw, and now it was just a matter of
working out the minor details, such as the price. We
hassled back and forth for a while, and finally I nailed
him down on the third call-back and was just getting
ready to hang up when he insisted on talking about the
plot of the picture. It turned out that he was going to
do one of those "Good Old Days" things—not a biog,
but a general story on Hollywood in the 1920s. "We
were going to work it up as *The Mack Sennett Story*,"

he told me. "Only you know what would happen. We'd put out a big buck for rights, and then we'd have to change the whole thing anyway. So we'll just sort of keep the feel of the period, get me? Lots of slapstick stuff, and we may hire Chester Conklin or a few of the other old-timers who're still around. But the guy I'm really trying to get hold of is Artie Ames."

Something clicked then, and it wasn't the receiver. I took a deep breath. "Artie Ames?" I said. "Why, he happens to be in my office right now."

"You handle him?"

"Why not?" I said, which wasn't really an answer, either way.

"Can you get him over to Semple in Casting tomorrow morning?"

"Why not?" I said again.

"It isn't really much of a deal, just a bit," he told me.

"What do you mean, it isn't much of a deal?" I revved the motors just a trifle. "You want Hollywood in the 1920s? You want the spirit of slapstick comedy? The genuine spirit, the authenticity, the whole soul of the era can be summed up in just two words—Artie Ames. And you say it isn't much of a deal."

"We may go five grand," he answered.

"Talk about that later," I assured him. "You tell your man Semple to expect Artie Ames at nine."

I hung up fast, buzzed my girl, and told her to admit Artie Ames in three minutes. Then I sat back to do a little fast exercise in total recall.

Because I *still* didn't remember Artie Ames. Oh, the name rang a bell, once it was associated with the silent slapstick comedies. But I couldn't place the face. I scanned flickering images of all the two-reel clowns—Lupino Lane, Billy Dooley, Larry Semon, Lloyd Hamilton, Bobbie Vernon, Charlie Chase. I thought of the other mustached comics, like Jimmy Adams and Jimmy Finlayson, and Conklin, of course, and that great little Englishman, Billy Bevan. I came up with Al St. John before he turned into a western stooge, and Hank Mann, and even Max Davidson. I even conjured up a picture of the old trademark of Educational Comedies—*The Spice of the Program.*

But it wasn't until I thought of the music that I remembered my man.

They used to play jazz accompaniments for the comedies in the old silent days. Things like "Running Wild" and "Barney Google" and "Raggedy Ann" and "Don't Bring Lulu": jerky, syncopated rhythms to synchronize with the jerky, syncopated antics of Jack Duffy or Snub Pollard or his sister Daphne. I don't know what they played for Buster Keaton, but Langdon usually drew "I'm Just Wild About Harry," and Harold Lloyd was associated with "Collegiate" after *The Freshman* came out. Chaplin, naturally, had "Charlie My Boy."

Artie Ames usually had "San."

I placed him now. Artie Ames—two-reelers during the late twenties. Just before talkies came in. A little guy—they were all such little guys, Stan Laurel and Monty Banks and the rest—with a peculiar make-up. He always looked like the political-cartoon figure of Mr. Taxpayer or the Average Man—balding, bespectacled, bemustached, bewildered. Carried an umbrella and wore a stiff high-crowned derby. And as he raced around the organist played "San." Sure, I remembered Artie Ames.

Then he came in, and I didn't remember him at all.

I don't know just what I expected to see. Certainly I'm aware that a performer looks different off-screen and out of make-up. I wasn't anticipating the exaggerated eyebrows, the unnatural dark circles under the eyes, the pasty-white complexion, the sagging shoulders, the shuffling walk, the nervous flutter of the fingers.

On the other hand, I was more or less prepared to greet an elderly man, possibly even a shabby one. As far as I knew, Artie Ames went out with the talkies almost thirty years ago, and I expected that time would have taken its toll.

But Artie Ames was a complete surprise: he was a total stranger.

To begin with, he wasn't nearly as short as I'd remembered him to be. He held himself erect; he was neither hangdog nor fidgety, and he was wearing a suit made by my own tailor, who turns them out at $200 a copy. On top of all that, he wasn't old. Oh, you wouldn't peg him as a youngster, but he could pass for a man in his forties. And a well-preserved man at that, with a full head of graying hair and a face devoid of wrinkles or pouches. He didn't resemble his screen characterization of thirty years ago, and he didn't appear to be ready for a nursing home either.

When he opened his mouth to greet me by name I got the biggest surprise of all.

Artie Ames had a basso profundo voice.

Then it all came back to me, of course. The voice—that's what killed him. It was wrong for talkies, wrong for a slapstick comic playing a Timid Soul character. Sound slaughtered his career, just as it eventually slaughtered the career of a great artist like Buster Keaton. Now I remembered.

He told me all about it during the next few minutes. How he did bit parts, went out with tab shows during the early thirties, how he made a whole series of films in Europe—for, he hastened to assure me, he was still popular abroad. "After all," he said, "I was only twenty-nine when sound came in. And a man has to do something."

"A man has to eat too," I suggested.

He didn't like my suggestion. I could tell from the way he drew himself up stiffly in his chair. "That's never been a problem," he answered. "I own a block of lots down near Long Beach. No buildings on them— just oil wells."

Which, of course, explained the $200 suit. But it didn't explain what Artie Ames was doing in my office today. He cleared that up himself immediately.

"Suppose you're wondering what I want with you," he said. "I'll make it short and sweet. The grapevine tells me that Metromount is casting for a flick about silent pics. And the word is out that they want Artie Ames. Think you can represent me?"

I didn't waste time stalling. "I already represent you. Report to Semple, in Casting, at nine tomorrow."

He didn't even blink. "I heard you were a bright boy," he said. "I guess I heard right."

"You'll test," I told him. "But don't talk contract until you check with me. It's some kind of a bit, and they mentioned five. Maybe we can raise the ante."

"Don't worry." He nodded. "The reason I came to you

in the first place was because I found out you're handling young Nolan on the same deal. I know you've got an in there. But perhaps I can help matters along in my own way. Wait and see."

He bowed out, and I spent the next forty-eight hours waiting and seeing.

On his next appearance Artie Ames was wearing another $200 suit and a high-priced grin on his face. He told me just what the grin was worth.

"Twenty-five grand," Artie Ames exulted. "That's what Melvin said he'd go for. And he called in Sid Belter, right after he saw the test, and told him to build up my part. In fact, I'm going to work with him on the movie sequences and fatten the part myself. Use a lot of my old routines. And Melvin says he's got an idea for building all the promotion around me—make a comeback vehicle out of it. Said I didn't have to worry about my voice either. Engineers can handle that now. You should have seen them in the screening room! They were crazy about me—I had 'em rolling in the aisles!"

Well, I've heard that kind of talk before. But the next day, when we went to Melvin's office to sign the contract, I found out that Artie Ames was telling me the truth. Dick Melvin *was* excited. And they were going to angle their publicity around the old-time comic.

When I saw the actual contract, made out for the $25,000 figure, my respect for Artie Ames went up several notches. He was nobody's fool. And who knows?— perhaps I had myself a valuable property. Once in a while those has-beens make a big comeback.

Artie Ames seemed to think so when he signed for the deal. "Give me that pen," he said. "This marks the beginning of a new career."

I nodded.

How could I know that he was signing his own death warrant?

It's a standing gag in the industry that Hollywood people are the biggest suckers for their own publicity. That's why they believe their own ads in the trade papers and their own puffs in the columns.

Maybe so. And this may have contributed to my respect for Artie Ames in the month that followed. He certainly got a big enough build-up. Melvin and his crew of hired assassins at the studio went all out. Ames was interviewed; he was quoted; he was profiled; he was shoved into guest appearances—all carefully staged so as to get in a mention of the forthcoming picture, of course. But there was plenty about just plain Artie Ames too. The name was getting around to a new generation. And after seeing his picture pop up all over the place, and reading copy on him day after day, I couldn't help but be aware of him.

Still, I like to believe that part of my growing affection for the man was based on his own personality. I came to know him fairly well. He dropped in at the office frequently; we managed a few luncheons together, and I even spent a couple of evenings out at his big house near Malibu.

I found out that Artie Ames was lonely. In spite of his money—and he really had it—he'd never married. And unlike many of his age group, he didn't care to associate with his contemporaries. Not for him those little social gatherings where former stars sit around and reminisce.

"Who needs those horses' necks?" he scoffed. "They're washed up, finished." Ames always lapsed into the slang of the twenties when he got excited. "Why should I waste my time listening to the sad story of how they faw down go boom? Far as I'm concerned, life is just a bowl of cherries."

That's something else I found out about Artie Ames. He had never retired. In his own mind he was still a star. He had never stopped being a star. He showed me his press books. The clippings were up-to-date. The fact that most of the rave reviews of the past twenty-five years were printed in French or Spanish or Italian didn't faze him a bit. All he knew was that somewhere people still enjoyed his work. Whether they called him "Artie" or "Arturo" didn't matter. He was a comedian; he worked for an audience, and laughter knows no language barrier.

"I'm going to show these smart alecks around town how wrong they were," he insisted. "When they see the routines I've worked up for this picture, they'll be sorry about passing me up all these years. Comedy doesn't change. The good stuff is always good. And there isn't much competition any more. What have they got today? They got Lou Costello! Jerry Lewis!"

Here he went into an impromptu imitation of the latter, and for a moment I was amazed by the startling transformation in the man. He aped Jerry Lewis perfectly. His miming captured Lewis's gestures and facial expressions precisely but caricatured the caricature. He managed to burlesque Lewis's burlesquing. And all done so easily, so assuredly.

He could discuss the theory of comedy with the same ease and assurance. Of course he talked about the old days, but he did so with complete authority. He spoke about the grotesques—Kalla Pasha, who was too hairy, and Mack Swain, who was too fat, and Slim Summerville, who was too thin, and Ben Turpin, whose eyes were too crossed. He explained the difference between the exaggerations of a Ford Sterling and the unappreciated subtlety of Charlie Chaplin's brother, Syd. His conversation was spotted with allusions to half-forgotten figures—Charlie Murray and Louise Fazenda and Mabel Normand and Babe Hardy, when he worked with Jimmy Aubrey. This is the kind of priceless information which seldom knocks anyone off his barstool.

Still I was interested, and more interested when he demonstrated some of the comedy bits he'd planned.

So was the studio.

I was on hand when they started filming. Artie Ames had been assigned to the First Production Unit, because they planned to shoot his stuff in advance of the rest of the picture. He wasn't in the "story" of the film itself: he merely appeared in the scenes revolving around the old-time movie making.

Seeing him in action took me back thirty years. Oh, the studio was new, and the sound stage was modern, and the technicians used the latest equipment—but Artie Ames was unchanged. In costume and make-up he was the comic of 1929, and the routines he'd worked out were definitely of that vintage.

The amazing thing about it was that he was funny. Not only to me, but to everyone on the set—to the props, the grips, the gaffers, and the bit players. More important, he was funny to Dick Melvin and to Sid Belter, the writer. Several times during the first day's shooting he "broke up" the rest of the cast, just by his ad libs. It was all strictly pantomime stuff, you understand, but with the perfect timing and the deft precision common to many of the silent comedians who worked without benefit of a crew of gag writers or even the assistance of a written script.

"Wonderful!" Melvin exulted to me. "At this rate he'll steal the picture." Then he scowled darkly. "Have to do something about that," he muttered to himself. "Miss Swivel-hips won't like it."

Sid Belter chewed his pipe. "Don't worry, sweetheart," he said. "You saw the script. She's all taken care of. Plenty of close-ups, lots of nice, simple, two-syllable dialogue. The audience will know who's the star."

"Well, they're not going to remember her when this character is on the screen," Dick Melvin said. "Maybe we made a mistake, letting him build up those routines."

"Forget it," Belter answered. "He's great. Just what we needed. Besides, he works fast—we'll have all his stuff in the can before the week is out, except for the one scene with Miss Swivel-hips. And we can always chop it up later."

I didn't say anything. I was beginning to worry a little, because I'd forgotten that this was supposed to be a starring vehicle for Miss Swivel-hips, as they called her.

Perhaps it would be safer if that's what I called her too.

Actually her real name doesn't matter—she never used it anyway. None of the Miss Swivel-hips of Hollywood ever use their real name. It's part of the pattern.

Miss Swivel-hips was a gorgeous blonde. She used a screen name, and like most Hollywood blondes, she was originally a brunette. Her history was standard too. Product of the usual broken household, violated at the age of nine, or was it ten?—her astrologer would probably know the exact date—and married in her teens to some Okie motorcycle cowboy or the equivalent. A few years of knocking around, some dubious experiences as a model, and then—Hollywood and the golden transformation.

Now, of course, Miss Swivel-hips had already arrived. Her every word, opinion, or wisecrack was dutifully chronicled in the public prints, her manifold romances detailed, and her acting skill extolled. The fact that words, opinions, wisecracks and even the romances were mainly the creations of press agents didn't really matter. Nor did her acting skill, which was virtually nonexistent. What did matter was that Miss Swivel-hips commanded $150,000 per picture. Her contract was real—possibly the only real thing about her, except a thirty-nine-inch bust and a torso that was rapidly becoming a trademark.

So, when the day's shooting was completed, and Artie Ames gave me a perspiring welcome in his dressing room, I was more concerned about Miss Swivel-hips than I was with my client's immediate reaction.

"How'd you like it?" he greeted me. "Wasn't it the cat's pajamas?"

I nodded, wincing a little at the dated slang. Maybe Artie Ames was the cat's pajamas, but I couldn't help thinking of another pajama-clad cat who wouldn't much care for his performance.

"Told you I could do it," he said, as he applied cold cream to his face. "Wait'll you see what I've got lined up next. We're going to do one of the old chase sequences. You know—twelve guys in a tin lizzie, running up the side of buildings—everything. Melvin's all excited. He's worried because he thinks I'm too old to take those prat falls, but he doesn't know me. I've still got plenty of tricks to show him."

I wondered if Artie Ames was acrobatic enough to take another kind of a fall, in case Miss Swivel-hips decided to pull the rug out from under him.

And as he hurried through a change of clothes I decided to broach the subject tactfully.

"You're doing a swell job," I said truthfully. "But don't forget, they may do a little cutting later on. After all, you're not officially the star of this picture."

He grinned at me. "Don't you worry about the star of the picture," he told me. "I met her yesterday, when we went over plans for the scenes we'll be doing together."

"What did you think of her?" I asked.

"Great gal. A real trouper, that kid. Of course, she needs a little polishing, but she's got the real savvy— and she's willing to learn."

This was news to me. "Glad to hear it," I said. "It's important to get along with her, so play it diplomatic."

Artie Ames grinned again. "Don't you worry about that part," he murmured. "I'm doing all right. Reason I'm changing in such a rush is that I've got a heavy date with her tonight for dinner."

"Business?"

"Who said anything about business? Believe me, this is strictly for pleasure." He managed a third grin for himself in the mirror. "And if you don't believe it, read Lolly's column tomorrow."

Then he dashed out.

And the next day, like a good little boy, I read Lolly's column. And Hedda's and Sid's and all the others.

Artie Ames hadn't been kidding. He and Miss Swivelhips had done the town. One of the tabs even carried a picture of the two of them dancing, and I must admit they didn't make such an incongruous couple. He was close to thirty years her senior, but the picture didn't show it. And in many a Hollywood calendar the months of May and December are juxtaposed.

During the next ten days I didn't see anything of my client, but I got plenty of reports. Melvin kept me informed of Artie Ames's progress on the set—"Terrific, sweetheart, absolutely terrific!"—and the gossip columnists kept me informed of his progress around and on the town.

By the time the ten days were up they were printing direct quotes from Miss Swivel-hips herself. Romance? "No comment." Engagement? "We're very good friends." What had happened to Miss Swivel-hips's supposed marriage to a wealthy Texas promoter? "Artie Ames has taught me that a laugh is worth more than a million dollars any day."

I couldn't quite believe it, but I had to. And I stopped worrying about Artie Ames. One of the movie magazines ripped out its inside spread and substituted a hastily written article titled "Old Hollywood Meets the New" and filled it with pictures of the twosome at the beach, at her house in Bel Air, at the races. AP and UP were running squibs now, and it was getting to be news. Plenty of human interest in it, of course—even better than the days when Chaplin used to squire around some young leading lady. Because Miss Swivel-hips was an accepted celebrity and Artie Ames was making a comeback. It was quite a story while it lasted.

And all the while they were fattening him up for the kill.

When the ax was sharpened, the victim couldn't see the blade for the glitter.

He came running into my office, all excited. "Did you hear about it?" he demanded. "Did you hear the news?"

"What news?" I swiveled around, facing him. "Tommy Nolan tells me the picture's almost finished, if that's what you mean. It'll be in the can before the end of the month."

"Never mind that," Artie Ames panted. "I'm talking about my footage."

"You still have a couple of scenes to shoot with your leading lady," I said. "Is that what you're so hopped up about?" I hesitated. "Or are you two planning a little announcement of some kind?"

He almost blushed. "Well, I really shouldn't say anything," he mumbled. "She wants to wait until the picture's finished, see? Oh, she's a great kid—the cat's meow! You ought to see us Charleston—"

"This is an announcement?" I inquired.

"Oh, I forgot." I could see the excitement mount again. He was practically dancing across my carpet. "It's the Sullivan show—they're going to do a special preview bit on the Ed Sullivan show next month! It's all set. And they're using one of my scenes!"

I stopped swiveling and sat up straight. "Big deal," I said.

"It must be, or else Melvin wouldn't have gone to all that expense. Know what he did? He had my scene processed in advance—stuck on the sound track and a special musical score, just for TV showing. This is *it*, kid!"

This was indeed it, if true.

"They're running the print tomorrow morning at eleven for Dick Melvin and all the big shots," Artie announced. "You be there?"

"I wouldn't miss it for the world," I assured him.

And I didn't.

The next morning at eleven I was sitting in one of those nice soft executive chairs in the Producer's Screening Room. Melvin had a cigar; Artie Ames had a cigar; I had a cigar—everybody had a cigar except Miss Swivel-hips. But she was there, big as life, at Artie's side, to witness his moment of triumph.

The lights went off; the projector began to hum—and the ax fell.

You know what the poet said? "This is the way the world ends—not with a bang, but a whimper."

Well, the poet never worked in Hollywood, or he'd have changed his story. If he'd been sitting there in the projection room with us, he'd have seen the end of Artie Ames's world and heard the sound that came with it.

Artie Ames's world ended that morning with a squeak.

It ended with a squeak; it ended with a blat; it ended with the idiot music you hear accompanying the cartoon antics of a half-witted dog.

We stared up at the vaunted chase sequence that Artie Ames had told me about, and we heard the sounds: the squeals, the brays, the barks, the cackles. When the driver of the flivver pressed the horn, some genius in the engineering department had put the blat of a foghorn on the sound track. When Artie Ames climbed out, the very pathetic picture of Mr. Average Man faced with insuperable difficulties, and cranked the motor—explosions, machine-gun fire, and the ironic mockery of an atomic-bomb explosion. Ames faced the camera to deliver one of his rare lines of dialogue, and I wondered how they'd corrected that bass voice of his. I found out as his mouth opened and a squeak emerged.

It was the nasty, subhuman vocalization of a tape recorder run in reverse.

No words emerged—just an insane gibberish.

And the gibberish continued throughout the sequence. The sequence itself was cut drastically, and some clever craftsman had speeded up the action until what remained was a frenzied flicker of paranoid distortion. Artie Ames's pantomimic bits were projected in a lightninglike fashion that gave him the appearance of an epileptic in full seizure. And all the while out of his mouth came this *Silly Symphony,* this *Loony Tune* noise.

Funny? Yes, it was funny—the way a four-year-old child thinks it's funny when the mouse puts a cannon muzzle in the cat's ear and blows the top of his head off. It was funny-grotesque; it was funny-idiotic, and most of all it was funny-cruel.

The sequence was mercifully short, much shorter than the originally filmed version, and I remembered Melvin's remark about "chopping." Only he hadn't chopped—he'd butchered. He'd ripped out the close-ups, torn out the pantomime, and given the victim the voice of a pig, squealing in slaughtered agony.

When the lights went on again I didn't look at Artie Ames. Nobody wants to see the face of a murdered man.

And Artie Ames had been murdered. They'd killed him up there on the screen. They'd killed him and his art and the whole genius of silent comedy. They'd laughed at the laughter, burlesqued the burlesque, ridiculed the ridiculous.

"How about that?" Melvin boomed. "Pretty tricky stuff, eh? The boys did a good job. This ought to slay 'em."

I didn't like to hear that talk about wanton destruction.

And neither did Artie Ames.

"Hey, what's the big idea?" he demanded. "You massacred a perfectly good scene."

"Massacred?" Dick Melvin's eyebrows were twin half-moons of arched astonishment. "I thought it was funny as hell. How about you, Sid? Dave, what did you think? Eddie? Mike?"

Sid and Dave and Eddie and Mike and all the others on Dick Melvin's payroll chorused together that in their personal opinions the scene was funny as hell.

Nobody bothered to ask how funny hell was, even though the hell was there in Artie Ames's eyes.

"You double-crossed me," he said. "You cut out all

the good stuff. You speeded up the film. You put in those noises. You took out all the sympathy, all the audience identification. You made me into a goof."

"Now don't get salty, sweetheart," Dick Melvin said. "This is the picture business, remember? I'm handling production, and I know what I'm doing. I've seen the rushes we've shot so far, and I'm working for a balance. Had to cut out a lot of your stuff, Artie, because it made the picture top-heavy. Put too much emphasis on that old-time atmosphere." He put his arm around the comic. "Tell you a little secret, sweetheart. You're just too good, that's all. Too damned good. Now if we were making like, say, a documentary about the silent movies, what you did was just fine. Hit the whole spirit of the times—just like they did it in 1927. But we're filming a story, see? A story about this boy and this girl, and how they get together and have a fight and get together again. Got to keep the emphasis where it belongs."

"But couldn't you let what you did use alone?" Artie Ames was pleading now. "Even if you cut me to one or two scenes, couldn't you let the stuff stand?"

Dick Melvin shook his head. "You didn't listen to me, sweetheart," he said patiently. "I told you we weren't making a documentary. You do 1927 comedy, but this isn't 1927. Today's audiences, they don't care about that old-time stuff. To them it's cornball, something to laugh at. So we're giving it the treatment—showing we can laugh at it too. Don't think I can't appreciate your kind of talent. Lord knows, I wish we had the kind of audiences who appreciated real comedy when they see it. But we can't take that chance. Got a million and a half tied up in this little epic. So I have to keep an eye on the old B.O. And I can't take the story line away from Miss Swivel-hips either. Can I, darling?"

He turned to her, but Artie Ames cut in ahead of him.

"What do you think?" he demanded. "Don't you agree with me?"

She fluffed her curls. "Well, I don't know, Artie. After all, Mr. Melvin *is* the producer. *He* can tell what's best for the production."

Artie Ames stared at her. "But, honey," he blurted, "you know what this is going to mean to me. We talked it all over. This could be my big chance—my comeback vehicle. It can make me a star again, a big star. Then you won't have to be ashamed of me. And after we're married—"

What had Artie Ames said about Miss Swivel-hips? Something to the effect that she was "the cat's meow"?

Well, the cat was meowing now.

"Never mind that! We're talking about the picture, and Mr. Melvin is right. You can't go around hogging scenes in my picture—"

"*Our* picture," Artie Ames said. "Remember how we talked about it, honey? This is going to be *our* picture."

The cat had claws too.

"Come off it! I've got a career to protect, and I'm not going to let them pad out scenes for some sawed-off little nobody in a funny hat." The cat was spitting now. "Grow up, Artie! We had our kicks, but you ought to know the whole deal was a publicity setup. You're a swinger, old buddy, but the party's over. Take a good look at yourself in the mirror sometime and then you'll see why that marriage stuff is definitely out."

Artie Ames couldn't have faced a mirror then. He couldn't face anybody. He turned to Dick Melvin, but the producer stared down at the floor.

"I get it," Ames said, and his voice was never deeper. "The old build-up routine. And I suppose that stuff you've been handing the papers about my comeback is just a lot of hooey too."

"Well." Dick Melvin cleared his throat. "You know how it goes, Artie. We figured we had a good angle to tie a story to, and we used it. Did a great little job, too— look at all the ink we got! And don't forget, we have played up your name, plenty. Maybe you'll get yourself another couple of deals out of this after the picture is released."

"You mean after they see me in scenes like the one you just ran?" Artie Ames shook his head. "Don't try and kid me. I'm washed up, really washed up."

Then came the moment I dreaded. He looked at me and said, "Well, what about it? Are you going to let them get away with it? I've got a contract."

I opened my mouth, but Dick Melvin cut in ahead of me. His voice was harsh. "Damned right you've got a contract, Artie, and a good one. Twenty-five grand we laid out, for a job any walk-on could do with a little make-up and coaching. But we bought your name, so we could use it for the publicity angle. Your contract doesn't entitle you to write, direct, produce, cut, or edit. It calls for you to be on the set when we want you— and to do what we want you to do. So stop trying to push us around. This isn't 1927, like I said before."

Artie Ames shrugged. "All right," he said. "It's your nickel. But I'm walking out."

"Go jump, for all I care," Melvin snapped. "But remember this—you've got one more scene to shoot. The pie-wagon bit. You said you wrote it, and we want it, and we're going to shoot it. What we do with it after that is our business. But next Tuesday you be on location in Malibu, bright and early, and no tricks either. You're going to give us exactly what the contract calls for."

"Forget the scene," Artie Ames said, and he was begging now. "Just go ahead and do whatever you like. But leave me alone. Please."

"We want that scene," Melvin told him. "It'll make a sock finish."

Artie Ames nodded and shuffled out. It wasn't the comedy shuffle he used when he worked. This was a different kind of a shuffle—a blind one. He walked out of that screening room like a zombie.

Dick Melvin sighed and looked at me. "Sorry we had to give him the business," he said. "But he ought to have figured how it would be." He frowned. "Guess he took it pretty hard. Maybe you better go after him. He might be, you know, in a mood."

"Maybe he'll kill himself," Miss Swivel-hips said, and her voice held more excitement than concern.

I stared at her. "How could he?" I asked. "You can't kill a corpse. And he died here half an hour ago."

"Cut the melodrama," Melvin muttered. "Just see that I have a live actor on location Tuesday morning. He's got to come through with that sock finish for us."

Now I know what the score is. Maybe Dostoevski or somebody like that could get away with a murder yarn about killing a man's soul. And maybe he could peddle a bill of goods about how more than a man's soul was killed—how a whole golden age of entertainment was slaughtered by a new era. But I can't. And if that's all there was to the Artie Ames bit, I wouldn't waste your time and mine by trying to tell it.

But there's more to it. Not much more—just *enough*.

You see, I went after Artie Ames. I went after him, and I kept after him, and I stayed with him all during the long weekend.

It wasn't easy. He wanted to drink, and I wouldn't let him. He wanted to take sleeping pills, and I hid the bottle. He wanted to cry—and this he did.

"They're all against me," he said. "I haven't got a friend left in the world."

"I'm here," I reminded him.

"Sure. You're here. Because you want to protect that precious contract. Not for the money, but because a deal is a deal, and you can't afford to let your reputation as an agent suffer."

"That's not true," I told him. "I understand. I'm all for you, Artie. To me you're one of the all-time greats."

"What's the use?" He blinked at me. "I might as well stop kidding myself. For more than twenty years I've been sitting around, giving myself the needle, telling myself that I was still a star. Banana oil!" He grinned wryly, and it was not a pleasant thing to see. "Banana oil! They stopped saying that in 1929. Forgot it, just like they forgot me. This is a new generation, isn't it? A generation that likes Miss Swivel-hips and her kind of talent. I don't belong here. You want comedy, see a cartoon. Let the little animated pictures hand you a fast boffola."

I gave him a drink then but just one. "Now listen to Uncle," I said. "Stop this self-pity stuff right now and get hold of yourself. You're Artie Ames. Maybe you're forgotten, maybe you're getting kicked around, but as long as I believe in you—as long as you believe in yourself—you've got a chance. There's just one thing you must remember. You're a trouper. A real trouper, out of the old school. The show must go on, that sort of thing."

"Laugh, clown, laugh!" he said bitterly.

"All right, make fun of it. But the tradition's real.

And sometimes the laugh backfires. Look at the way they sneered at Al Jolson—a beat-up old guy with a collapsed lung, box-office poison, all the rest of it. He showed them. And you can show them too. You want to win their respect? Then keep your own self-respect. Go out to Malibu next Tuesday and play it straight. Give them the scene, just as you wrote it. Give them everything you've got. You're Artie Ames—always remember that. And don't let yourself down."

Well, it sounded like the old college try, and the funny part of it was, it worked.

He perked up. I checked on him Sunday, and Monday night after I closed up shop I dropped in on him, just to see if he was in shape.

What I saw scared me at first. In a three-day weekend he looked as if he'd aged twenty years. No, his hair hadn't turned white and his face didn't show any new wrinkles. It was just his expression—the way his eyes stared and the way he twisted his mouth. He was definitely an old-timer, now, riding a one-way ticket.

But his deep voice was vibrant, and his gestures were animated, and he greeted me as if he was really living again. When I heard him speak I was fooled completely. I'd forgotten that you're supposed to be afraid of a suddenly animated corpse.

"All set," he said. "Been running through the routine this afternoon. And you know what I'm going to do tonight?"

I shook my head.

"I'm going to bake me some pies," he crowed.

"Pies?"

"Sure. You know the way the bit goes, don't you? Your juvenile, Nolan, has just quarreled with Miss Swivel-hips, see? He's her director, and to make her sore he casts her in this Keystone-comedy thing, where she does this scene with me. I'm the comic driving the pie wagon and she's after me with an umbrella. I'm heading for the old cliff, but I'm too sore to notice—I quit driving, climb in back of the truck, pick up a pie, and let her have it. Right in the mush."

"The old custard-pie routine, eh?"

"Melvin said we had to have one, to make it look like real slapstick. But it isn't custard, of course. It's blueberry. Photographs better. They've got to be real gooey to splatter just right—prop man was asking me what kind I wanted, and I told him I'd make up a batch myself. Always did in the old days."

He couldn't stop talking now, any more than he could stop twitching his mouth. "I can still hurl 'em too. Been practicing up. I used to be one of the best in the business. Almost as good as Arbuckle. Old Fatty—he was tops. He could sail two at once, one in each hand, and never miss."

I nodded. "This I've got to see," I said. "Tell you what. Suppose I pick you up tomorrow morning and drive you out to Malibu and watch the shooting."

He twitched his mouth at me, and I guess it was supposed to be a grin. "I get it. Want to show Melvin you're delivering the goods, eh? Well, why not? Come on along."

"It's not that," I said. Then I paused. "You sure you feel all right?"

"Of course. Feel great! Snapped right out of it. You gave me the word, didn't you? No sulking. Laugh, clown, laugh. The show must go on. Give Melvin his sock finish."

There was nothing else I could say, so I went away. But I worried all night, and when I showed up next morning I wasn't sure he'd be there.

But he was ready, and when I honked the horn in the driveway he came out, carrying his big box of pies. He even clowned a bit for me, balancing the box ever so delicately as if it contained the crown jewels. And he bowed.

"Artie Ames rides again," he said. "The Last Roundup. On to the guillotine."

He never was any good at dialogue, I told myself. He was a silent comic. Or had been. Now he was just an animated corpse, a grotesque little old man who chattered frantically and twitched his mouth at me as we drove out to the roped-off location area at the edge of the big bluff overlooking the beach.

"Funny feeling," he said. "This is it, you know. The end. I'll never do it again after this one is finished. Today I'm putting on my make-up for the last time."

"Stop it," I muttered. "You'll get another break. When

the picture is released I can line up plenty of work for you."

He shook his head. "Breaks ran out for me years ago. Melvin was right. This isn't 1927 or even 1929. The new gang is in the saddle. Assembly-line producers like Melvin. Cheap dialogue writers like Sid Belter. Blondes with box-office busts like Miss Swivel-hips. All they need me for is a sock finish."

But I was still worried. Dick Melvin was very cordial, very glad to see me and Artie Ames. He was busy with the location-unit director and the studio police, and he didn't seem to notice how Artie Ames looked when he arrived. I was glad of that, because I was sweating it out, wondering if the comic was really on the verge of a crack-up. I only hoped he'd do the scene right on the first take and get out before there was any trouble.

Miss Swivel-hips was ready, emerging from the make-up tent, and somebody drove the pie wagon into position while the cameramen lined up their shots. The scene called for Artie Ames to drive the wagon slowly toward the edge of the bluff while Miss Swivel-hips pursued him with the umbrella. Then he'd appear at the rear of the wagon and hurl the pie. Actually, of course, the wagon would have a driver up front. They'd stop action then and shoot another scene where the pie wagon apparently went over the cliff. That would come this afternoon.

Dick Melvin explained it to me and to Miss Swivel-hips, who seemed calm enough. And then Artie Ames came on. The old Artie Ames, in make-up, carrying his pies over to the wagon and loping back in a way that got a laugh out of the camera crew.

His painted mouth smiled at Melvin and Miss Swivel-hips and me. They didn't notice anything wrong. I was beginning to feel a bit better too. Maybe he'd carry it off yet.

Melvin must have felt the relief, too, because he patted Artie Ames on the shoulder and said, "How about it, sweetheart? Want to take a dry run, or should we just roll 'em right away?"

Artie Ames gave him his clown's grin. "I'm ready if you're ready," he said. "I always did it in one take back in twenty-seven. Don't worry—this one will be right."

So they lined up, and Miss Swivel-hips ran into camera range, whacking Artie Ames over the head with a big old-fashioned umbrella. And he gave little hops, wincing comically—the Beast belabored by Beauty—and then he floundered into the pie wagon as it started to move.

Miss Swivel-hips chased the wagon, brandishing the umbrella. The wagon headed slowly for the edge of the cliff.

Then something odd happened. A body dropped out of the cab of the wagon. I recognized the regular driver. He fell easily, as though pushed off-balance, and picked himself up at once. He hadn't been hurt.

Still, it was enough for the director to yell, "Cut!" And the cameras stopped turning.

But the wagon kept on rolling, and all at once Artie Ames appeared at the rear. He stood there grinning, balancing a pie in one hand. Miss Swivel-hips stopped and stared up at him. She looked statuesque and lovely.

Artie Ames peered down, as the wagon rolled away toward the cliff edge. The direct sunlight hit his face, and I could see the white, clownlike make-up. Beneath it I could see his lips twitching, and I could see his eyes.

There was nothing funny about the way he looked.

Then he said something. I guess I'm the only one who heard it, because a moment later he hurled the pie, and a moment after that the pie wagon went over the cliff and Artie Ames went with it.

That was the end. The end of the scene, the end of the picture, the end of Dick Melvin's production, and the end of Miss Swivel-hips's career. But Artie Ames had the last word.

"To hell with that laugh, clown, laugh business!" he yelled. And then came the pie—the pie that hit Miss Swivel-hips in the face, the pie that Artie Ames had made himself—and carefully filled with TNT.

He gave them their sock finish all right.

THE ACTING OF A DREADFUL THING

by Lionel Booker

*"Lionel Booker" is the pen name of a Hollywood actor
who has also published other mystery and crime stories
under other names. Since he prefers to keep his identity
private, this is all we can say about him!*

"Believe me, this series has a great chance to make
it," said my agent. "They've got a top star, the format
tested well in questionnaires, and it's a Carl Spencer
production. What more could you want?"

As a matter of fact, all I wanted was work in a television series. *Any* series. What actor doesn't? It's the
closest thing to a steady-paying job in our profession
and a chance for instant stardom. Many unknown (and
often untalented) performers have risen to become su-
perstars simply by speaking witless jokes in weekly
sitcoms.

Most series start out as a pilot, which is a fully produced opening episode that introduces all the regular
characters and gives an indication of what kind of format future episodes will follow. It also gives the network executives a chance to appraise the salability of
the idea to the viewers.

What causes a pilot to be made has nothing to do
with the originality of the idea, the entertainment value
of the script, or the availability of good performers as
much as the three points ticked off by my agent when
he informed me of the audition, particularly the last
point.

"Spencer has a great track record," he went on. "The
networks all trust him. Practically every one of his
shows winds up in the top ten. Lately he's had a couple
of duds because he tried to get too arty, but this is more
in line with what's selling right now."

The series was to be another of those half-hour sitcoms about a gruff, macho widower who was trying to cope with a petite, fetching, and somehow worldly wise teenage daughter with a penchant for one-liners.

To me the real value of the project was a chance to work with one of my heroes—Jerome Barkley. Barkley was a legend in theatrical circles because he had earned his considerable reputation without ever stepping in front of a motion-picture or television camera. He was accounted one of the greatest stage actors of the century, and everyone was shocked when it was announced he would risk his unique status by starring in a television situation comedy.

Some put it down to the economy giving Barkley little opportunity to display his talents on the financially risky Broadway stage, but credit also had to be given to the remarkable Mr. Spencer who had started in the business as an assistant stage manager in one of the star's earlier triumphs. He accomplished the doubly difficult task of selling his lifelong idol on doing the show and convincing the network to risk a major investment on an élite stage actor who was revered in his own circle but had no mass following to insure the cost.

"You got it," phoned my agent a few weeks later, his voice reflecting his own excitement. "You're playing Barkley's best friend. They're sending you the script tonight and the call is for ten o'clock tomorrow morning at Stage Five."

The studio had once been the location for countless wartime epics, South American-set musicals, and colorful historical romances during the heyday of motion-picture supremacy; but when I entered the cavernous structure of Stage Five that morning I saw the changes that progress had made.

On one side, comprising about one third of the entire area, were elevated rows of seats because the pilot was to be taped before a live audience. This left the floor on the opposite side for the main permanent set; cameras and microphone booms would be placed between the performers and the spectators who would mainly view the action from huge color-television monitors hanging before the seats.

That morning there were no cameras and the air

resounded with carpentry sounds as the set was still being constructed. A long wooden table stretched along the middle area, covered with pencils and scripts. A craft's union man tended a refreshment table nearby, heavy with bagels, cream cheese, fresh fruits and vegetables, pastry, and a large electric coffee urn.

Barkley, a graying, middle-aged man who still preserved the trim physique and rugged good looks of his salad days, suddenly came into my vision. He wore a ratty sweater, held a paper cup of black coffee, and smoked an ancient briar pipe. After the initial palpitation that even actors feel when they meet a legendary star, I took his proffered hand and countered his kindly "Awfully glad to have you with us" with a stammering "It's a great honor for me to work with you," which he received with a broad smile, sensing my sincerity.

Spencer, as befitting his status, wore the only suit and tie among us and came across as a gracious and literate chieftain. He radiated pride whenever he gazed toward Barkley as if Barkley's presence reflected his own status as a producer who had not settled into the typical Hollywood herd of flesh merchants but sought instead for some element of excellence.

My attention then went to a small blonde young woman who sat conspicuously silent at the table, her eyes locked on her script. Her name was Alison Conroy, the actress playing Barkley's daughter, and I learned she was a recent graduate from some drama school and had no professional experience, having been selected by Spencer for both her cuteness and her innocence.

She treated Barkley with such reserve that it charmed him completely. Soon he was hovering over her like the father he was supposed to be, explaining every word of instruction from our youthful director, Dick West.

"My lord," he chortled after she successfully read her first line. "She's a miniature Ethel Barrymore. I shall have to be on my toes."

The read-through, some blocking, and individual health-insurance examinations took up our first day. Expecting all proposed series to run at least seven years, the network likes to make sure the cast is physically able to last that long.

My car was assigned a space in the studio parking

lot next to Alison's, and after she bid farewell to Barkley I said to her, "Well, it looks like we're all going to have a great time. It's a wonderful company."

She nodded vacantly, watching Barkley's disappearing Jaguar for a moment, then muttered disdainfully as she climbed into her own VW, "It's too bad our star can't act."

That was the start of one of the most horrendous rehearsal periods I have ever experienced. Barkley soon became aware of Alison's opinion of his abilities and stopped trying to show even a veneer of tolerance for her inexperience. There were never any overt arguments, no shouting matches on the set, but the frigid atmosphere belied the loving father-daughter relationship they sought to convey.

To make matters worse, West, only a few years older than Alison and more attuned to her values, sided with his contemporary in the small war that began to rock Stage Five. Always soft-spoken and polite with Barkley, his lack of praise or enthusiasm and his doting consideration of Alison's growing number of problems made it plain where his sympathies lay.

Spencer tried to be diplomatic both because of his investment and his innate gentility but I felt he leaned toward Barkley. After all, the success of his pilot depended a great deal on the actor's appeal, and he still retained much of the hero-worship of his younger days.

My position was of one caught in the middle. Alison did not consider me a hopelessly outdated relic since I had once attended an acting school and had seen a DeNiro movie, so I was privy to some of her comments.

"Dear God, he's too much, isn't he?" she whispered to me as we sat watching Barkley do a scene involving neither of us. "I mean he's ruining the inner truth of that moment with his old hoke. My agent says this series could finally make me a star but look what he's doing with it." Quietly I mused that the length of her career hardly warranted the impatience and resentment I heard in her tone.

As for Barkley, he was aware that, outside of Spencer, I was the only one old enough to know who he was and soon he began inviting me after rehearsals to join him in a drink in a small bar near the studio.

"She pretends to be above such mundane things as technique like the rest of us poor mortals," he snorted over a Scotch and soda, "but the little fool doesn't even know how to open a door. I don't intend to let a little wet-nosed brat mess up a show of mine, even in this God-forsaken medium."

The final confrontation was not long in coming. The rehearsal period for a half-hour pilot is usually from one to two weeks, and just before the taping in front of a live audience, a special preview is given for the executives of the network as proof we haven't been wasting their money and also as an opportunity for them to pull out if so inclined afterward.

West decided to add the idea of actually taping the preview, which is not usually done. I think he was worried about Alison, whose small voice and tiny gestures had trouble reaching the seats, while Barkley's stage-trained resonance could probably have been heard in Glendale without the aid of a microphone. Barkley sensed a conspiratorial ploy in placing cameras and sound equipment between him and his audience, but he kept his own counsel, at least until we met at the bar after rehearsals.

"So the two of them think they can get the best of me, do they?" he chuckled ominously. Then he raised the glass in a mock toast and added in the voice he once used as Brutus, one of his best roles, "She will learn. *'Between the acting of a dreadful thing and the first motion, all the interim is like a phantasma, or a hideous dream.'*"

And hideous it was for poor Alison as we prepared the next day to perform for the powers who would decide our fate. Sitting ashen in front of her makeup table, she trembled so badly she had trouble holding still while liner was applied to her terror-filled eyes. I thought for a moment she was going to upchuck when the floor manager informed us that we were only five minutes away from showtime.

Barkley, as was his custom, slept peacefully in the darkness of his dressing room until the call and rose with an exuberant air, stimulated and elated by the coming presentation. He grinned maliciously at Alison's petrified condition and made a florid gesture toward the direction of the seats, declaiming, "Our audience awaits, Madame Barrymore."

West gave him a murderous glare and tried to speak soothingly to Alison, who snapped at him in hysterical rage, "I'm all right! Leave me alone!" The great man's laughter was heard as he walked toward the set.

The audience consisted of network executives and their wives, all of whom knew their futures depended on the success of the series. Thus, they were an extremely receptive, almost desperately eager audience, and the half-hour script ran almost forty-five minutes because of their enthusiastic responses.

Barkley stole the show. He sneeringly gazed once at the rampart of electric machinery intruding between him and the spectators and then seemed to physically rise above it. Even when he couldn't be seen his powerful presence made itself felt to the point where nobody looked up at the monitors.

With me he was most generous, setting up my jokes to the point where they couldn't possibly fail, then stepping aside to give me full credit. This was my reward for the after-rehearsal drinking sessions.

At first he dealt mercilessly with Alison, overriding her restrained performance until it became obvious that the contest was tragically uneven. Then he backed off and feigned an exaggerated attempt to support her pitiful delivery. When it was over she ignored the charitable smattering of applause to retreat tearfully into her dressing room, leaving Barkley to savor the thunderous ovation he received. During the traditional period of congratulations he circled the tiny room set aside for refreshments like a conquering hero.

The next day everything appeared to have returned to normal, but there was an unmistakable attitude of condescension in Barkley's relationship with Alison and West. The youthful director, however, exhibited no resentment and went quietly about his work as if nothing had happened. Alison was withdrawn during the reading of the script changes, and when we broke for lunch I walked her to the food wagon parked outside the sound stages. After a bit of small talk we got down to the situation at hand and for a moment I thought her tears would return.

"I guess this isn't going to make me a star after all," she said lightly, her lips trembling. "Maybe I should just get out of the business."

I sympathized with her, remembering my own dismay at her age when I realized the American theater had not been eagerly awaiting my arrival. We returned to the sound stage to find it almost deserted. The union man had just prepared a fresh batch of coffee for this afternoon's session and I saw West sitting by himself in the corner going over script changes.

By this time Alison had sufficiently recovered to the point where she was ready to attempt a reconciliation with Barkley.

"Do you think he'd let me bring him a cup of coffee?" she asked timidly.

"I'm sure he'd love it," I smiled and watched her fill a container. It was such a nice gesture of recognition and respect that I decided I liked the girl very much as she disappeared inside Barkley's dressing room.

West turned in his chair and regarded her as well, his face taking on a resigned expression. Perhaps he felt sadly betrayed by her submission to their common enemy, or maybe he was wearily accepting it as part of Barkley's triumph. Just for a moment I detected a sense of victory in his manner as well, but before I could wonder about it I heard a familiar voice behind me.

"The show looked great yesterday, Lionel." I turned to see the beaming countenance of Carl Spencer as he came onto the stage from the outside. "The network loved it."

I nodded with appropriate enthusiasm but before I could reply he turned away abruptly and went over to West. "Hello, Dick. I didn't see you over there."

I left them in what appeared to be an important discussion of a production problem as Alison came out of the dressing room without the coffee container. "He was asleep," she told me in answer to my look. "I just left the cup on his table for when he wakes up."

Spencer paid her no attention and I guess she was glad of it, after yesterday's performance. Technicians came back and in about five minutes it was time to start the afternoon rehearsals.

West looked at his watch impatiently and barked to his assistant, "Go get the great man."

"I'll do it," I said quickly and moved off before he had time to object, which he appeared ready to do. Perhaps he was angry at my countermanding his order but I wanted to inform Barkley who had left the coffee and why before he came out.

When I entered I found the room in complete darkness, but I had been in there many times before and knew where the few sticks of furniture were located. As I headed in the direction of the lamp I was surprised to find myself colliding with what later I learned was a chair and falling helplessly to the floor. My temple struck the corner of the low table and a blaze of pain went through my head. The darkness was accompanied by a shower of flashing stars and all sounds ceased until I faintly began to hear a babble of voices and feel warm coffee being forced through my lips.

"He's coming around," echoed a voice and I dimly perceived Spencer kneeling over me, a look of concern on his face. I gulped at the liquid he offered and looked around at the commotion which surrounded me. After answering repeated inquiries about my health I was finally told that I had disappeared inside Barkley's dressing room for so long that West's assistant came to see what had happened. The man was more cautious than I was in finding the lamp, and when he turned it on he shouted in alarm, seeing me sprawled unconscious on the floor and Barkley apparently still asleep on his sofa.

The cry brought a crowd of people into the dressing room. West went to Barkley while Spencer, seeing I was injured, got me coffee. Then Alison began screaming. Barkley was not asleep. He was dead.

West carried her out of the place and over to the refreshment table where the union man was indifferently slicing carrots. Spencer promptly took charge and told everyone not to leave, or touch anything—he would call the police.

Their subsequent investigation put Barkley's death down as the result of poison—poison which was found in the coffee container that still rested on the table in his dressing room, half consumed. The police, as a matter of routine, had already taken samples of the electric coffee urn or what was left in it because practically everyone took a swig of the steaming brew immediately after the discovery of the body. That alone, besides their laboratory analysis, told them that the poison couldn't have come from the urn. It had to have been put in the cup after it was filled, and I don't have to tell you in what an unenviable position this placed Alison.

The investigators ignored my recounting of her reason for taking him the coffee and only considered what had been reported of her attitude before and immediately after her disastrous experience at the preview. To make matters worse for her, all of us who were present on Stage Five before the discovery of the body confirmed the fact that no one else went into the dressing room after Alison came out and that no one else touched the poisoned cup.

Then, to clinch matters, the union man, an individual of perception and good memory, swore that Alison had to break the unused plastic bag that held the coffee containers in order to select the one for Barkley, making it impossible that the poison had been planted in the container before the coffee was poured.

All in all, it came down to two theories, neither of them really satisfactory. One, that Barkley had taken his own life, waking up after Alison's departure, finding the coffee at hand, and administering the poison to himself. Even if such a sequence could be accepted, what possible reason could he have had for suicide? He was starring in what promised to be a spectacular success, with enthusiastic support from the network, and he had just vanquished a rival with a performance which all of us who saw it had to agree was superb.

The second theory held that Alison, in rage and hysteria over her professional humiliation, had killed Barkley for revenge, having obtained the poison the night before. Under the guise of seeking a reconciliation, which she hoped would remove all suspicion from her, she slipped the poison into the coffee on her way to the dressing room. Whether or not Barkley was awake or woke later was immaterial because the weapon had already been primed.

As for the idea that I poisoned the coffee, forced it

on Barkley, then bopped myself on the head in the few minutes I was alone in the dressing room, I'm glad to say it was quickly dismissed, if ever entertained.

"Nobody knows what they're going to do about the series," my agent told me later, voicing what he considered the most important facet of the situation. "You'd better get a copy of the tape for your reel."

My reel is my personal video tape of past performances, and I had to agree that a scene between myself and Jerome Barkley might be very impressive. It was shortly after I got a copy of the taped rehearsal that the networks announced the reports of the insurance examinations had come in and showed that Barkley had suffered from an incurable disease that was expected to take his life within the year. His own doctor confirmed this and said that the actor had been living with this knowledge for some time.

The news removed the main barrier against a verdict of suicide and it was decided by the authorities that the despondency of imminent and painful death finally got the better of Barkley, and he chose to go out by his own hand during a moment of personal triumph. It cleared Alison, who was again a marketable commodity for her agent. So it came as no surprise when I got a call from my own agent telling me that the pilot was on again. Spencer had found a suitable replacement for Barkley, a well-known television star without half of Barkley's credentials or talent but sufficiently "hot" to regain the network's faith in the project. The rest of the original cast, including Alison, was being asked to honor their contracts.

This was why Spencer was requesting I see him that afternoon, according to my agent, to get my full commitment. My performance had tested well with sample audiences who had seen the tape and I was on my way to my heart's desire—a regular role in a TV series. Even so, I faced the meeting with dread, having hoped that the situation would never arise.

Spencer's office was located in one of the rough wooden bungalows in the studio, with an interior that was plush and prosperous-looking, gleaming with plaques and statuettes that testified to the success of Spencer's past endeavors and cluttered with photographs of stars, political figures, and entertainment executives all in the process of shaking the producer's hand. Spencer was as gracious as always, calling me Lionel and commanding me to call him Carl.

"Jerry Barkley worked so hard to make this show a reality," he said in a subdued tone after we were seated, "that I feel it's a sort of tribute to his memory that we get it on the air. And now that things have cleared up for Alison, we'll have almost the same team. She's a talented actress and will someday be a big star. I'm sure of it."

"Yes," I answered quietly. "I saw the tape of the show and she comes across much better than I thought."

"I agree," he smiled. "I've been giving the matter a lot of thought since..." He sighed and shook his head as if to clear it. "You know, I just can't get that awful day out of my mind."

"Neither can I," I said pointedly. He sensed an extra meaning in my tone and looked at me sharply. I took a deep breath and plunged. "In fact, I keep going over it to find some logical explanation."

He stiffened and regarded me with cold eyes. "Explanation for what?"

"The coffee," I answered. "The coffee you gave me to drink after I passed out. I didn't think much of it at the time, but it was warm. Almost tepid. I had no trouble in gulping it down."

"What's that got to do with anything?"

"The union man had just finished making a new batch when we got back from lunch and it was steaming-hot when Alison poured out Barkley's cup. The urn was still hot after we found the body, even when the police took a sample to test for poison. Yet the cup you gave me was only warm."

He tried to look impatient and his voice had a tinge of enmity. "Lionel, I don't know what you're getting at, but I have—"

I interrupted him, something that would have caused my agent heart failure if he had been present. "Everyone has gone under the supposition that the cup Alison brought into Barkley's dressing room was the one that was poisoned. But what if there were *two* cups? What if one had been brought in *before* Alison's? The fact that a chair was out of place indicates that Barkley had a previous visitor who pulled it up to the sofa to talk to him.

"Let's say this visitor slipped the poison into a cup of coffee when Barkley wasn't looking and quietly left, being careful not to let anyone see him. He had made sure his own fingerprints were not on the cup, and when Barkley's body was found the circumstances would point to suicide, even without a motive. Perhaps that could be supplied later—from an insurance report."

I glanced up at him but he wasn't moving a muscle now, or making any attempt to hide his hostility.

"The first visitor, having circled around and re-entered the stage, rushed into the dressing room with everyone else when West's assistant let out a yell. He must have been on the edge of panic because I had gone in earlier and never reappeared. On entering the dressing room, most of the attention was on me and Barkley, but there was one person who would take special interest in the fact that there were now *two* cups of coffee on the table. Where could the extra one have come from? Who put it there? Alison wouldn't have noticed it because the room was dark when she left her cup there.

"Well, our friend was now in a state of terror that something had gone wrong with his plan and all he could think of was that one of those cups, the full one, Alison's, had to be got rid of. During all the commotion he grabbed it and rushed back to the refreshment table on the pretext of getting some coffee for me. But the union man was standing right there, so he couldn't throw the cup away without being seen, and since it was full, he couldn't shove it into his pocket. So he pretended it was empty and faked filling it from the urn. Then he rushed back to me and poured the liquid down my throat.

"He could now do what he liked with the container, having established a reason for its presence. Later he learned how lucky he had been because nobody noticed there had been two cups on the table. The only thing that went wrong is that the coffee had begun to cool down, but who would notice that except the guy who drank it?"

There was a long pause. Then Spencer shook his head and sighed. "Lionel, you must be crazy. Why on earth would I want to kill Jerry? He was giving me my first hit series in two years. You saw how well he went over at the preview."

"Yes, but I also saw the video tape. It's a funny thing about acting. Its quality depends a great deal on where it's done. Barkley gave a brilliant *stage* performance that day for the audience in the bleachers, and they loved it. But it's what the camera picks up that counts in this business, and with the lens only a few feet away his acting seems embarrassingly exaggerated and gross. Yet Alison, who looked awful from a distance, steals the show on camera. Her tiny gestures and quiet voice are exactly the right level and even her nervousness and ineptness become endearing. *He* looks like the amateur in those circumstances."

To my surprise he merely nodded, all pretense gone now. "Yes. I felt terrible when I saw the tape that night. I wanted so much for Jerry to succeed but the network said they'd never pick up the show unless he was replaced. Unfortunately for me he had signed an ironclad contract, and we couldn't do a thing without his consent."

He looked up at me and tried to put a tone of appeal in his voice. "Lionel, you have to understand my position. We're being allowed fewer and fewer mistakes in this business. It's become too expensive. I had gone over my limit, and they all looked at my hiring of Jerry as proof I was finished, washed up. It was only because I was also responsible for Alison that they decided to give me one more chance, but only if I got rid of Jerry.

"I went to his dressing room after you all broke for lunch. I thought the stage was empty. There was no one at the refreshment table, so I poured out a cup of coffee for Jerry and took it in to him. When I pleaded with him to let me break his contract he became enraged. He said he wouldn't give West and Alison the satisfaction, that we were wrong, that TV was an illegitimate theatrical medium but he'd never pull out. What could I do?

"For the past year I've been dreading the end of my career and secured some poison I was going to use on myself if things got too bad. I had it in my pocket then, and I began to think: why should I die when it's all *his* fault? When he wasn't looking I slipped the poison in the cup and wiped off my fingerprints. He had started to drink it as I was leaving. I guess he then put out the lights and died in his sleep, never realizing what I had done. I hope so.

"Believe me, I never wanted to hurt anyone. That's why I got rid of that extra cup. I couldn't imagine where it had come from but I didn't want anyone else implicated, certainly not Alison. His death was supposed to be taken as a suicide and when they started to suspect her I didn't know what to do. I didn't know about the insurance report then. It had been a sudden impulse, and I thought I could work out some motive later. Thank God the report supplied one. I needed Alison for the series."

He laughed mirthlessly. "The irony is that his health problem was the very cause I needed to break his contract. And I suppose it explains why he was so anxious to stay with the show, why he switched to TV in the first place. He wasn't a wealthy man, and he needed the money a year's run, plus re-runs and syndication, would have given his family." He shrugged. "Of course I'm looking after them now. It's the least I can do."

Suddenly he straightened in his chair and faced me in a businesslike manner. "Now, what about you, Lionel? What's it to be? More money? Better billing? Have your agent contact me."

I looked at him in amazement. "Are you serious?"

"Lionel, everyone says this series could really take off. Dick West certainly realizes that. I saw him when I re-entered the stage after...after seeing Jerry. Dick knew I was going to try to fire Jerry. After all, that was his whole purpose in taping the preview. To show him up. I tried to find out if he saw me enter Jerry's dressing room since he was in that corner during the entire lunch period. It turned out he had, but he's a smart boy. He's never said a word, even when Alison, for whom he has some affection, was in danger. That's why Dick is going to go far in this business."

I turned and started out the door but the strident, vicious sound of his voice stopped me.

"Don't be a fool, Lionel. It's just your word against mine. And don't forget, everyone wants this series to make it. Even if the police believed you, where will you be? Out of work. Finished. A ruined career. Think about that, why don't you?"

I hadn't turned around but merely paused. Suddenly I was out the door and down the broad streets of the studio lot until I reached the little bar where Barkley and I had spent so much time. Sitting there, I mulled over Spencer's words. He was right. It was just my word against his. It might start inquiries in his direction but the industry was never cooperative when one of their own was being investigated. And they rarely forgave the one who blew the whistle, especially if he was an actor.

I did nothing that night, telling myself it was too late to begin anything. But when morning came I had come to a decision. Slowly, regretfully, I was reaching out to phone the police from the breakfast table when the news came over the radio. Carl Spencer, head of his own production company, had been found in the early hours by his housekeeper, shot through the head, apparently a suicide. On his desk he had left a full confession to the murder of Jerome Barkley.

There are two ways of looking at it. It could have been that his better nature had taken control of him, the one that admired Jerome Barkley's artistry and sought to create a worthwhile production bearing his own name. With this came a realization of what had happened to him during his drive for power and success, and in this one act he sought to clear away the unhappiness he had caused.

Or maybe he was just scared—scared of a struggling actor who shared the same ambitions but who, when faced with the same choice between success and self-respect, might not reach the same decision. Perhaps Spencer came to believe I would not hesitate in taking the harder but more honorable path. If that's true, all I can do is try to pay him the same respect he had shown me and believe that both these theories are correct.

But I *did* hesitate. Nothing can change that, and even if I tell you that I am positive I was going to phone the police, I'll never be able to prove it—to either of us. Barkley had quoted the line about the interim between acting a dreadful thing and its first motion being like a phantasma or a hideous dream, and I guess I'm stuck in that interim from now on.

BAD ACTOR

by Gary Brandner

*Gary Brandner grew up in Seattle, graduating from the
University of Washington with a degree in journalism.
Although he intended to be a sportswriter, he never got
near an actual newspaper—instead, he drifted through
public relations, advertising, and technical writing before taking up full-time free-lancing in 1969. He is the
author of seventeen novels, more than fifty short stories,
three nonfiction books, and several articles. Perhaps his
best-known work to date is* The Howling, *which was
made into a movie in 1980.*

Young would-be actors filled the waiting room of the
Bowmar Talent School. They paced the carpet or perched
on the chairs, sizing up the competition. I walked
through the crowd to the reception desk and gave the
girl my phony name.

"I'm Alan Dickens. I'd like to enroll in an acting
course."

The girl smiled without really looking at me and
answered in a voice like a recorded message. "Fill out
an application and leave it in this basket. You will be
called for an interview."

I took a blank form from a stack on her desk and
went over to a table where a couple of beach-boy types
were struggling with their spelling. In this room full
of eager kids I felt about a hundred years old.

I had felt much younger the day before when I rang
the doorbell at Frank Legrand's house in San Gabriel,
where the suburban greenery was a refreshing change
from my dull office.

Legrand himself answered the door. A narrow-shoul-
dered man in his mid-forties, he wore a dark business
suit and a worried expression.

"Thank you for coming out, Dukane," he said. "I—
I've never done business with a private detective before."

73

"Not many people have," I told him.

After inviting me in, he got on with the business. "As I told you on the phone, I want you to investigate this Bowmar Talent School."

"You said your wife and daughter were involved," I prompted.

"Yes. A month ago Tina, that's my daughter, acted a small part in her high school play. A couple of nights later a man from this Bowmar outfit came to the house and said he'd seen Tina's performance, and wanted to enroll her at the talent school. I was against it, but Tina got all excited and Esther, my wife, said it couldn't hurt to go down and talk to them. So the next day she and Tina drove into Hollywood, and *both* signed up for acting lessons. The cost seemed way out of line to me, and it sounded like those people had made some questionable promises about putting Esther and Tina into the movies."

"If you think there's fraud involved you ought to get the police in on it." I lit a cigarette and looked around for an ashtray.

Legrand jumped up and said, "Here, let me get you something." He left the room for a minute and came back with a china saucer. "You can use this. When Esther and I quit smoking she threw out all the ashtrays in the house so we wouldn't be tempted."

I took the saucer from him and dropped my burnt match into it.

He said, "I don't really have anything to go to the police with—just a feeling. Anyway, I don't care about prosecuting these people. The important thing to me is my wife and daughter. I don't want them to get their hopes built up and then be hurt."

Legrand's eyes strayed to a pair of silver-framed photographs on the mantel. One was a dark-haired woman with dramatic eyes. The other was a pretty teen-ager with a face unmarked by emotion or intelligence.

"What makes you suspect that the school isn't on the level?" I asked, tapping ashes into the saucer.

After a moment Legrand said, "Dukane, I love my wife and daughter. There is nothing I wouldn't do for them. But I know them both very well, and believe me, they are *not*, and never will be actresses."

I had accepted a retainer then and gone home to prepare for my entry into show business.

Now I waited in the lobby of the Bowmar Talent School while the receptionist worked her way down through the completed forms to mine. Then I almost blew the cue by not reacting when she called my new name. When the girl repeated it, I came to and hurried up to the desk.

"Miss Kirby will talk to you," she said, indicating a tall female seemingly made of styrofoam and vinyl.

I followed Miss Kirby through a short hallway with several doors opening off it, and into a small office with walls the color of cantaloupe. She sat down and I took a chair facing her.

"Well, Alan," she said, scanning my application form, "so you want to become an actor, I see."

"I hope so," I said bashfully.

Miss Kirby leaned toward me, and the shadow of a frown marked her plastic features. "I hope you won't take offense, but you *are* just a tiny bit, er, mature to be starting out on an acting career."

My face stretched into what I hoped was a boyish grin. "I suppose I am starting a little late, but I just decided last month to have a fling at it. If it doesn't work out, I can always go back to the bank."

"Bank?" Miss Kirby's interest picked up.

"My father owns a bank back home in Seattle. I'll have to take it over eventually, but in the meantime I'd like to try what I've always wanted to do—acting. Unless you think it would be a waste of time."

Her tiny frown erased itself. "You know, Alan, now that I look at you more closely, I think you're just the type the studios are looking for these days. There are plenty of handsome juveniles around, but rugged leading men are hard to find. Yes, you're definitely the Burt Lancaster–Kirk Douglas type."

I lowered my eyes modestly.

"Come along now and we'll get some pictures of you."

"You want pictures of me?"

"Right. To send around to the studios and agencies. You want to get your face known in the business as soon as possible."

"Oh, sure," I agreed.

Miss Kirby led me across the hall and into a room where a man with orange hair and a big nose sat gloomily smoking a cigarette behind a desk. Photographic equipment cluttered the room, which smelled faintly of developer.

"This is Lou Markey," Miss Kirby said as she left me. "He'll take good care of you."

"Have a seat," Markey said, studying me without enthusiasm.

I put on an eager look and returned his gaze. There was something familiar about the bright little eyes, the comical nose, and the orange hair of the photographer. He used the glowing stub of his cigarette to light another, then jammed the butt into an overflowing ashtray. He offered the pack to me, but I saw they were triple-filter menthols and declined.

"Your nose is going to give us trouble," Markey said.

"It's been broken a couple of times," I admitted.

"They can straighten it, I suppose, but it won't help us now with the photos."

"Sorry," I said.

Markey sighed wearily. "Don't worry. I can light you so it doesn't look too bad, and later I can hit it with an airbrush."

"That's good," I said, feeling foolishly relieved.

He stood up and walked around the desk. "Let's get you over here by the curtain first."

When I saw the up-and-down bouncing motion of his walk I knew why he was familiar.

I said, "Are you *Beano* Markey, by any chance?"

He smiled for the first time. "Thanks for the present tense. Most people ask if I used to be Beano Markey."

"It was the early fifties; wasn't it, when you made your movies?"

"That's when it was. I must have been in two dozen low-budget teen-age epics. I was the comical kid who always lost his pants at the prom."

"Do you do any acting now?"

"Not since my voice changed. Of course, the critics said I didn't do much acting then either, the ones who bothered to review those pictures. And they were right. I never could fake reactions that I didn't feel, so I was always playing myself—the comical, clumsy high school kid."

Markey sat me down in front of a dark curtain, told me to turn this way and that, look up, look down, while he snapped away with a small, expensive-looking camera and kept up a low-key conversation.

"You seem like a fairly intelligent guy," he said at one point. "Why do you want to be an actor?"

The question surprised me. "I don't know, I guess it seemed like it would be fun and exciting."

"Yeah, exciting," Markey said in a flat voice. "Let me tell you something—"

Whatever he was going to tell me was interrupted when the door burst open and a young man with a thousand-watt smile bounced in.

"Hello there," he said, "you must be Alan Dickens. I'm Rex Bowman, president of Bowmar. How are you coming, Lou?"

"I just got started," Markey grumbled.

"You can finish up later," Bowman said airily. Then he turned to me. "Miss Kirby has been telling me about you, Alan. Let's walk on down to my office and we'll lay out a program for you."

He hustled me out of the photographer's room and into a large office walled with pictures of show business celebrities. A mountain of a man with blond curls was just leaving as we entered. Bowman took a seat behind an acre of desk and pushed a legal form across the polished surface toward me.

"That's our standard contract," Bowman said. He lit a long greenish cigar and blew the smoke toward the ceiling where an air conditioner sucked it out.

I ran my eyes down the paragraphs of fine print and saw that the contract implied much, but promised little.

"What's this 'career assistance'?" I asked, pointing to a line near the bottom.

"We make every effort to launch our graduates into successful careers in movies and television," Bowman said smoothly. "And I don't mind telling you that my personal contacts in the industry are a big help in landing that first part."

"What contacts are those?" I asked, as innocently as I could.

He chuckled indulgently. "The names probably wouldn't mean anything to you, but I'm in constant touch with the men who run things in Hollywood from behind the scenes." He walked quickly to a pair of filing cabinets and slid out one of the top drawers. He dipped into a row of manila folders and drew out several 8-by-10 glossy photographs. "Now, these are a few of my graduates whom you're probably seeing a lot of on the screen these days."

The attractive young folks might or might not have looked like somebody on television. All the stars under thirty seemed to come equipped with the Standard Face.

Bowman stuffed the pictures back into the file drawer. "That will give you an idea of the help I give my people to get them in front of the camera."

It gave me no such idea, but I nodded and said nothing. So far, though Rex Bowman appeared pretty fast on his feet, he didn't seem to be breaking any laws.

He took a look at his jeweled wristwatch. "If you want to sign the contract, you can start right in with classes this morning."

"Fine," I said, "I'm anxious to get started. But if it's all right, I'd like to take the contract home tonight and read it over."

Bowman's eyes narrowed a millimeter. "Ordinarily we don't let a student into one of our classes without a contract. You can understand that."

"Well—" I began.

He dazzled me with a smile. "But I'll make an exception in your case. That's how positive I am that we are going to have a long and profitable association."

"I appreciate that," I said.

Bowman touched a button on his desk and the plastic Miss Kirby floated into the office.

"It's almost time for the morning break," he said, "but Miss Kirby will take you in to catch the last few minutes of theatrical speech class."

In the classroom some twenty students sat on floor cushions listening to a young man who was mumbling something unintelligible. I spotted Esther Legrand and her daughter Tina near the front of the group. Both wore flared jeans and tie-dyed shirts. Esther had a loop of beads around her neck, and Tina wore a hammered silver ankh. The kid looked pretty good, the mother would have looked better if she dressed her age. I carried a cushion up front and sat next to them.

For several minutes I listened to the mumbler without understanding a dozen words. To start a conversation with Esther Legrand, I said, "There's a guy who really needs speech lessons."

She gave me an icy look. "That," she said, "is our instructor."

With that conversation out of the way I returned my attention to Mushmouth. Just before I dozed off he must have adjourned the class because my fellow students began standing up and chattering among themselves.

I turned to try again with Esther Legrand, and found her staring back at the doorway where her daughter was in animated conversation with Rex Bowman. He looked over and gave us the big smile and started in our direction. Tina frowned as he walked away from her.

Bowman said, "Glad to see you're getting involved, Alan. It will be about twenty minutes until the next class. You're welcome to sit in."

"Thanks, I'd like to."

"Most of us go up the street to a coffee shop for the break. Would you like to come along?"

"No, thanks," I said. "I'll stay here and look around."

"We'll see you later, then."

When Bowman and the students had trooped out I wandered back into the office part of the building, trying to look inconspicuous. The lobby was still full of aspiring stars. Through the open door of the photography studio I could see Lou Markey arguing with a chubby blonde about which was her good side.

As soon as I had a chance I slipped into Rex Bowman's office. His desk was clean except for the ashtray filled with cigar stubs. I moved to the filing cabinets and started pulling out drawers. Other than the one he had opened for my benefit, they were empty.

A bookcase gave me nothing until I came to a file folder wedged in at the end. The papers inside concerned the financial aspects of Bowmar. I hadn't read very far when I heard the voices of the returning students.

I was heading back toward the classroom when Bowman came in. He answered my smile with an odd look, but said nothing.

According to a schedule pinned on the door, the next class was going to teach us how to walk. I wasn't too surprised to see that the instructor was my friend Mumbles from Theatrical Speech. Before I had a chance to learn much about walking, the bruiser I'd seen leaving Bowman's office came to the door and waggled a finger at me. I walked back to see what he wanted.

"Mr. Bowman has a special class he wants you to take a look at," the big man said.

He led me down the hall toward the back of the building and held the door open while I walked into another room. At that instant I sensed that something was wrong—half a second too late.

The sap hit me high on the back of the neck, in just the right spot and with just enough force. Curly was an artist.

I landed hard on my hands and knees, and tried to shake the buzzing lights out of my head. The room was small and bare with nothing to look at except the blond giant standing spraddle-legged in front of me.

He said, "Mr. Bowman thinks you ought to have a special class in minding your own business."

As I tried to push myself up, he leaned forward and tapped the point of my shoulder with the sap. My right arm went dead and I kissed the floor.

Curly was enjoying himself. He grinned and laid the sap along the side of my jaw. Pain clanged through my head like a fire gong.

"This class is just for private snoopers, Mr. Dickens-Dukane." He leaned over to let me have one in the kidney.

Curly stopped talking then and just moved around me picking his spots. My head had never cleared from the effects of the first blow, and every time I tried to get into some kind of fighting position he would hit me with the sap, just hard enough to put me down again.

After a while Curly tired of the game. Or maybe I wasn't showing enough life anymore to make it interesting.

The last thing I remember was the big blond face saying, "Nightie-night, snooper. Don't come back." He swung the sap at my temple and the lights went out, suddenly and completely.

I awoke to a sound like the surf. Then the sound grew louder and I got a whiff of diesel exhaust. I opened my eyes to see I was parked on a dead-end street next to the Hollywood Freeway. My head and body felt like I'd rolled down a mountain, but nothing seemed to be broken and there were few visible bruises. My wallet and watch were still with me, but the Bowmar contract was gone from my pocket.

As I reached for the ignition I saw that my registration slip had been rotated from the underside of the steering post where I kept it. Bowman must have got suspicious and sent the muscle man out to check my car.

I kicked the engine to life and drove painfully home to my apartment. From there I called a friend on the staff of *The Hollywood Reporter*. She did some checking for me and learned that nobody of importance in the entertainment industry had ever heard of Rex Bowman. He had been a member of the Screen Actors' Guild a few years back, but was dropped for nonpayment of dues.

With a glass of medicinal brandy within reach, I eased my aching frame into a hot tub to soak and think. It was questionable whether Bowman was breaking any laws at his talent school, but at least I had enough information to cause him some trouble with the state licensing board. Also, I had a personal grievance now. Tonight I would pay him a visit and persuade him to let the Legrand ladies down easy, and then we would discuss my bruises.

Rex Bowman's house, I found, was small by Bel Air standards, which means it had something less than twenty rooms. It was after ten o'clock and the streets were empty when I pulled to the curb behind a gray sedan.

I climbed out of my car and started up the walk. When I was halfway to the house the front door opened and a woman ran out. When she saw me the woman stopped, looking around as though for an escape route.

"Hello, Mrs. Legrand," I said.

She went past me with a rush, swinging at my head with something on the end of a silvery chain. I made no move to stop her. She ran awkwardly across the lawn to the sedan, jumped in, and drove off with a shriek of rubber. As I continued up the walk to the open door of Bowman's house I had a feeling I wouldn't like what I found inside.

I didn't.

Rex Bowman sat in the center of a furry white sofa, his head sagging forward as though he were examining the bullet hole in his bare chest where the silk robe gapped open. One hand rested on the back of the sofa while the other lay in his lap with a burnt-out cigar between the fingers.

In front of the sofa was a glass-topped coffee table bearing a heavy ceramic lighter, a clean ashtray, and today's edition of *Daily Variety*. A molded plastic chair was pulled up to face Bowman across the low table.

I went to the telephone and dialed Legrand's number. I told him he'd better get hold of a lawyer and get him out there tonight. Then I called the police.

When Sergeants Connor and Gaines from Homicide arrived I told them as much as I knew, including how I ran into Esther Legrand on her way out. They let me come along when they left for Legrand's house in San Gabriel.

Legrand's lawyer was there when we arrived. He stood protectively behind Esther's chair, advising her whether or not to answer the detectives' questions. Tina, who had been summoned home from a party in Beverly Hills, sulked on the couch next to her father.

Esther Legrand admitted being at Bowman's house, but she refused to say why. Her story was that she found the man dead on the sofa, then ran out the door and panicked when she saw me.

Legrand, in something like shock, said he had no idea his wife had gone to Bowman's place. She had told him she was going to a club meeting, and he spent the evening alone watching television.

While Sergeant Connor questioned the family, Gaines went out to check the gray sedan. In a little while he came in and called his partner aside for a conference.

Gaines handed something to Connor, who came over and dangled it before Esther. It was the silver ankh I'd seen Tina wearing earlier.

"Do you recognize this, Mrs. Legrand?" Connor asked.

Esther turned to the attorney, who shook his head negatively.

The detective turned to me. "How about it, Dukane, is this what Mrs. Legrand swung at you when you met her coming out of the house?"

"It could have been," I said.

Connor returned to Esther. "It was found tucked under the driver's seat of your car."

"I don't know anything about it," she said in a monotone.

Tina spoke up then from the couch. "Oh, Mother, it's no use. They'll find out sooner or later." To Connor she said, "It's mine. I was at Rex Bowman's house tonight. I slipped away from the party and went there—it's only a five-minute drive. We were...in the bedroom when somebody came to the front door. Rex didn't want us to be found together, so he told me to go out the back way. While he slipped on a robe to answer the door, I gathered up my clothes and ran out. I must have dropped the ankh."

"Did you see who was at the door?" Connor asked.

"No."

"It wasn't me," Esther put in. She brushed aside the protests of her lawyer and went on. "Rex and I were..." here she forced herself to look at her husband, "having an affair. When I found out he was seeing Tina too, I went over to have it out with him. When I found Rex dead and Tina's ankh lying on the floor, I was afraid she had killed him. I picked up the ankh and ran out. I still had it in my hand when Dukane saw me."

Sitting motionless on the couch, Frank Legrand looked like he'd just taken a shot between the eyes with a poleax.

While the Legrand family talked themselves into deeper trouble, I got out of there. I wasn't helping anybody, and there were some unformed ideas in the back of my head that I wanted to pull up front and examine.

It was the middle of the morning, and I was on my

third pot of coffee and the last of my cigarettes when I figured it out. All I had to do was prove it, and I thought I knew how.

I drove out to the Bowmar Talent School. The death of the boss hadn't slowed the operation. I found the lobby as full of applicants as the day before. I walked past the reception desk to the office area. Through her open door I saw the plastic Miss Kirby in worried conversation with the mumbling speech teacher. As I continued along the hall, the big blond sap expert rounded a corner in front of me. He put on a weak grin and stuck out his hand. "Hey, no hard feelings, Dukane. Okay?"

I hit him twice in the belly before he could tense his muscles. The big man's mouth flopped open and he turned the color of raw modeling clay. I stepped back and planted my feet for leverage, then let him have my best shot on the hinge of the jaw. His face jerked out of shape and he hit the floor like a felled oak.

"No hard feelings," I said.

Lou Markey looked up from behind the desk when I walked into Bowman's office. His hair was uncombed and his cheeks were sprinkled with orange stubble. The ever-present cigarette smoldered in his hand. It took him a moment to place my face.

"Oh, hello, Dickens. Were you looking for someone?"

"My name isn't Dickens," I said. "It's Dukane. I'm a private investigator."

"Are you here about Rex Bowman?" he asked.

"You know what happened last night?"

"I heard it on the radio early this morning," he said. "I thought I'd better come in and start getting our papers straightened out. There's a lot to be done."

"Does that include changing the name back to the Markey School of Acting?"

"How did you know that?"

"I ran across it in some of Bowman's papers. It looks like he kind of took over your operation."

Markey shrugged. "Rex knew how to make money, I didn't. The new name, Bowmar, was supposed to be a combination of his and mine, but most people thought it just came from Bowman."

"What was he going to do next, phase you out completely?"

Markey's forgotten cigarette singed his fingers and he jumped to light another. "It doesn't make any difference now, does it? As the surviving partner I'll take over the school."

When he had his lungs full of smoke I snapped, "Give me the gun, Markey."

"What gun?"

The words popped out immediately, but Markey's eyes flickered down and to his right.

I got to the desk drawer before he moved, and lifted out the .32 automatic that lay inside. Markey sagged back in the chair and aged ten years before my eyes.

"I didn't go there planning to kill Rex," he said. "But I couldn't let him push me out of my own school the way he planned. I hated what he turned it into, anyway. Sure, he made money, but all the lies he told the kids who came to us. I told him it was wrong to lead them on like that, but Rex wouldn't listen to me. He wouldn't give an inch." He blew his nose, then looked up at me. "Where did I slip up, Dukane? How did you tumble?"

"It was the way you left things in Bowman's living-room after you shot him. Something was wrong, but I didn't pin it until this morning. Bowman was smoking a cigar when he was shot—it went out in his hand. Yet the big ashtray in front of him was empty. Wiped clean. It had to be the killer who cleaned it—not to get rid of Bowman's ashes, but his own. Neither Esther nor Tina Legrand is a smoker. Frank Legrand either, for that matter. But you light one after the other, a distinctive cigarette that would point straight to you."

He stared down at the desk top for a long time, then looked up with the ghost of the crooked smile that belonged to Beano Markey, the comical kid in the high school movies. He said, "You didn't really know I had the gun here, did you?"

"No," I admitted, "but I figured you came straight here, not even going home to shave."

"And you tricked me."

"I just counted on your honesty. You told me you never could fake reactions."

"The critics were right," Markey said. "I'm a bad actor."

THE LITHUANIAN ERASER MYSTERY

by Jon L. Breen

*The humorous short stories of Jon L. Breen are in-jokes
for the mystery enthusiast. Parodying the styles of famous mystery writers such as John Dickson Carr,
S. S. Van Dine and Ellery Queen, they betray the fact
that their creator is a scholar of the mystery story.*

The theatrical season of 1968 began in a disconcerting manner. E. Larry Cune went to a play. For E. Larry
was an unabashed sentimentalist who loved to return
to the scenes of his past detectival triumphs.

Witness, for example, his periodic visits to the small
town of Wyattsville, the New England village that had
the highest per-capita murder rate of any incorporated
community in the world, including even St. Mary Mead,
England. Since murder seemed to follow E. Larry, he
had taken on the aspect of a Jonah, or so some thought;
but the police department of Wyattsville was never sorry
to see him since they had a 100 percent record of so-
lutions to their homicides, a record also unmatched by
any community anywhere.

But this is not a tale of Wyattsville, disappointing
as that may be to the many Wyattsville fans everywhere; it is the story of E. Larry's return to the old and
revered Greek Theatre (the one on Broadway, not the
one in Hollywood), the scene of his first great triumph,
the solution of the vicious murder of Mr. Anagopolous,
an asthmatic but otherwise inoffensive member of the
audience—a case known to the world as *The Greek
Coughin' Mystery.*

That was many years ago, in 1929, when E. Larry
had been in his early thirties, and his father, Inspector
Richard Cune, had been the elderly and respected birdlike bulldog of Centre Street. Now almost forty years
had slipped by, wars had come and gone, skirts had

lowered again and risen again, *pince-nez* and Duesenbergs had gone out of style, science had advanced and humanity deteriorated. Now, in 1968, E. Larry was in his late thirties, and his father, Inspector Richard Cune, was the elderly and respected birdlike bulldog of Centre Street, having survived one serious bout with retirement.

Nostalgically, E. Larry surveyed the huge playhouse from his orchestra seat. He and a full house of first-nighters were waiting to see the premiere of Orson Coward's new musical comedy, *Gold,* a one-man tour de force with book, music, and lyrics by Orson Coward, who had also produced and directed. He had also planned to star as the show's youthful hero, but advancing years and a spreading waistline had led him to retire as a performer, for this production at least. The new show was a musical version of Frank Norris' turn-of-the-century novel, *McTeague.* Many scoffers doubted that this grim naturalistic story of greed and tragedy would make suitable musical comedy material, but after all hadn't Orson Coward made musical successes of Theodore Dreiser's *An American Tragedy* and John Steinbeck's *The Grapes of Wrath*? (It's not true, however, that he paid two million dollars for the theatrical rights to *How To Avoid Probate.*)

Shaking hands with the famed writer-director-producer-composer prior to the curtain, E. Larry was conscious of an edginess in Orson Coward's manner, something he had never seen there in the many years he had known Orson Coward, dating back to the thirties when the then-boy wonder could have played teen-aged heroes with ease. Thus, tonight's nervousness could hardly be ascribed to opening-night jitters.

As they parted, E. Larry to return to his seat and Orson Coward to return backstage, the great man (Orson Coward, not E. Larry) said, "The show must go on, you know."

Must go on.

In spite of what?

Had that been fear in Orson Coward's demeanor?

What had he to fear?

E. Larry, of course, realized that his very presence at any function put the fear of sudden death in all those around him. He hadn't attended a play, sports event, or party in years without having to solve a murder at some time during the festivities, perhaps because so many potential murderers (and, in fact, their victims) leaped at the opportunity to match wits with him. But why was Orson Coward so sure he'd be tonight's victim? This would bear watching.

The curtain rose.

E. Larry had seen from his program that the first musical number was to be an ensemble titled "Be a Friend to Your Dentist." So he was surprised to see the show's ingenue, Pat Alison, come onto the stage and immediately begin to sing "Never Been Kissed," a sentimental ballad that was scheduled to close the first act.

"E. Larry, that's not right," squealed Nora Redcap, his companion of the evening.

"I know," said E. Larry. And as he watched the lovely young Pat Alison sing the words of the haunting melody, he thought he noticed an expression of puzzlement on her face, as though this change in the program were a surprise to her too.

Apparently the script had been rewritten sufficiently so that the opening number seemed naturally placed. Although several actors were somewhat unsure of their lines, the story progressed well enough until the time came for the second song. It proved to be "Alone in My Solitude," sung by the show's star, Van Washington, portraying the young dentist McTeague.

"E. Larry," Nora implored him, "that song isn't supposed to come until the second act! And it doesn't make sense to have two pensive ballads in a row. I don't understand this at all."

"Nor do I," said E. Larry pensively.

Van Washington was in good voice, but his face also betrayed a lack of understanding.

For some reason Orson Coward had changed the order of the musical numbers, E. Larry told himself.

Why? What did it mean?

Closing the initial scene, Washington appeared again, lustily singing the show's biggest potential hit, "I Know the Score Now."

"E. Larry," Nora almost screamed, "that's supposed to be the finale!"

"You're right, Nora," E. Larry said.

"He's ruining the show, E. Larry."

Orson Coward ruining a show? A man with his sense of showmanship, with his dedication to the theater? E. Larry told himself it could not be. Somehow, subtly, Orson Coward must be improving the show.

After the first three, the songs came in their proper order and the actors seemed more at ease, as though playing the show as rehearsed. By the curtain of Act One the enthralled audience had almost forgotten the curious early events of the evening.

During intermission a man E. Larry recognized as Hugh Vivyan, a backer of the show and longtime friend of Orson Coward, rushed up to E. Larry's aisle seat, saying breathlessly, "Mr. Cune, you must come backstage at once! Orson Coward has been murdered!"

Grieved but scarcely surprised, E. Larry followed the distraught "angel." He found Orson Coward's body lying in a hallway off the dressing rooms. The writer-director-producer-composer had been murdered by a heavy blow to the head, obviously the work of a blunt instrument. A volume entitled *The Complete Wit of Orson Coward,* found near the body, appeared to be the weapon.

Standing over the body were Pat Alison, the ingenue; Van Washington, the star; Millicent Grady, the wardrobe lady; Alfie Tanager, the stage manager; Flossy Blore, a Broadway showgirl romantically linked with Orson Coward; and Victor Towne, the assistant producer.

Washington was saying, "This is a calamity, Towne! What a loss to show business!"

Victor Towne nodded gravely. Flossy Blore wept quietly into her crocodile bag. Millicent Grady's beady eyes darted back and forth. Alfie Tanager looked truculent. Pat Alison looked ingenuous.

"Mr. Cune, who could possibly have done this terrible thing?" Towne asked.

"I don't know, Mr. Towne. Yet. But I know this: Orson Coward expected to be murdered tonight. He left me a clue to his murderer's identity."

"A clue?" said Pat Alison. "How?"

"By his rearrangement of the musical numbers in the show," E. Larry reasoned.

"So that's it!" exclaimed Van Washington. "We couldn't understand why he did that. Five minutes before curtain he handed each of us a revised script."

"Each of us" included 89 principals and 203 singers and dancers, most of whom were now milling around behind the great Greek Theatre curtain, since there was not enough room to join the suspects in the hallway.

"Mr. Tanager," E. Larry told the stage manager, "check with the unions and see if one of your men can call Centre Street. Have him ask for Inspector Cune, the birdlike bulldog. I expect to have this case wrapped up before dad gets here, though."

"Mr. Cune," said Vivvan, the backer, "why didn't Orson say something if he expected to be murdered? Why did he simply allow it to happen, do nothing to prevent it?"

"When he saw me in the audience," E. Larry admitted sadly, "he knew there was no hope; he was doomed. Showman that he was, he knew his role now was to leave me a dying message, or a pre-dying one in this case, to help me deduce the murderer."

"Can't you solve a murder without a dying message?"

"Yes, but it usually takes me a whole novel to do it. I should wrap up this one in a few thousand words."

"I hope so," Van Washington said fervently. "The curtain for Act Two is already overdue."

"Yes, indeed," said E. Larry. "So let's get on with this at once." Suddenly E. Larry's keen silvery eyes spotted something on the floor near the body. He stooped to pick it up. "Ah, just what I've been looking for!"

"What's that, Mr. Cune?" Towne asked.

"A rubber eraser." He turned it over. On the less worn side was clearly stamped: MADE IN LITHUANIA.

"Is that a clue, Mr. Cune?" Pat Alison asked.

"We shall see, Miss Alison," E. Larry replied, slipping the eraser into his pocket. "Now to the message: what do those three songs in sequence mean?

'Never Been Kissed'
'Alone in My Solitude'
'I Know the Score Now'

How do they apply to the people here? I seriously doubt that any of you has never been kissed. One or more may be lonely, but that seems tenuous as a clue. Was anyone here ever an athlete, amateur or professional?"

"I played football in college," Vivyan admitted. "Second string all-American."

"Are you lonely?"

"Well, I guess so—but no lonelier than the average Broadway show backer."

"Have you ever been kissed?"

"Really, Mr. Cune, is this necessary?"

"Have you ever been kissed?"

"Yes, frequently. I've been married four times."

"All right, Mr. Vivyan. No need to get excited. Let's take a different approach. The letters of the first words of each of these songs—do they spell anything?"

"N-A-I," said Nora Redcap, who had joined the group backstage. "I don't see any meaning in that, E. Larry."

"Try the last letters."

"D-E-W. That could mean something. But what?"

"Early morning, I suppose. How about spelling it backward?"

"W-E-D."

"And the first letters?" exclaimed E. Larry, triumph rising in his voice.

"I-A-N."

E. Larry whirled to face the other ladies present. "Has any of you ever been married to a man named Ian?"

"No, no Ian," Flossy Blore said. Pat Alison and Millicent Grady shook their heads.

E. Larry struck his forehead with the heel of his hand. "Who is this Ian? Whom did he wed? If we can find a woman who has been married to a man named Ian, we'll have the killer!"

The assembly seemed impressed. E. Larry was in the fervor of creative ratiocination that his intimates knew so well.

"Imagine Orson telling us so much," Van Washington marveled, "simply by changing the order of the numbers."

Suddenly E. Larry stopped in his tracks.

"Numbers. Numbers. Of course! I'm an idiot, a moron, a gibbering imbecile. I should have seen it at once. How could I have been so blind? Numbers!"

"Numbers, E. Larry?" A small birdlike man had appeared on the scene.

"You're just in time, dad. I've cracked the case."

"It's just like 1929 all over again!" said Inspector Cune, beaming.

Hugh Vivyan appeared thunderstruck at the remark. "My God! I must call my broker at once!"

Inspector Cune, his face mirroring puzzlement, watched the backer's retreating back. "Why's he in such a hurry, son? Is he the killer?"

"No, let him go, dad, he's not the culprit. Mr. Tanager, I'm going to address the audience. Open the curtain. The rest of you come out, too, and we'll wrap this thing up the way Orson Coward would have wanted."

CHALLENGE TO THE READER:*Who killed Orson Coward? And how did E. Larry know? What was the meaning of Orson Coward's pre-dying message? All the clues are now in your possession, so match wits with E. Larry Cune.*

The stage manager shrugged resignedly and signaled for the great Greek Theatre curtain to open, to the surprise of hundreds of extras. E. Larry then walked onto the stage, raising his hands for silence, and the others filed quietly out behind him, even the star Van Washington content in this instance to play a supporting role.

"Ladies and gentlemen, I regret to announce that there has been an unfortunate occurrence—"

Immediately men with black bags began making their way to the aisles all over the massive playhouse.

"No, we don't need a doctor. I must tell you that Orson Coward is dead." A startled roar from the audience. "Murdered." This came as an anticlimax, since most of them had already recognized the famous E. Larry Cune.

"Fortunately, Mr. Coward left behind a clue to his murderer's identity. You may have noticed that the first three musical numbers in tonight's performance were not in the order indicated on your program. This was devised by Mr. Orson Coward to tell me who he *knew* was planning to kill him.

"Note the titles of the three numbers, ladies and gentlemen:

> 'Never Been Kissed'
> 'Alone in My Solitude'
> 'I Know the Score Now'

What does each of these suggest?

"Each suggests a number," E. Larry italicized. "For instance—sweet *sixteen* and never been kissed."

The crowd gasped at the revelation.

"Now, what number does 'Alone in My Solitude' suggest?"

"One!" shouted a voice from the balcony.

"Right! And the third title, 'I Know the Score Now'?"

Silence.

"Score, score!" E. Larry insisted.

"Twenty!" Inspector Cune exclaimed.

"Exactly, dad," said a proud son. "Twenty. Now examine the three numbers—16, 1, 20. What do they tell us?"

Silence.

"It's a simple code. *The numbers represent the letters of the alphabet.* A equals 1, B equals 2, C equals 3, and so on. Thus the sixteenth letter is—"

Suddenly Pat Alison was running across the stage, but her flight was interrupted when she became trapped in the hammy hands and beefy arms of Sergeant Healy.

The audience was on its feet giving E. Larry Cune a standing ovation in recognition of the long established fact that he, like Orson Coward, was a great showman.

As the tumult subsided, Inspector Cune said, "But, E. Larry, will we have a strong enough case to stand up in court?"

"I don't know, dad. Thank God I'm not the District Attorney."

"I must tell you something," said Millicent Grady, the wardrobe lady. "I'm her mother; Orson Coward, my ex-husband, was her father. She hated him for keeping me on in such a menial position, but I really liked it for I still loved him. And I can reveal now that she was once married to Ian Fellmer, the spy-story writer."

"Now I know we have a case that'll stand up in court," said Inspector Cune with birdlike satisfaction.

"I'm relieved, dad. I hate to have my cases end in messy suicides." E. Larry did not know at the time that Hugh Vivyan had just leaped nine stories to the sidewalk below from his broker's office on Wall Street.

"I have just one question, Mr. Cune," said Victor Towne, the assistant producer. "What did the Lithuanian eraser have to do with the case?"

"Not a thing really. But doesn't it make a marvelous title?"

ON DIFFERENT TRACKS

by Michael Scott Cain

Michael Scott Cain is a writer and poet (he has published three volumes of poetry) who writes mystery stories because he loves them. He has published a novel, Jason's Song, *and is working on a mystery concerning television evangelism. "On Different Tracks" deals with rock and roll, reflecting another interest of the author. Mr. Cain says that he is planning a crime novel about the rock music industry but is having trouble coming up with a crime the industry has not yet committed.*

Richie was going over his royalty statements when I came in. Sitting crosslegged on the couch, a pile of papers on the cushion to his right, he frowned as he punched figures into his calculator. The scent of some expensive perfume hung lightly in the air. He must have chased a chick out just before he called me.

"What's up, Richie?" I said.

He held his hand out, signaling me to wait, and hit the total button. The figure disgusted him and he snarled under his breath, tossing the calculator aside.

"Damn it, I can't catch them," he said. "I don't know how they're doing it."

"Let it go, Richie. The auditors couldn't find a thing in the company's books. They aren't cheating you."

"Yeah, well, I guess you'd feel that way."

I wasn't used to the tone in his voice. "What are you talking about?"

"Burt was down at Wildwood over the weekend, doing the games on the boardwalk."

That figured. Burt, Richie's keyboard player, was a freak for amusement parks. A pinball machine could transport him to heights he'd never hit with his synthesizers.

"So?"

"Guess what he won playing pinball?"

"What?"

95

"This." He held up an album. The cover showed Richie, decked out in New Wave finery, holding his guitar in a Chuck Berry machine-gun pose. The title, *Madman in Love,* ran across the top of the cover. Richie's name, in the same typeface, balanced the cover across the bottom.

"Terrific," I said. "I didn't know they were ready to ship yet. The company rush them or what?"

Richie tossed the album onto the floor. "They *haven't* shipped yet. The covers haven't even been printed."

"Then where'd they get that one?"

"It's a pirate!" Richie shouted. "They're all over the East Coast! By tomorrow they'll be nationwide. Somebody ripped off the album."

"Oh, no."

These days a new album by Richie Clete was a big deal. You know him. You've probably got a couple of his records in your stacks. For years he was just another journeyman rocker; every album he cut was a total stiff and he barely kept alive by staying out on the road all year long, building up a following. His label dropped him and when Jeff Weiss, his manager, tried to line up another deal he found nobody wanted Richie. It took a while, but Jeff finally got a new label deal. Richie hired a new producer, and with the first album for the new company lightning struck. Now his albums ship double platinum—he sells about 100,000 units a day. With those figures, it was inevitable that pirates would start putting out counterfeit Richie Clete records.

I'd been with him from the beginning. He was my oldest friend in the world and when he went on the road I went with him as his sound man. I'm the guy you see in the back of the auditorium working a huge console. My job is to balance all the sounds coming out of those speakers and to compensate for lousy acoustics. If I'm not at the console, the guitars sound like cats scratching a post and the synthesizers sound like the death screams of a computer.

I also engineer the records. I enhance Richie's voice and keep the instruments sounding the way they're supposed to. When we're in the studio only two people touch the tapes we cut: Richie and me. That's why he was looking at me that way now.

"What do you figure happened, Carl?" he asked.

"Somebody at the label must be on the take. It wouldn't be the first time. Pirates have people in all the companies."

"I don't think it happened that way, Carl."

"Oh?"

"Even if they worked at top speed, going overtime around the clock, they'd need six weeks to get hold of the tapes, dupe them, master them, and press the records." He paused to let that sink in. "Where were the tapes six weeks ago, Carl?"

"At the mixing studio. We were polishing the mix."

"That's right. Under your supervision."

"Look, Richie, I wouldn't do a thing like that. We're friends, man. I wouldn't sell out a friend."

"I always *thought* we were friends, Carl. Now I'm not so sure."

"I'm telling you, Richie—I didn't do it."

"You're going to jail, Carl. And that's not all. I'm going to slap you with a lawsuit that'll have you spinning till you hit your grave."

"Listen, Richie—"

"Get out of here, man," he said. "You disgust me."

Once the word got out that Richie'd accused me of pirating, I'd be through in the business. Rock is a big-money game and when you're dealing with a product that has a multi-million-dollar potential you don't mess around with a man who's even been *accused* of dealing himself an extra hand. If I intended to stay in this business I had to find out what was going down. I took a cab to June Ameling's mixing studio, Electric Juniper.

June was on the phone. She waved at me and spoke into the receiver. She was a tall woman and the spiked boots she liked to wear made her tower over regular-sized people like me. She'd been doing PR for one of the major labels and noticed that the bands had to go out of town to find a first-rate mixing studio. When her marriage went down the tubes she needed a challenge, so she opened Electric Juniper. It had been a hit from the first day.

June was all business. When you rented time from

her, you showed up when you were supposed to and did your job. She wouldn't hold studios. The backlog was so great that if you were two hours late you found somebody else working at your console—she'd rerent your studio to the next person on the waiting list. Try not paying her—and you'd be surprised how many people in this business try not to pay—and she'd confiscate your tapes, holding them for ransom. She could afford to be autocratic because Electric Juniper was the best there was, a state-of-the-art studio all the way.

She told the record-company heavy on the phone that she didn't care how much he was going to make. "Make a billion for all I care but if you don't come up with the seventeen thousand you owe me you're going to have to make it without those tapes."

She hung up while the heavy was still telling her what his lawyers were going to do to her. Turning to me, she said, "How's it going, Carl?"

"Somebody ripped off Richie's new album."

Her face whitened. "From here?"

"I'm afraid so."

"You know, Larry split a while back." Larry was her engineer. He worked as assistant on our records. "No notice or anything. He just didn't show up one morning and he hasn't been in since."

"About six weeks ago?"

She checked her calendar. "Yeah."

"That's it then. Did he have access to the safe?"

"He wasn't supposed to, but he could have gotten hold of the combination. It's possible."

"You sound a little dubious."

"Every studio here has its own safe. I change the combinations with each job. You know how carefully musicians guard those tapes. If my place isn't secure I'm out of the business."

"But still Larry disappeared at the same time our tapes did."

"Too strong for coincidence, isn't it?"

"I'll go by his place. If he shows up here, hold him for me, will you?"

I left June watching her studio's reputation go down the drain.

* * *

Larry didn't answer his door. I checked around and the super told me he hadn't seen him for a month or so. "Tell him if he wants his stuff," he said, "he can come up with the rent."

I told him I'd pass on the message and went home. A short barrel-bellied man waited by my door.

"You Carl Boswell?" He had big sad eyes.

"Yeah."

He followed me inside. I didn't resist.

"My name's Sherill. David Sherill." He flashed a badge. "I'm with the F.B.I."

"Richie called you guys in already?"

He looked puzzled. "Richie?"

"Richie Clete."

"Oh, the guy who made the record? No, the record company alerted us this morning. You work for Clete, don't you?"

We stood in the center of the living room. I told him to sit down. "Richie fired me this morning," I said. "He thinks I duped his tapes."

"He thinks you did what?"

"Duped. Had a duplicate made."

"I see." He frowned. "And did you?"

"No. I think Larry Boucher did it."

He looked at me doubtfully. "Larry Boucher?"

"An engineer at the mixing studio."

"The what?"

"You don't know a whole lot about record-making, do you?"

He shrugged. "This is my first record-piracy case."

I sighed. "Look, there are a couple of things you have to understand about the way records are made. Every studio has its advantages and drawbacks. Some do voices well, others are good for guitars, others are keyed to synthesizers."

"You use different studios then?"

"Yes. Records are made on different tracks. We use up to twenty-four. We put the lead guitar on one, the voice on another, the rhythm guitar on track three—like that. Since we record at different times in different studios you can imagine how the whole thing sounds when it's first played back together."

"Rough, huh?"

"Exactly. So we take it to another studio and mix it. Get all the instruments in balance, bring the voices out, all that. Mixing is to a record what editing is to a film. We take all the tapes into the studio and come out with one finished tape. An average record can be turned into a killer. Blow the mix and a killer can turn into a stiff."

"That's the last part of the process?"

"The last part of the *recording* process. After that, we turn them in to the company. They master the tapes and press the records."

"You're losing me again. Master the tapes?"

"Records are pressed from a silver disc called a master. It's a printing plate for a record."

"The tapes would have to be mastered before they could be pirated, wouldn't they?"

"No, anybody who can get his hands on the tapes can get a master made. There are thousands of mastering plants in this country, a dozen right here in the city. They'll do business with anybody who comes through the door."

"And this Boucher had access?"

"He worked in the mixing studio."

"There's something wrong. If you were still mixing the tapes, how could he steal them?"

"We were just sweetening. For all practical purposes, they were ready to go."

"Sweetening?" There was a pained look on his face.

"Punching up the sound. You know, highlighting a little, for the real sound freaks."

"I see. I have one other problem with this Boucher though," he said dryly.

"What's that?"

"The record company gave me a list of suspects. Boucher's name was there. I checked them all with the police. Boucher's dead."

"What?" Had Sherill been playing with me? Did he suspect me?

"They fished him out of the river a few days ago. The body had been in there for a while and you know what that can do. They just nailed down the ID this morning." He frowned. "Somebody bashed in the back of his head."

"His partners killed him?"

"Possibly." He stood and stretched. "Considering the time frame, it's a safe bet the mastering was done in the city. I'll need you to help me find out where."

"If Boucher's dead, why do you need to know that?"

"Because we have a murder now. Whoever did this with him—that is, if Boucher was involved at all—killed him. I want that person."

I put my coat on. "Let's go then."

Sherill drove a plain brown Ford so nondescript it could only have belonged to him.

We started hitting the mastering plants. At the fifth one we got lucky. The owner, a balding little man who spoke through a cigar clenched between his teeth, glared at us when Sherill asked about his recent jobs.

"Hey, who knows from anything?" he said. "Guy comes in wants a job done, I do the job. I'm a businessman."

"Then you mastered the Richie Clete album."

"Who's to know? Maybe I did, maybe I didn't. When did it come in?"

"About six weeks ago."

He flipped through his ledger. "Nope. No Clete here."

"Wait a minute," I said. "Richie Clete's the artist, not the guy who brought the job in."

"Who's to know from artist? I got customers, not artists."

Sherill said, "It would probably have been a rush job, wouldn't it?"

"It would have to be," I said.

He stepped nearer to the cigar-smoking man. "Do you do rush jobs? Maybe at premium prices, while the customer waits?"

"Damn right. This is a competitive business. Why? You got one?"

Tapping the ledger book, Sherill said, "Check it out. Five, six weeks ago."

He ran his fingers over the pages. "Here's one."

"What's the name?"

"Sam Oakley."

Sherill didn't react until we were outside. Neither

did I. When we were in the car Sherill said, "You know the name?"

"Everybody knows Sam Oakley's name. He's connected, isn't he? Look, I didn't realize this was mob stuff."

"What did you expect? Record piracy's big business. About a quarter of the records and maybe half the tapes on the market are counterfeit."

"You figure Boucher went to Oakley?"

"Maybe. But there's another factor here."

"What's that?"

"Sam Oakley's brother was married to June Ameling. He's her brother-in-law. We might just have a family affair here."

"How do you know that?"

He started up the car and checked to see if the street was clear. Pulling out into the traffic he said, "It's my job to know stuff like that."

We watched an F.B.I. crew go over the studio.

"I should have known Sam would be messed up in this," June said.

Before I could answer, an investigator over near the safe called out to Sherill, who walked over to him.

After an uncomfortable silence June said, "I didn't do this, Carl, you know that. I've got a good thing here. Why would I mess it up?"

Sherill came back in time to pick up what she'd said. "Greed's always a possibility," he said. "Miss Ameling, there's what looks like dried blood and a whole bunch of disinfectant stains on the carpet near the safe there. It looks like your man was killed right here. Probably by whoever was opening the safe."

"Larry died *here*? That's terrible!"

"You're going to have to come down to the office with me."

"You've got it wrong, Sherill," I said. "June wouldn't do a thing like this. It doesn't make sense."

"From where I'm standing, it does. I'm sorry, Miss Ameling, but I'm going to have to take you in for questioning."

As he led her out, I tried to tell myself he was right, she'd killed Larry and sold the tapes. I watched him close the car door behind her and figured I'd better go see Richie.

I caught up with Richie at The Pit. Up-and-coming bands showcased there, so whenever he was in town Richie fell by to check out the competition.

He was at a table with three girls. I tapped him on the shoulder and when he turned I shouted so he could hear me over the music.

"Get out of here, Carl," he said, turning his eyes back to the stage.

A singer wearing pancake and black eyeliner moaned out minimal lyrics in front of a four-piece group. I knew Richie hated that stuff, but he pretended to be engrossed in it.

"We have to talk," I said.

"We got nothing to talk about, creep."

"It's important, man. I know who ripped off those tapes."

He stroked one of the girl's shoulders. "So do I, creep."

"The F.B.I. just busted June Ameling."

He looked up at me. "You putting me on?"

"Come outside so we can talk."

He flashed the girls a grin and followed me out into the street. The night was chilly. I pulled up my collar and leaned against a parked car. We could still hear the throbbing of the music.

"The feds got June?" he said.

"Richie, Larry Boucher's dead. Somebody bashed in the back of his head."

"You're kidding! June wasted Larry?"

"No," I said. "I figure *you* did."

His face turned mean. "You'd better get out of my sight, man."

"What was it, all of Jeff's paranoia about the record company ripping you off? You figured to pick up a little extra money at their expense?"

"I'm warning you, Carl."

I ignored him. "I think you got greedy. You felt the label was cheating you so you figured why not pick up the difference by pirating your own record."

"You're crazy! That would be like stealing from myself!"

"Not if you thought you were already being stolen from. You'd see it as a way of recouping. You took the tapes, Larry saw you, and you wasted him. What'd you do, hit him with a reel of tape?"

"Look, I don't know what this fantasy of yours is, but I don't want to play."

"You knew the cops would be nosing around about Larry—after all, he wouldn't stay at the bottom of the river forever—so you set me up. I don't know how you could have done it, man. I thought we were friends."

"I told you, I don't want to play! What makes you think I wasted Larry? Whoever hit that safe could've done it."

"Not just anybody. Larry got the back of his head crushed. There was no struggle, nothing messed up. June just figured he'd split—that's how calm it was. It had to be somebody he knew, somebody he trusted enough to turn his back on. He got his head bashed in by a friend."

"You're crazy, man. I didn't waste anybody. It had to be June. The feds got her, didn't they?"

"I thought about that. But June wouldn't ruin her business for a quick buck. You and I are the only other people who could have gotten that safe open. I didn't do it. That leaves you."

"Yeah, well, that's your fantasy. You can't tie it on me."

"I don't have to. An F.B.I. man named Sherill's going to do that. You're through, Richie."

"And you came to gloat? Is that it?"

I shook my head. "I came here," I said, "because until this morning I thought we were friends."

I turned and walked away, huddling inside my coat for warmth. As I walked home, I remembered the old days on the road, the hustling and scrambling years with Richie, and felt very much alone.

MURDER IN THE MOVIES

by Karl Detzer

The author of more than one-thousand articles and stories for a wide variety of magazines including the Saturday Evening Post and Collier's, Karl Detzer served as an editor at the Reader's Digest for more than forty years. Among his many awards are the Distinguished Service Medal, earned in World War II, the Gold Medallion of the Freedoms Foundation, and an honorary doctorate from the University of Indiana, received in 1979. Although fiction represents only a small proportion of Mr. Detzer's tremendous output, most of it, like the story you are about to read, was of the highest quality.

Jack Harter was murdered; no argument there. He died of a .32-caliber bullet through his heart. That's in the record. The murder took place on sound stage Number 21 on the Titanic studio lot in Hollywood, the night of April 13th. The time was somewhere between eleven o'clock and eleven-five, which is close enough.

This much is history and nobody denies it. So why do I bring it up? Because this month the Hollywood fan magazines began picking the case to pieces again, saying the whole story hasn't been told; ran pictures of Jack Harter, and Marie Fleming, and Sam Masterford, and Joe Gatski, and Joan Nelson, and Rose Graham, with question marks all around them. One of the magazines even used my picture. It said, "Has property man told all?" Think of that!

The writers of a Hollywood fan magazine have to have something to write about, I suppose. But there isn't any mystery in the Jack Harter case, and never was, except between eleven o'clock that night and four in the morning. By the time the city police got there (and I admit we were a bit slow in calling them) all the cops needed to do was write the answer down in the book.

I'm telling it now, just the way it happened, so that

there needn't be any more pictures surrounded by question marks.

To begin with, there were thirteen of us on Stage 21 at the instant the murder occurred, on the night of the thirteenth, and maybe that had something to do with it, and maybe not. Thirteen on the stage, and one man guarding the door.

It had been a tough day on Joe Gatski's unit. Gatski was the supervisor, what's called an associate producer on some lots. He was the big shot on this particular production, understand, responsible to the front office for bringing it in under schedule and holding down costs and making it good box office. He picked the story, and the writers, and the director, and the star, and the extras, and the camera and sound crews, everybody. It was his baby.

This was a fourteen-day job, according to the production charts, which means that from the time the camera first turned over on it till the last retake was in the cutting room, would be two weeks. And not ten minutes over. What's more, it looked as if we'd beat the schedule, too.

We started grinding the morning of the first, and here it was the thirteenth at eleven o'clock at night, and only one shot to finish before midnight, and we'd wrap it up in thirteen days. Thirteenth of the month, thirteen days of shooting, and thirteen people on the sound stage, and up pops a murder. Quite a combination of cause and effect, if you believe some people.

That morning the call board had us booked for a location shot out in Cahuenga Pass at eight o'clock. We had that shot in the can before eleven, and were at the studio and through with lunch and all set up to go on the back lot at one o'clock. This was a trucking shot in the Paris street, a retake of one we'd done the week before. Joe Gatski had picked it to pieces in the rushes, and ordered Sam Masterford to shoot it over.

Then we went back to the sound stage and worked in a couple of added comedy gags that Gatski had figured out which couldn't have got by the Hays office, but we shot them anyhow. Everything going fine, you see, until three o'clock, and then Gatski came out on the stage and began to cause trouble. He didn't think we were putting our heart into his gags, so he turned on the old temperament. That was easy for Gatski.

You'd think from the way he hollered and swooned and swore that this was a million-dollar opus we were shooting. But it wasn't. It was a little item called *Back of the Boulevard*. Maybe you remember it, that mystery piece laid in Paris where an American detective saves the life of the Park Avenue girl. If it cost a nickle over a hundred grand to produce, well, the business manager must have been cheating again. Just an ordinary Class B flicker, for double runs in the nabe houses—that's all it was intended for.

Marie Fleming was the star and Jack Harter played opposite her. Funny coincidence, too, because Jack used to be her husband, and not so long ago, either. She married him in 1931, when they both were just a couple of contract players. By the next year her name was in the lights on the marquee, a full-time star. And in 1931 she met Clem Batting, and she divorced Jack and married Clem before you could say Joseph B. Mankiewitz.

Jack never was a star and never would be. But everybody figured he was good for male leads for ten more years and for good character parts the rest of his life. He was a good actor, you see, but not one of these pretty boys.

I say it was a coincidence, Marie and Jack playing opposite each other. But nothing more than that. They didn't get hostile to each other the way a lot of people do after the divorce. It was always "Hi, Jack!" when she met him, and he'd answer "'Lo, Marie!" and they'd act glad to see each other. Why, one night the newspapers got pictures of them dancing together at the Troc.

You'd think that it would be easy to handle them in a love scene, then, wouldn't you? Well, it wasn't. Sam Masterford, the director of this opus, had plenty of trouble whenever they got together. And in this fade-out shot, it was a real headache.

Oh, they went through all the motions of falling into each other's arms; they followed the book on dialogue; and he planted the kiss on her lips for a good long ten count. But somehow, it didn't jell. It was phony, if you get what I mean. The customers wouldn't believe it in a thousand years.

So here we were, on the night of April 13th, making the fade-out again. It was a simple dolly shot, of the two of them going into the clinch, while the camera trucked forward on them. Do it right once, and the picture'd be finished.

It's always a tough proposition, in the last hours of any production, whether it's a colossal super-super or just a plain quickie. Like an orchestra winding up faster and faster for the final big um-pah. Nerves are ready to snap, and the emotions come right up to the skin where it's worn thin. It takes only one small drink to get a man drunk on the cleanup night. You get mad easy, and you find yourself laughing like hell at something that really isn't funny. And you're just as like as not to fall in love with anybody that happens to be around.

I can't explain it exactly. But ask anybody that's ever worked in a studio. Grover Jones should have written a piece about it.

To make things worse this night, here was Joe Gatski being a general nuisance and giving bad advice and getting in everybody's way. Sam Masterford, the director, was trying to hold things together. He was sweating and pale. It was like trying to drive a four-horse chariot with Joe Gatski scaring the horses. We started shooting the fade-out at eight o'clock, and had made two takes on it, neither of which satisfied Masterford, and were in the middle of the third when Gatski hollered, "Cut!"

"What's wrong with that?" Jack Harter asked.

"Everything," Gatski answered. He could have an insulting voice when he wanted to, and this night he sure did want to. "There's two ways of doing that scene, Harter," he said, "Clark Gable's way and your way. And strange as it may seem, the people like Gable's way best. You better try it."

Sam Masterford said, "I thought they were going through it pretty well that time, Joe."

Joe didn't even look at him. He just said, "*You* thought, did you? You better tell it to Louella, so she can put in her newspaper column. 'Sam Masterford has a thought.'"

Sam started to answer, then he put his hands in the pockets of his slacks and walked slowly out into the lights. Sweat was running off his long, thin nose and his lips were moving in and out, but he wasn't saying anything.

"What about it, Sam?" Marie asked.

"We'll rest a few minutes," the director answered. "Then we'll do it again."

The gaffer—he's the chief electrician—hollered "Save 'em!" and the light operators up on the scaffolds threw their switches and the big floods and stone lights went out, and the spots and baby spots on the floor dimmed. Marie was still in Jack's arms all this time. He sort of pushed her away now and crossed to his dressing table and sat down and began to pat his forehead with a piece of cotton, very carefully, to take off the perspiration without smearing the make-up. And Joan Nelson, the hairdresser, came up behind Marie and started to fix her back hair where it had got mussed up in Jack's arms.

Marie's stand-in was over by the bulletin board, and Marie called to her: "You run along home, honey. I'll not need you again tonight."

Her voice seemed to startle Joe Gatski, for he got up quickly and walked out to the middle of the set.

"Listen, you two!" he yelled. "You, Fleming, and you, Harter. I'm sick of this. Me, spending all this money to get a fade-out right, and you double-crossing me! Now, when you put on that scene, put it on hot! What I mean, hot!"

Gatski was a little man, about forty years old, with a bay window like a basketball and a voice like a baseball umpire's. He began tramping up and down now, and his heels, hitting the floor, made echoes up against the roof, in spite of the acoustic lining. And as soon as he was through with Marie and Jack, he turned on Masterford.

"You call yourself a director?" he hollered. "A director! Why, you couldn't direct a dog and pony act! You know this is costing me money? You know what money is? Or don't you know anything?"

Masterford didn't answer, just kept on sweating, all over his pale, high, narrow forehead, and blinking his gray eyes behind his thick glasses. A good director, Sam Masterford, even if he did get his start in horse operas. He looked at his watch after a while and called, "Ready, Marie? How about you, Jack? Okay, then. All ready, everybody. This is going to be the one we print."

He always said that when things weren't breaking right, and he had to shoot a scene over and over. Sort of pep talk. All directors use it. It's their idea of psychology.

Well, we all were hoping he was right this time. Rose Graham, the script girl, held her script book up so no one could see her yawn, and went back to the little folding chair in front of the camera and sat down.

The three men on the scaffolds got set, and when Otto Schmidt, the gaffer, yelled "Lights!" they threw on the heat. The set wasn't much, just a plain interior with a window and a sunlight arc shining through it, and a table with some books on it down left, and this door. In the previous scene Jack had come in the door and halted, and then the camera panned around to show Marie looking at him. She lifted her arms to him slowly while the camera trucked forward, and then the script called for a cut to this dolly shot of the two of them.

We started in on it again, the fourth take since supper. Some directors would have been boiling, but Sam stayed cool, on the surface at least. The cameras were grinding, and everybody was hoping this would be the last one when Gatski began to yell again.

"If I wanted Ann Harding in this production, I'd hire her," he said to Marie. "Who ever gave you the idea that the fade-out was supposed to cool off the audience? The idea is to send 'em out heated up!"

Marie answered, in a voice everybody could hear, "You're a worm, Joe."

"After how I build you up!" he screamed. "Talking to me like that! Why, you little—" But he choked up trying to find a word.

"Hold everything, Mr. Gatski!" Jack Harter hollered. "Don't say it to her!"

"Oh," Joe answered, surprised, because featured players aren't in the habit of speaking up to supervisors. "So you don't want us to pick up your option, eh?"

"I don't give a damn," Jack told him, and you could see he meant it. "I'm through with pictures."

"You said it," Joe snapped.

"And with you potbellied leeches that—"

Sam Masterford broke in.

"Come on, everybody. Our nerves are shaky. Let's rest again. Get out and take a breath of air." He hesitated and added quickly, "But no liquor, understand that!"

"Give us fifteen minutes, Sam," Marie begged.

"Sure," he answered, and the gaffer yelled to save 'em and the lights went out again, and Joe Gatski groaned, remembering he was paying the grips and the camera crew and the sound men overtime.

"I'll go over to Charley's and get a cup of coffee," Marie explained. "Come on, Jack."

We watched them leave the set, Marie and her ex-husband, arm in arm, and I couldn't help thinking what a screwy business the movies turned out to be. How anybody can keep his senses!

When they had gone, Joe Gatski said to himself, "A worm, eh? After all I done for her! And that louse thinking he could get away with taking her part!"

He started to walk again, back beyond another set, at the other side of the sound stage, and his heels hit the floor, bang, bang, bang. Marie and Jack were gone about fifteen minutes, maybe twenty. It was five minutes to eleven when they got back, according to Murphy's watch. Murphy was the studio policeman at the stage door who checked every last person in and out.

The way we knew they were back was that we heard Marie laugh. It was a genuine laugh. Not one of those things they turn on for the sound track. I remember thinking, "Well, it did her good to get that crack at Gatski off her chest."

When they came in, Lanny Hoard, the writer, was with them. This *Back of the Boulevard* was his. Lanny had a soft spot in his heart for Marie... everybody who read the gossip columns knew that. She wasn't his big moment, or anything like that, but he liked to write pictures for her. And didn't often get the chance.

Marie played triangle stories usually, because she'd got typed that way, and Lanny wrote mysteries. And nothing else. There's a gag around the studio that he had a special key on his typewriter with "Gunfire!" on it. You know the sort of stuff. Melodrama.

He was a young fellow, around thirty-one or two, and not bad-looking for a writer.

Marie and Jack were in the middle of the set by now, after looking in their mirrors, and Sam Masterford yelled, "Burn 'em!" The gaffer lifted his hand and the lights all went on in a blaze, and Lanny ducked back into the shadows.

At that moment, according to Archie Murphy, the cop at the door, there were twenty-two people on the set. No one could get in or out without passing him, and he had a reputation for keeping an accurate list.

Well, Masterford looked around and saw that everybody was ready, and then he asked Rose Graham, "Okay?"

You see, the script girl is responsible for any holes in the picture. It's up to her to make sure that one scene hooks up to the rest without any change in costume, or the way the players have their hair combed, or in the length of the ashes on their cigars. Detail, you understand. Script girl has to see everything, and remember it.

Now, when Masterford asked her if this scene was okay, she studied Jack carefully, then Marie, and finally she nodded sort of uncertainly. Masterford followed her eyes. He was a good director, remember, and I guess he saw the same thing she did. I know that I noticed it right away.

It wasn't anything you could put your finger on. But there *was* a change. Not in Jack, but in Marie. She was prettier, if anything, and it wasn't make-up, either, and it wasn't the lights. She was just naturally prettier.

Of course, there isn't anything you can do in a case like that, except pray that it will hold out till you get the shot made. But Masterford didn't seem to be in any hurry.

"Well, are you going to shoot the scene?" Gatski wanted to know.

"Sure," Masterford said, and looked around again.

The gaffer called, "Lights okay."

"Sound okay," came the loudspeaker in the sound booth.

Assistant Director Bill Cook hollered, "Everybody quiet!"

"Look here a minute, Marie," Sam interrupted. He sounded troubled, all of a sudden. Marie looked at him, and now she wasn't pretty. I don't know why, but when she took her eyes off Jack, she just wasn't.

"Okay," Sam agreed after a minute, so she smiled at Jack again, and Jack smiled, making the prettiest two-shot you could imagine.

"Turn 'em," Sam said in a peculiar tone, like a sound track that's picked up an echo.

The camera chief pressed the button and answered, "She's turning."

"Camera," Sam called. "Action."

So there were Marie and Jack, under the lights, slipping closer and closer together, with the sound mike swinging over them to pick up their words.

"Jack!" Marie whispered. That was her final line, okay. You see, Jack Harter was playing a character named Jack. The script had him answer, "You, Judy! You, forever!" as they clinched.

But Jack didn't say, "You, Judy!" He said nothing. He just took Marie and held her close while his lips met hers. The camera chief was counting, wagging his finger like a referee for this ten-count fadeout. Only it went more than ten. It went about fifteen before Sam Masterford yelled, "Cut!"

Lanny Hoard whistled and called, "Atta boy!" He was a little fellow, not much taller than Joe Gatski, and he had a shrill voice.

"We do it over," Sam said. "You blew your line, Jack."

Lanny yelled, "What the hell if he did! It's a natural the way he did it. Leave the line out! I wrote it, and I admit it doesn't belong. His way, it's a natural!"

"A natural," Sam repeated. "Oh, yes."

"It's okay," Gatski called. "Wrap it up and go home!"

Sam stood a minute, rubbing the side of his nose, and I looked back at the stage, just to see what he was looking at, I guess, and there Marie and Jack were, still in each other's arms, as if they hadn't heard a word. I tell you, it made even me laugh, it was so comical. I wondered, "Why did she ever quit him for a lug like Clem Batting?"

Of course she wasn't married to Batting, now, either. That had lasted only a year, when Clem walked out on her, so, I thought, maybe Jack's on the inside track again.

I ran to my lockers, along the rear wall, where I keep my properties. You don't dare turn your back to properties without putting locks on them. The mixer opened the door of his sound booth and came down the steps, lighting his pipe. Lanny Hoard called, "Marie, can I speak to you?"

But she still wasn't listening. I was standing where I could see everything, Marie and Jack still on the set, the chief pushing his camera aside, and the script girl still sitting. The stage was dim.

Jack Harter wasn't talking now. Neither was Marie. They were just looking at each other. Hungrily.

Sam Masterford had walked off the set, looking back and sort of shrugging, and I saw him head toward the hooks on the east wall, where we hung our wraps. In the dark he bumped into Joe Gatski, but I was only twenty feet from them, and didn't hear Gatski say a word. Sam told the police afterward that Gatski mumbled, "Excuse me," which doesn't sound like Gatski.

Joan Nelson, the hairdresser, snapped shut her curler and eyelash box, and started toward the exit without saying good-night to anybody. Lanny Hoard saw her go and walked quickly after her, as if he had an idea. The second camera man and one of the grips, a stage hand who'd been pushing the camera truck on the trucking shot, were at the door in plain sight of Murphy, the cop, when the shot sounded, so they were out, as far as suspects went. But where the gaffer went, nobody knew. And when the time came, he wouldn't tell.

I still was facing Jack Harter when it happened. It just went *plop,* not very loud. I couldn't even tell which direction the report came from, whether from the floor or the scaffolds overhead.

For ten seconds nothing happened. Neither Marie nor Jack moved an inch. Then Jack started to bend forward. Doc Herring, the studio night surgeon, said Jack died instantly. But he didn't fall instantly. I guess he was looking too hard at Marie for that. He bent a little, then straightened, and slid to the floor. His head bumped the table, and he lay quiet on his back.

Still nobody hollered. Marie dropped to her knees, whispering, "Jack! Oh, Jack! Speak to me!"

I didn't move. Couldn't. Just looked. So did Rose Graham. Only she listened, too. And saw and heard more than the rest of us. Being a script girl, that was second nature to her.

Lanny Hoard came out of the shadows with a strained, peculiar expression on his face, both mad and surprised. He was holding up his right hand, and I saw he had a coin in his fingers. It turned out to be a nickel.

"What happened?" he asked. I heard Joe Gatski's heels slapping the floor behind Lanny, and of course Joe took charge. He's good at that. Maybe that's how he held his job so long.

He asked, "Why did the damn fool shoot himself?"

Marie looked at him, and if I ever saw hate, it was in her eyes. But she didn't answer; not with words. Just picked up Jack's head and put it gently in her lap and kissed his forehead, and the tears made zigzag lines down her yellow make-up.

By this time Gatski was hollering. "Don't leave nobody get out! Where's Sam Masterford?"

"Coming," the director yelled, running forward, trying to get his arms into his topcoat sleeves, and looking astonished and scared.

Gatski hollered, "Call Infirmary! Doctor! Police! No, no! Studio police! Come quick! Tell 'em Joe Gatski says so. Lights! Watch your dress, Marie—that blood will spoil it! It's charged to this production."

Nobody else said a word. But we were all there, thirteen of us. Twelve living, and Jack dead. Murphy the cop didn't leave the door, just blew five blasts of his whistle, over and over, calling help.

The gaffer threw some switches, and about a dozen lights flashed on, all seeming to point at Jack Harter's face. There was plenty of excitement.

Cap Wright, the night police chief, came at Doc Herring's heels, with a brace of studio cops behind him. Doc didn't even take out his stethoscope, just opened Jack's eyes and looked at them, then dusted off his hands and pulled Marie to her feet.

"Chair," he said quietly, and when I brought it, "Sit down, Miss Fleming. He's dead, of course. Who—" The doc didn't finish.

Cap Wright did that for him, though, right away.

"Who knocked him off?" he asked. He was a big man, ugly, with bug eyes. Honest, everybody said, but not exactly jolly. He'd fought off too many gate crashers, trying to meet the stars, to have a nice personality.

Joe Gatski answered him, and what he said shocked most of us. "Who knocked him off?" he repeated. "Why, Marie did it."

Cap Wright grunted, "Hell to pay! Why'd she do it?"

Then I spoke up. I said, "She didn't."

"Oh," Cap Wright answered, sort of relieved.

Joe Gatski got mad and hollered at me, "What the hell do you know?"

Cap shushed him and asked, "Where's the gun?"

That hadn't occurred to us. We all looked around the floor, but no gun. Gatski told Cap to find it quick, but Cap didn't bother to answer. He lined us up, all except Marie. She still sat there, pinching her fingers and not looking pretty anymore. Joe Gatski started to walk away, but Cap hollered, and he turned, sort of surprised, and came back.

Cap asked Rose Graham, "Just where were you, miss?"

"Sitting in that chair, right here," she pointed with her foot.

"That's right," the camera chief agreed. "All the time she set there."

Cap turned on him and asked, "Where was you, Dutch?"

"Pushing my camera, here, like this," the chief answered.

I said, "That's right. I could see them both."

"Could they both see you?" Cap asked suspiciously.

Rose spoke up. "I could," she said.

"Did he have anything in his hands?" Cap wanted to know.

She nodded. "A whisk broom. He was brushing his coat."

Cap laughed, it striking him funny I had a brush when he was thinking of a gun. He asked Rose, "Did Miss Fleming have anything in her hands?"

"No," she answered. "Miss Fleming didn't shoot him. Neither did the prop man nor Dutch. And I didn't. The shot came from back there." She pointed toward the corner of the stage, past an unfinished set of a library interior, with a statue of some kind on a bookshelf.

"How'd you know?" Joe Gatski asked.

"The sound came from there," she answered.

Doc Herring asked her to repeat that, and she pointed again.

"Where was Harter standing?" he inquired, and when I showed him, Doc said, "She's correct. The course of the slug is from left to right. Whoever shot him stood over there—" he pointed, too—"some little distance."

We all looked toward the corner, which was light enough now, but had been plenty dark when Jack was shot. The two cops came back from prowling around and said nobody was hiding on the stage, and they could find no gun.

Cap Wright said, "Well, one of you did it. For the moment we'll count Miss Fleming out. And you, miss—" he nodded to Rose—"and Dutch and this prop man—" he pointed at me. "That leaves eight." He began to count them off. "Mr. Gatski, Mr. Masterford, the gaffer, this detective writer, this fellow." He pointed to the grip.

Murphy, the cop, interrupted: "He's okay, sir. Him and the second camera man were right inside the door when it happened. It wasn't them."

"Um," Cap answered. "There's still six to pick from. Guess I'll have to question all of you."

"Of course," Sam Masterford answered sensibly. "That's only right. Start on me."

But Cap didn't. He started by looking at the gaffer. I looked, too, and what I saw surprised me. For the gaffer was drunk. Extremely. Liquor was sticking out his ears, you might say. He hadn't been drunk when we wrapped up the picture fifteen minutes ago. We'd have known it, for he was a guy you had to watch; he'd even been warned that he'd lose his job if he brought another bottle on the lot.

Cap said, "What's wrong, Otto?"

"Hell with you," the gaffer answered, and Cap had his men search him, and while they searched, Cap asked, "Where were you, Otto, when the shot was fired?"

But the gaffer just said, "I don't like studio cops."

They found no gun on him, but something else. In his billfold was a thing you'd not expect to find on a studio technician. A picture from some fan magazine. A picture of Marie Fleming.

Cap asked Marie politely, "He a friend of yours?" and pointed to the gaffer. She shook her head. But it set Cap to wondering about the rest of us, and when his eyes came to Lanny Hoard, he frowned and remembered what the gossip columns were saying about Lanny being that way about Marie.

"Where were you, Hoard?" he asked Lanny suddenly.

Lanny answered sarcastically, "Mr. Pinkerton grills suspect. Well, I was about to phone."

"No dirty cracks necessary," Cap told him. "You're so good at figuring things out, figure this one! Who saw you phoning?"

Lanny looked startled, and said, "Why—no one." He turned to Joan Nelson, and I remembered—he had followed the hairdresser off the set.

"He was talking to me," Joan backed him up. "Then he walked toward the phone and I started for the door."

"What did he talk to you about?" Cap asked.

Hoard answered, and you could see him getting red: "I borrowed a nickel of her. Hadn't a cent in my pants and wanted to phone for my car."

"That's right," Joan admitted, and Lanny held up the coin.

"I'd just got studio operator," he said, "and she told me to deposit five cents, and I heard the shot. I didn't put through the call."

Cap grunted, and went and whispered to his two cops, and they left the set, one going outdoors and the other starting to hunt inside again. Gatski was getting nervous. He said impatiently, "Well, do something!"

"All right. What were you doing?" Cap asked him,

but Gatski had no time to answer. Marie, who hadn't spoken yet, answered for him.

"He was pulling the trigger," she said in a flat voice.

Sam Masterford went right over to her and began to talk soothingly, and Gatski tramped up and down and swore, and asked Cap Wright to search him, and called Marie names. So Cap got the story, prying it out of us, about the argument between Gatski and Marie and Jack.

"Well, where were you, Mr. Gatski?" Cap asked again.

"He should ask a supervisor where he was!" Gatski answered sort of jerkily. "I was by the water cooler. Taking a stomach tablet. I had the heartburn."

"Alone?"

Gatski yelled, "Of course alone! Do I ask for the spotlight when I take a stomach tablet?"

Cap said to himself, "Mr. Gatski alone at the cooler, this writer alone at the telephone, the gaffer nobody knows where, but drunk."

Masterford broke in quietly, "I was alone, too. I'd gone for my coat and hat and stopped to put on my rubbers. They went on hard. I was still working on them when I heard it."

Cap went and looked at the hooks where the wraps hung, and then asked Sam, "Did you pass anybody, going toward that corner?"

"Just Mr. Gatski," Sam said, and he told about bumping into Joe, and Joe's "Excuse me."

Cap said, "Uh-huh," and looked at the sound mixer. He was the only one that hadn't confessed to being alone in the dark somewhere. Cap asked, "What's your name?"

"Battinger," the mixer answered.

Cap repeated, "Battinger?" He thought it over, still was thinking when Lanny Hoard spoke.

"Wasn't Clem Batting's real name Battinger?" he asked.

Then I remembered. When Marie divorced Jack to marry Clem, the newspaper columnists had dug up Clem's real name.

"Clem's my brother," the mixer said.

Marie looked at him quickly, with a scared expression, as if that were a secret she hadn't meant to tell. But Joan, the hairdresser, spoke up again at once. "Mr.

Battinger was ahead of me on the way to the door when the shot was fired. I could see him. I'd just left Lanny."

While Cap was thinking this over, the cop he'd sent offstage came back and whispered to him, and he nodded and looked at Lanny, then back at the mixer.

"So Clem's your brother," he said. "But the girl claims she saw you heading toward the door when the shot was fired. If you didn't do it, it's a good thing you've got an alibi."

He didn't seem satisfied, however. When the cop came back still without the gun, Cap searched us all, regardless. He got the three women to help him search each other, even, but there wasn't any gun. All this took time. It was three o'clock and we were getting nowhere fast, when suddenly Rose spoke up.

"You're running in a circle," she accused, and Cap said:

"Yeh? You could do better?"

Rose blushed easy, but she stuck to it. And everybody listened. Everybody around a studio knows about script girls and what kind of eyes and ears they've got.

"You know already it's one of us," she said, "and you yourself limit it to one out of six."

"That's right," Cap agreed.

"Of those six, let's start with Otto, then," Rose said. "He's got a picture of Miss Fleming in his pocket. But regardless of that, he's just plain drunk."

"Not drunk," the gaffer denied.

"He'll not tell us what he was doing at the minute," she admitted, "but that's explainable. He was drinking on the set and didn't want to lose his job."

Cap argued, "We can't find any bottle."

"I saw Otto hide a bottle once before," Rose said. She walked back along the wall, where a battery of lights stood ready to work on the rose trellis set in the morning. She looked into the barrel of each light and finally called Cap. "He spilled it, you see," she pointed out as Cap lifted an empty bottle from the light. "Didn't put the cork back in. There's the liquor, running down inside the light."

"My bottle," Otto grunted, and Cap asked:

"What does it prove?"

"Why, that he was drinking when the shot occurred,"

Rose said. "The sound scared him, and he dropped the stopper. There it is, on the floor. It was too dark to find it, so he did the next best thing. Put the bottle away open."

Cap admitted, "It's possible. That would put the gaffer at the opposite corner of the stage from the murderer, in spite of the picture in his pocket."

"That leaves five," Rose said. "As for Battinger, he has Joan's alibi." She looked at the sound mixer, and he tried to smile. "That's enough, isn't it? In spite of his being the brother of Marie's former husband?"

Cap didn't like to count the mixer out, but at last he said, "For the time being, okay. That leaves—"

"Joan herself," Rose said, "which is ridiculous. And Mr. Gatski, and Sam Masterford, and Lanny Hoard."

Lanny cried, "You're crazy, Rose. You've got to show a motive."

"Yes, when writing a melodrama," she answered, without looking at him. "But this isn't a script. It's facts. The sort of things I'm used to, day in and day out."

Lanny started to storm, and Cap told him to shut up.

"Lanny either talked himself into a hole or out of it a bit ago," Rose said. "He claimed he had the receiver off the hook, with the operator listening for the sound of a nickel hitting the bell, when the shot was fired."

Cap smiled. "Smart girl," he said. "I thought of that, too. Hoard told the truth. My man checked with the operator. She heard the shot, and Hoard saying, 'What the hell!'"

"That leaves two," Rose went on, holding up two fingers, "Mr. Gatski and Sam Masterford."

Joe Gatski began to holler all over again and nothing could stop him this time. He said he'd get the girl's job, and he talked about his lawyers, and walked up and down, banging his heels on the floor. At last Cap got him quiet, telling him what this girl said wasn't important. But Joe went on giving her filthy looks just the same.

She said, "Sam was putting on his rubbers, over by that wall. The murderer—" she hesitated, as if she didn't like the taste of the word on her tongue, then in spite of herself she repeated it—"the murderer was standing somewhere near the end of that unfinished library set there, and Sam was in behind it. And Mr. Gatski was back near the rose trellis set you see over there."

"Why, that's right," Gatski yelled. "I couldn't shoot around corners!"

"How do you know where Gatski was?" Cap asked.

"My ears told me," Rose said. "Haven't you heard him walk? He runs the same way, hitting the floor first with his heels. I think he'll drive me crazy sometimes on a set. To get to the place from which the shot was fired, and back again, in that short time, he'd have had to run. But he didn't run. I was listening."

Sam Masterford looked sort of astonished.

"So you put me behind the eight ball in your calculations?" he asked.

Rose answered, "No. Behind the pistol. You shot Jack."

Sam didn't say a word. Not a word. Just blinked his gray eyes behind his glasses and looked at Marie. She got up to her feet, slowly, and if a woman ever had suffering in her face, she did at that moment.

"So it was you, Sam," she whispered. "Sam, I understand now. All this talk about you loving me!"

Gatski grumbled, "It's screwy, perfectly screwy! Sam Masterford wouldn't shoot a—"

"Mr. Masterford saw the same thing I did," Rose went on, speaking to Lanny Hoard. "The reason Jack blew up on his last line was that there wasn't any line. They were just falling in love all over again." Marie sobbed out loud, but Rose couldn't stop. "It wasn't acting at all," she explained. "Someone called the scene a natural. It was. Sam recognized it. He tried to change it. Didn't like it, and didn't even want to shoot it. He put it off as long as he could. But Marie kept right on looking at Jack the same way."

Still Sam didn't say a word.

"He has his rubbers on," Rose added. "Remember, he called attention to them, said he had a hard time getting them on. You can't hear a man run in rubbers."

Lanny broke in, half-defending Sam. "You didn't find any gun on him!"

"That's right," Cap agreed, "we haven't found a gun."

Rose looked toward the library set, with its bookshelves half-full. She said, "Did you look back of the books?"

The two cops began to tear down the books. There the gun was, on the top shelf.

Rose said, "Sam and I worked on a quickie together, six or eight years back. One of the first sound-effect jobs. He ran in a scene then of a fellow hiding a gun in the bookshelves of a library. I've always remembered it."

"Oh," Sam said, and sweat began running again off his long, thin nose. "I see. That's where the idea came from," and then he asked the only question in his own defense. "Why didn't Gatski put it there? Or Hoard?"

"They weren't near enough," Rose answered, "and besides, they couldn't reach that high shelf, Sam."

"They could throw it up," he sort of argued.

"Not without me hearing it," she reminded him.

Cap turned to her. "Thanks, miss," he started to say, but Joe Gatski had pulled out his watch by this time, and he interrupted:

"Four o'clock!" he exclaimed. "And we haven't called the city police!" He started for the phone, but turned around quickly. "Remember, holding you here was none of my doing. I'm paying no overtime after eleven o'clock. Charge it up to Masterford."

Sam just shrugged, and didn't say anything. He never was much of a hand to talk. He didn't even take the stand at the trial. Claimed he didn't remember anything about it. He didn't of course, but the public couldn't believe that. Never will. Somebody's hiding something, they think, but the reason for that is, they've never been on a set on a cleanup night. Anything can happen to anybody the last hours of any production. Like I said before, somebody ought to write a piece about it.

CLIFFHANGER

by Georgiana Eidukas

Georgiana Eidukas is a new writer, and "Cliffhanger" represents her first published story. Prior to her efforts as a fiction writer she worked for Blue Cross/Blue Shield in Chicago, her hometown, writing technical and training manuals and working as part of their management staff training new employees. She describes herself as a member of the post—World War II baby-boom generation, and is currently in the process of making her own contribution to the much-heralded "new" baby boom of the 1980s.

It was the worst influenza outbreak of the season but I have no complaints, because it was that particular bout with the flu that saved my life. Not *my* life exactly, but the life of Clarissa Evans White, the character I play on *All the Livelong Day,* the Number Two rated soap opera of the past several seasons, and one of the last live, untaped soaps still running. And if the flu hadn't struck our set last Thursday I'd be standing in the unemployment line this very minute.

I'd like to say this treachery began that Thursday, but in truth it's been a long time coming. When your character's been lying in a coma for the last nineteen weeks, and the only lines you've been given are occasional sighs—well, I ask you, isn't it pretty clear what's going to happen?

For all these years I've played that shrew—complaining, cajoling, whining. I've been married thrice and divorced twice, with numerous illicit liaisons in between. My last husband—a sweet handsome man, and no match for me—died nineteen weeks ago, the same day my coma began. There were suspicious circumstances surrounding his death but the police were unable to question me because of my very convenient coma.

But that Thursday—well, on that Thursday the

writing was on the wall, or should I perhaps say, on the script.

I came to the studio on time, even though I've not had a word of dialogue for ages, while Ruthie Maynard, that blankety-blank, who plays Mary Grant—"good ol' Mary"—was late, as usual. All these weeks I've been on time, gone to makeup and hair-styling, donned my hospital gown, run through the script, and then done my scene. I say "done" rather than "acted" since it's pretty hard to act out a coma, but I must say I've been *very* believable, considering the circumstances.

Complaining to the producer had got me nowhere. He's been happy with our ratings and our writer has introduced several new characters into our story using *young,* new actors. *Very young* new actors.

Une femme d'un certain âge apparently has no appeal these days with the younger viewing audiences and when Clarissa's coma became a weekly feature with no end in sight, I began to wonder—and to worry.

That Thursday, after our regular live broadcast, I went to my dressing room, changed clothes, ate the sandwich I'd sent out for, and went to pick up my Friday's script. We usually spend at least two or three hours after our live air-time rehearsing our scenes for the next day, getting fitted for wardrobe, and getting our lighting and camera angles set up; but there were no scripts that day.

At first I thought that because we'd had such a bad outbreak of flu and both Paul Scott, our producer, and Joe Hester, our director, were out sick, that maybe there was some foul-up with the printing; but Robbie Sullivan, the assistant director and son of our sponsor, Robert Sullivan of Sullivan Soap Flakes fame, called us together and announced that we were all to show up early the next day and we'd be handed our scripts shortly before air-time.

Now, normally, Friday's show ends with a cliffhanger—will Betty marry Bob? Will Freida tell Arnold about her long-lost son? Will Frank ever remember who he really is? Or is his amnesia hiding a deeper secret? But once every year or so we have our regular Friday cliffhanger *and* a major plot resolution, and for those scenes the cast is not given the script until just before air-time—so the word won't get out to the public and because Joe, our director, likes the spontaneity involved in acting a scene moments after reading the script. Needless to say, we all had to be quick studies.

Well, when that clod, Robbie Sullivan, told us all to come in early Friday for our scripts, everyone's eyes were on me. I could feel people physically backing away from me, afraid to be tainted by that pariah, the soon-to-be-unemployed actor; and I didn't blame them. You can't have a character lie in a hospital bed in a coma for nineteen weeks without everyone suspecting what's going to happen, and now they all surely knew.

I stayed in my dressing room until quite late. I wanted to avoid the other cast members. I'll admit it, I was feeling pretty bitter. I'd given twenty-two years of my life to *All the Livelong Day,* and now I was getting the sack, while that Ruthie Maynard would stay on forever, playing safe, solid Mary Grant, everyone's friend. It just wasn't fair.

I left my dressing room expecting to hear nothing but the silence of an empty studio, and instead I heard thumping and banging coming from down the hall, near the offices. A light shone in the corridor, cast from the open door of the Writers' Room, and a steady stream of very unfeminine swearing was coming from a very feminine mouth.

Lilly Sullivan, our all-purpose pinch hitter and Robbie's cousin, stood in the midst of a confusing muddle of papers.

"Aaah!" she screamed, waving her arms about her head like some comic-strip character. "I'm going crazy!" Her hair was hanging in her eyes, her hosiery was torn, and her pale suit was smudged with still-damp printer's ink.

"Need help?" I offered.

"Oh, golly, Liz, yes, but you really can't help me. I can't let anyone see the scripts before tomorrow. That jerk Robbie was supposed to stay and help me but he had to meet one of his cuties. With everyone out with the flu we're so short-handed, I don't know how we'll make it to the weekend."

"How about if I don't peek?"

"Huh?"

"Why don't you sort the pages and hand them to me upside-down. That way I won't see the script."

"Gee, thanks, Liz," she said, "but I really can't let anyone near these pages. I haven't even read the script myself."

With her last words a lofty tower of papers slid off the edge of her desk, and she sent up another howl. As she bent to scoop up the fallen pages, she never even saw the sure swift hands of Liz Snyder, a.k.a Clarissa Evans White, slipping a copy of Friday's script into her purse.

My worst fears were justified.

I read the script through that night, several times, in fact. There was no changing the words that were swimming before my eyes. In the third and final scene of Friday's show Clarissa Evans White, with her faithful young doctor by her side, dies in her coma, never regaining consciousness. Now, her doctor is the one who sighs as he lifts the edge of the sheet up and over the face of his dead patient, ending a career of almost a quarter of a century. The more I read, the more I stewed, the angrier I got. There was a way, a way to change the future, and I had to take the chance.

I spent several hours rewriting the second and third scenes and making fairly professional-looking copies.

In the first scene, two of our newest characters merely introduce a newly formed relationship, and it had little bearing on my future. The second scene was with Ruthie Maynard. When Mary Grant, her character, learns by telephone of a blackmailer's mysterious threat, she panics and tries to kill herself by putting her head in the gas oven. This scene was to be Friday's cliffhanger. At the last moment Tom Dawes, an actor playing the role of an old friend, comes to the kitchen door and sees through the window what is happening. He calls out Mary's name and bursts through the door at the last moment. Kneeling at her side, he pleads with her to live, to keep on breathing, to hang on till help comes.

Of course Mary will live. I know that because Clarissa Evans White doesn't. No writer would kill off two of his most well-established characters in the same segment. The fans wouldn't stand for it. Besides, Mary

Grant got sacks and sacks of fan mail every week, while poor Clarissa, the evil shrew, has been getting less and less mail each week she's been comatose.

I got to the studio extra early the next morning. Lilly Sullivan came in shortly afterward and gave me my copy of the script. There was a forlorn expression on her face that told me she'd read the script. I did my best to ignore her sad eyes.

Breezily I asked, "Need a hand, Lilly? I'd be glad to help you pass out the scripts."

"Thanks, Liz. Anyone down at your end yet?"

By "my end" she meant the actors' dressing rooms. "Just Tom Dawes and that young actor Bob Coombs who plays the doctor. Shall I give them their copies?" I was safe there; it was only a minor lie.

"Would you, Liz? I know I shouldn't but I'd be really grateful. With everyone sick I'm really rushed. Mike Vannet called last night and said the bug's got him, too. Looks like it'll be Robbie's show today."

Mike Vannet is the writer of *All the Livelong Day* and a more fortuitous illness could hardly have been arranged. That meant one less person for me to worry about.

I waited by the side entrance to the studio and as Tom and Bob came in I gave them "their" copies of the script. Robbie was running a little late when he finally arrived but I managed to pull him to one side.

I gave a discreet smile and whispered confidentially, "There's an attractive young girl downstairs in a booth in the coffee shop who asked me to tell you, 'Remember three months ago.'"

His face blanched, drained instantly of his usual ruddy color, and he nodded dumbly.

Robbie is notorious in his attentions to the younger members of the opposite sex. I don't know whom he was seeing three months ago, but I do know he's always seeing a woman or possibly several women. So the message I gave him was pretty certain to at least pique his interest; but I must say I was surprised at the initial reaction.

As he left to go downstairs I chuckled to myself, picturing a plump, reddish young man, anxiously hopping from booth to booth, peering into faces, looking for the one he would recognize, all the while wasting precious rehearsal time. Poor duped Robbie.

Now I was all set. I had nothing to do until air-time but keep Ruthie Maynard company. She behaved so solicitously toward me, cooing her sickeningly sweet platitudes till I felt I was approaching a state of hyperglycemia. At one point Tom Dawes began walking toward us, but I gave him a warning shake of my head and he veered off to talk to the wardrobe mistress who happened to be standing nearby.

Robbie returned in time to discuss camera angles with the cameramen and run through the dialogue with the two new actors doing the first scene. Seeing Ruthie and myself standing together he opened his arms and enfolded both of us. As he did so he gave me a peculiar glance, more closely related, I think, to his search in the coffee shop, than to commiserate with me about my imminent demise.

Lilly gave him a signal and he called for quiet and we all went into our respective sets and took our places. The music began as the cameras started rolling.

The first scene went exactly according to the original script. Too much so, in fact. The inexperienced actors were wooden, stiff. A lot of work would have to be done with them if there was any hope of continuing their roles.

After the commercial break Ruthie's scene went according to her original script, also. I was propped up in my hospital bed watching the scene across the studio. She ended her telephone conversation and went through an agonizing time trying to decide what to do. Her anguish was heartbreaking as she stuck her head into the oven and her limp body slumped to the floor. My heartbeat began to quicken as Tom Dawes beat on the door. Bursting into the kitchen, he knelt and held her flaccid body next to his. The camera moved in for a close-up of his emotion-wracked face. "Oh, no," he wailed. "I'm too late. *My dear friend Mary is dead!*"

I would have paid a fortune if the camera could have recorded that scene with a close-up of Ruthie's face as the eyes of the recently departed Mary Grant popped open and a glare of hatred shot wildly about the studio.

Pandemonium broke loose. As we cut away for a

commercial Robbie went racing over to Ruthie's set, thinking that Tom Dawes was writing his own lines; Ruthie was screeching like a peahen; the script girl, out with the flu, wasn't there to take the flak, but Lilly, still wearing the torn stockings of the night before, was looking faint.

No one had yet thought to look at me and all too soon the commercial was over and my scene began.

As my Clarissa lay in a coma I could hear the muffled threats as people tried to calm Ruthie Maynard and get her off the set. It wouldn't take long for everyone to figure out what had happened and who was responsible.

I could sense the tension next to my bed. Bob Coombs, whose only lines until now have been on the order of 'No change, nurse,' and 'We'll have to wait and see,' actually had a half page of dialogue.

He began, "Clarissa? Oh, my God! Clarissa!"

I fluttered my eyelashes gently and tossed my head from side to side. I could see the faint red light on the camera. I focused on Bob's face.

"Where am I?" I asked.

"The hospital! You were struck on the head. You've been in a coma for a long time."

"My husband...?" I gasped. I was giving the performance of my life.

"I don't suppose you remember anything?"

"Dead," I mumbled. "He's dead."

"Then you do remember?"

"Yes."

I nodded slowly and a huge and very genuine tear came rolling down my cheek as a harried cameraman tried to wing it and the organ music built to a vibrant crescendo. The entire cast and crew hovered in the shadows behind the camera. Robbie was shuffling through the pages of his script, trying to figure out where he'd blown it.

Again I nodded and gulped and the tiniest tremble shook my lower lip as I spoke.

"It was Mary," I said. "She did it."

And I smiled into the camera, a simple but noble smile for all my new fans.

Music. Fadeout.

THE DECLINE AND FALL OF NORBERT TUFFY

by Ron Goulart

The work of Ron Goulart has its roots in many genres. His science fiction has elements of mystery, his mysteries have elements of fantasy, and most everything is infused with wit. Under numerous pseudonyms he has written dozens of novels, short stories, novelizations, and comic strips. In 1971 he won the Mystery Writers of America's Edgar Allan Poe Award.

Twenty-six million people saw them die, and that's not counting reruns.

Real murder is rare on television, particularly on a talk show. If you weren't one of those who caught the actual broadcast, you probably saw the pertinent footage on one of the evening network newscasts. The killer, who also appeared briefly on the talk show, eventually did a lot of explaining and so most everybody, including the police, thinks they know just about the entire story. Actually, the murderer himself barely knew half of what was going on.

I knew the victims and the killer, although I didn't realize until too late that they were going to be the victims and the killer. Since the authorities have the killer in custody, and since I hate to get myself tangled in public messes, there's no reason for me to volunteer the information I have as to the true causes of the effect all those millions of viewers witnessed. Sometimes when we're filming a commercial with Glorious MacKenzie and I notice her between takes, staring forlornly into her cup of Wake Up! Coffee, I'm tempted to tell her all I know. But I resist the temptation.

It was because of the lovely Glorious, one of America's top five models, that Norbert Tuffy concocted his whole caper. We'd been using the stunning redhaired Glorious in our Wake Up! Coffee television spots for nearly a year, ever since the Wake Up! lab back in Battle Creek had made their scientific breakthrough and we'd been able to use the very effective slogan, "Wake Up! The only coffee that's 100% coffee free!"

Norbert and Glorious were living together in his mansion out on the Pacific Palisades when I'd first met him at a cocktail party that my advertising agency gave for all our commercial talent. Norbert, who was very good in a scrap despite his size, helped me out when the actor who'd just been fired from our Grrrowl Dog Grub account tried to bite my ankle. I'd been expecting trouble from the moment I noticed the actor had crashed the party wearing his Grrrowl policedog costume. At any rate, the small feisty Norbert and I became friends as a result of that incident.

It was several months later, over lunch at the Quick-Frozen Mandarin in Santa Monica, that he first alluded to the Blind Butcher affair. I was already in the booth when Norbert came scurrying in out of a hazy spring afternoon.

He was clad in one of those maroon running suits he was so fond of for daytime wear. "It was an omen." He plopped down opposite me and poured himself a cup of lukewarm tea.

"What?"

"When my house fell down the hill and into the sea last month."

"I thought the house only made it as far as the middle of the Pacific Coast Highway."

"The symbolism was there to be read by one and all. The decline and fall of Norbert Tuffy."

"Still haven't picked up a new scripting assignment?"

"I haven't had a TV script credit in four months. I am definitely on the proverbial skids."

"Maybe I can get you some freelance ad copy—"

"Ha," he said scornfully. "That would really finish me. It's bad enough my house fell into the Pacific because of a mud slide, it's bad enough my favorite Siamese cat was eaten by the pet wolfhound of a noted rock millionaire, it's bad enough Glorious is now living alone in a Westwood condo, it's bad enough I haven't won an Emmy in three years, it's bad enough I am virtually blacklisted because it's rumored I am suffering from writer's block, it's bad enough I'm being robbed of potential millions by a swine calling himself Macho Sweeze—and now you suggest I top it all by working in a cesspool such as that ad agency of yours."

"We pay as much as—"

"Forget it. I'd rather play piano in a bordello."

"You'd have to join the musicians' union to do that."

"Funny as a funeral is what you are," he observed as he snatched up the menu.

"Listen, you're letting a temporary setback cloud your whole—"

"Don't give me slogans. Do you realize Glorious and I may never get back together?"

"I wasn't even aware you two weren't living together. When we shot the last Wake Up! commercial with her the other day, she seemed happy."

"Sure, dumping me makes her euphoric," he said, summoning the waiter in the silk kimono. "Bring me the Number Six lunch, and pronto."

"Being on the skids sure hasn't helped your disposition, Mr. Tuffy," remarked the waiter. "And you, sir?"

I ordered a Number Five. "You and Glorious have parted before, Norbert, and always—"

"Oh, I'll get that incredibly lovely bimbo back," he assured me. "I know exactly how and when. When I collect the $54,000."

"$54,000?"

"Happens to be the exact sum I need to pay off my debts and get back on my feet again."

"Then you are going to get the assignment to do the pilot script for *My Old Man's a Garbage Man?*"

"Naw, they double-crossed me out of that gig, too, even after I laid an absolutely socko treatment on 'em," Norbert said. "I intend to acquire the $54,000 in question from Macho Sweeze. It's one half of $108,000."

"It is, but why's Macho going to give it to you?"

"You know that scum?"

"We had some commercials for 150 percent, the Headache Pill for a Headache and a Half on a movie of the week he wrote and I met him at the—"

"Wrote? That goon couldn't scrawl an X without help."

"I sense a bitterness in your tone."

Norbert fell silent until after our freshly thawed Chinese lunches had been placed before us. "Ever hear of a series of spy novels about a guy known as the Blind Butcher?" he asked me. "Allegedly penned by one Dan X. Spear. Published by Capstone Books."

"Vaguely." I poked my eggroll with my plastic fork and caused it to make a squeaking sound. "Why?"

"I created that series and wrote all six of the paperback novels."

"So you're Dan X. Spear?"

Norbert's teeth gnashed on his stir-fried tempeh. "Macho Sweeze is Dan X. Spear," he snarled. "See, this was all four, five years in the past, before I'd reached the dizzying pinnacle of success which I am presently toppling from. Macho had this vague nitwit idea for a series and he was going around with the granddaughter of Oscar Dragomann, the publisher of Capstone Books. A spindly broad of about seventeen summers, but Macho's always gone in for ladies with underdeveloped minds and bodies."

"What did you do, Norbert, sign some kind of agreement with Macho that gave him all rights in the project?"

He snarled again. "Norbert Tuffy doesn't, not ever, do anything dumb," he told me, pointing his plastic fork. "I was, let us say, injudicious. Something I have been known to be in moments of extreme financial deprivation. Some people get woozy when you take away oxygen, I get careless when I'm suffering from lack of money."

"Where does the amount of $108,000 come from?"

"The series was less than a hit," explained Norbert. "In fact, the final book in our series, *The Spy Who Broke His Leg,* never even got out of Dragomann's central warehouse down in Whittier." He paused to gobble a few bites of food. "We now dissolve from back then to now. Macho, lord knows how, is presently a dazzling star in the Hollywood writing firmament. Furthermore, he has become, possibly because of their mutual interest in young ladies who've only recently shed their braces, a close chum of ex-king Maktab Al-barid."

"Him I've never heard of," I admitted.

"Another reason I wouldn't let anybody chain me to an advertising agency—turns your brains to jelly. Anyway, Maktab Al-barid ruled the Arab country of Zayt until some fanatic holy roller led a revolt and took over that oil-rich little spot," said Norbert. "Before Maktab Al-barid skipped the country he managed to stash away something like a couple of billion bucks in various banks around the world. At the moment he resides in ex-kingly splendor in a Bel Air mansion once owned by a silent-screen lover and more recently by those rock poets of the platinum records, Honey and Hank."

"This Arab king is financing Macho in something?"

"The peabrain is going to make movies," replied Norbert. "His first motion-picture venture, announced but a few days ago in the Hollywood trades, is to be—we'll skip the trumpet fanfare—an adaptation of *The Spy Who Went Through the Meatgrinder*."

"One of the Blind Butcher novels?"

"One of *my* Blind Butcher novels, yeah. Second one in the series." The plastic fork suddenly snapped in his clenched fist. "See, under that dumb little agreement I injudiciously signed with him back then, Macho retains *all* subsidiary rights. All I ever saw was half of the paltry initial advances. Maktab Al-barid has paid Macho $108,000 for the screen rights and he's going to hand over an additional $216,000 for a screenplay."

"He seems to favor multiples of 54."

"That's the kind of sympathy I need."

I shrugged. "Norbert, you made a mistake," I said. "Maybe with a good lawyer you can do something."

"Good lawyer? There is no such being," he said. "No, to get my share—and Macho can keep the screenplay money—to get my share of that $108,000 I intend to start applying pressure. I may even drop in on Maktab Al-barid himself, although I hear he keeps himself very well bodyguarded because of a fear, perfectly legit, that terrorists from Zayt may be dropping in. Seems they'd like to have Maktab Al-barid star in a trial for treason and sundry other misdemeanors."

"I still think an attorney could—"

"I already talked to three of them."

"What did they say?"

"I haven't got a chance to collect."

As it turned out I phoned Norbert less than a week

later. Locating him was a little difficult, since his answering service had just dropped him for being three months in arrears on his bill. His agent swore he'd never heard of him, then offered me five other writers who were currently hot properties. Finally I got Glorious to admit she was still in contact with him and that he, having just checked out of the Beverly Glen Hotel in another economy move, was residing in the back half of an old duplex down in Manhattan Beach.

"Hello?" he answered that afternoon, using a completely unbelievable British accent. "You are speaking to Mr. Norbert Tuffy's confidential secretary, what ho."

"Hey, Norbert, listen," I said, and identified myself.

"Old chap, you're making a bally mistake. Mr. Tuffy—"

"The agency doesn't like me to waste too much time on personal calls," I went on. "But there's something I better talk to you about."

"Not a penny less than $54,000, if you're acting as go-between for your buddy."

"Macho Sweeze? Haven't even seen him since you and I had lunch last week." From my office window I could watch a handsome highrise building being constructed, its topmost floors lost in pale smog. "This has to do with a guy named Fritz Momand."

"What a sappo name. Who is he?"

"Don't you know?"

"I have no recollection of the name."

"Fritz Momand is a freelance commercial artist who specializes in fruit. I happened to—"

"In what?"

"Fruit. He's doing a series of ads for us for FrootBoms Cereal. That's the stuff shaped like little hand grenades which explode with flavor when you pour milk over—"

"What has this Fritz guy to do with me?"

"I was at his studio over on La Cienega yesterday, to okay his painting of an orange, and he got to talking about his wife. Her name is Frilly Jonah." I paused, anticipating a response.

"Anybody who'd voluntarily call herself that must have show-business aspirations."

"She does. She's a Country-and-Western singer who hasn't had much success."

"Probably sings on key, which is a great handicap," said Norbert. "You're not the greatest yarn spinner on the face of Los Angeles, pal. Not that I don't enjoy chit-chat and pointless blab—"

"You don't know Frilly? You haven't been seeing her on the sly?"

"Eh? Norbert Tuffy does nothing, absolutely *nada,* on the sly," he said loudly. "Besides which, my heart is still in a sling over Glorious MacKenzie."

"This is the truth?"

"Do I ever lie? Don't try to tell me this fruit vendor claims Norbert Tuffy has been fooling around with Frilly while he's slaving over a hot persimmon?"

I cleared my throat and turned away from the view, which was making my eyes water. "Fritz Momand is a big, violent guy who likes hunting," I began. "Very tough, extremely jealous. He's grown suspicious of late that Frilly has been seeing someone else. In the course of ransacking her room while she was off singing at the Back in the Saddle Club in Ventura, he unearthed a complete set of the Blind Butcher paperback novels. Each one was inscribed to his wife in glowing phrases. One such said: *To the apple-cheeked delight who's brought a new kind of love to me, with the passionate regards of the author.*"

"You actually thought Norbert Tuffy could write gush like that?" he asked. "Using a fruit image to woo the guy's wife is a nice touch, though. How old is this Frilly?"

"Never actually met her, but she's quite a bit younger than her husband. Probably about nineteen or twenty."

"So use your coco, chum. It's obviously that scoundrel Macho Sweeze who's putting the Dan X. Spear pen name to yet another sleazy use and giving the horns to your pushcart Picasso."

"But you wrote the books."

"True, true," said Norbert, "except, as I made perfectly clear to you when last we met, Macho loves to claim the credit. I am sure it's he who's using the books to impress this honkytonk bimbo now that one book is a movie-to-be."

"You're probably right. Just wanted to warn you to

watch out for Fritz Momand, since he seems the kind of guy who likes to do violence to those who fiddle with his wife," I said. "You haven't had any luck getting a settlement out of Macho, huh?"

"The amount of luck I've had in any area of late, pal, you could insert in a flea's nostril and still have room left to pack in an agent's heart," he answered. "I approached Macho and, politely for me, suggested he ought to do right by me. He was cordial, for him, and swore he'd see to it I got a little something. That is, *after* the film is released, which will be a good two years hence."

"You don't believe he'll do even that?"

"Most of Macho Sweeze's sincere promises could go on that list of the world's most famous lies, the one that commences with 'The check's in the mail.'"

"So now?"

"Since you are sincerely interested in my fate, unlike the circle of Judases I used to run with, I'll tell you what Norbert Tuffy has in mind. I have always been hailed, and justly so, as one of the most brilliant plotters in this nutty town. Even now, in my temporary exile, I have not lost the knack."

"You have a new movie idea in the works?"

"Naw, I'm working out a foolproof way to get the money Macho owes me."

The very next day I was stuck back on the Soy-Hammy account. That's about the only account in the shop, as you may recall, that I don't really enjoy. But this was a full-scale emergency and I had to fly to Chicago the same afternoon. It seems the head of Soy-Hammy's own advertising department had just been killed in a freak accident. He'd been having a drink at one of those revolving bars in a penthouse night club when the darn thing started to revolve three or four times faster than it was supposed to. When it suddenly stopped, he was flung clean off the terrace and fell to the street thirteen stories below.

His employers at SoyHammy had come up with the idea of giving his remains a lavish funeral, and since he had been associated with SoyHammy for many years, they figured it would be a nice touch to have all six pallbearers in pigsuits like the one the announcer wore on our SoyHammy commercials. To halt that before anybody in the media got wind of it, I was speeded eastward.

Talking all concerned out of the pigsuits and then sitting in while they interviewed candidates to fill the deceased's job consumed over two weeks. That spell in Chicago coincided exactly with Norbert's execution of his plan to get what he felt was owed to him.

Since I only spoke to Norbert once, very briefly on the phone, most of the details of his caper are what I got from the newspapers and television. Not that any of them knew who was really behind the scheme. He really was a good planner and the whole deal went smoothly.

What Norbert did was to kidnap Macho Sweeze. He then convinced Maktab Al-barid that the snatch was the work of Zaytian terrorists from his homeland and that unless the ex-king came up with $55,000 in cash for the Zayt Liberation Fund, he'd start receiving packages containing various choice cuts of his favorite author. That extra $1000, by the way, was to cover the expenses of the snatch itself. Norbert wore built-up shoes, a padded coat, and a stocking mask when he grabbed Macho, and even his rival author didn't recognize him.

"He was a tall skinny guy, must've been an Englishman from the way he talked," Macho told the police and the F.B.I. later.

Norbert gave Macho a shot of horse tranquilizer, something he'd swiped from the location of a Western film, and that kept him out cold for most of the twentyseven hours that Norbert held on to him. In a way I contributed—unwittingly, to be sure—to Norbert's final plan. He took Macho out of the parking lot behind that Country-and-Western club in Ventura where Frilly Jonah appeared now and then.

Maktab Al-barid was warned not to go to the law or Macho would be treated exactly as the Blind Butcher treated gangsters and subversives in the novels. To the ex-king, of course, $55,000 was nothing at all and he was even a bit puzzled as to why the fanatics asked for so little. It was a small price to pay for the safe return of one of his dear friends, and he paid it readily.

Once Macho was returned, his agent gave out the story. It was terrific publicity for the upcoming movie. There had already been a few small mentions in the trade papers about the movie, some of which had even mentioned that Macho Sweeze was Dan X. Spear. Now, however, the whole country was talking about the Blind Butcher and his brilliant creator, about how life had imitated art, and what a narrow escape he'd had. You could never really trust terrorists—they might well have taken the $55,000 and butchered Macho anyway.

The kidnaping made a celebrity of Macho. He began to show up on local talk shows, to get his picture in the magazines and the papers. The last time I ever spoke to Norbert was the afternoon the issue of *Persons* hit the area newsstands, with Macho's dark, roughly handsome face beaming from the cover.

"Did you see it?" Norbert asked.

I was fresh back from Chicago, suffering jet lag and what I suspect was a serious allergic reaction to nearly two solid weeks of SoyHammy for breakfast. My head was throbbing, my eyes were watering, and I didn't really respond very sympathetically.

"See what?"

"That smug leering face on the cover of *Persons*. Gosh, it's disgusting. When writers of real talent can't even get their pictures on a roll of—"

"Macho's had a lot of publicity lately," I reminded him, careful of what I said over the phone. Sometimes they listened at the switchboard. "Thanks, I imagine, to you—that was your touch I noted, wasn't it?"

"Who else?" I could almost hear his broad satisfied grin. "You going to inform on me?"

"None of my affair." I surveyed the pile of stuff that had gathered on my desk top in my absence; there was even a nine-pound SoyHammy. "Norbert, I have a lot of—"

"I'm back with Glorious," he told me.

"Good, I guess. Where are you living?"

"New place in Malibu. Very classy. Used to belong to Honey and Hank."

"So things are pretty much going okay for you again?"

"I have some bucks for the nonce, yeah. But I am not being bothered by the sound of eager producers pounding at my door to demand scripts. The only nibble I've had is from some guy who claims he's bought the rights to revive *Death Valley Days* on the tube," said Norbert, the momentary joy fading from his voice. "Boy, if I could've gotten all that publicity that Macho grabbed. After all, I wrote the books. Not him."

"Macho's new fame is a side effect of—well, of what happened to him," I said. "Look on the bright side. You and Glorious are back togeth—"

"That'll last about six minutes longer than my supply of loot."

"Still you ought to—"

"He's going to appear on the Mack Naydell Show tomorrow morning, live from Fish World in Laguna."

"That's one of the fastest rising talk shows in the country." I pressed my temple to try and control the throb. "But now, Norbert, I ought—"

"You bet it's a hot show. Naydell's going to knock Douglas, Carson, Donahue, Davidson, and Arends right out of the box any day now." Enthusiasm had returned to his voice. "They've been running teaser spots all day about Macho's appearance mañana."

"Don't watch, it'll only—"

"Remember that the Mack Naydell show is done absolutely *live,*" he said. "Meaning they can't edit it for most of their markets. I prevailed on one of my few remaining chums in Hollywood and got a ducat for the broadcast."

"You'll only upset yourself."

"Ah, tune in and see," chuckled Norbert.

Macho Sweeze appeared as scheduled the next morning. The show was broadcast live from the big outdoor amphitheater at Fish World. The day was clear, smogless, bright blue. There were some five hundred people circling the open-air stage where the prematurely gray Mark Naydell chatted with his famous guests. A very handsome setting the show had—the tree-filled hills around the outdoor theater framed it nicely.

Up in the forest, stretched out among the tall trees, was Fritz Momand. He had one of his high-powered hunting rifles with him, equipped with a telescopic sight. He also had a small battery-operated TV set, the earphone to his ear. Anything said down there on the stage he'd hear.

Frilly, early that morning, admitted she had indeed been having an affair with the man who had written the Blind Butcher novels. Fritz knocked her cold before she got to give him many more details. He left her sprawled, still in one of her fringe-trimmed cowgirl suits, on the living-room floor and took off for Laguna with his favorite rifle. He was a violent man who believed there was only one just punishment for a man who took advantage of his wife.

I watched the show from one of the screening rooms at the agency. My secretary was with me so I could dictate letters while I watched.

"Oh," she exclaimed just before a commercial break, "isn't that your friend there, in the second row of the audience?"

"Who?"

She pointed to the screen. "The belligerent little fellow who drops in for lunch sometimes."

By the time I looked up from my pile of papers they were showing a SoyHammy commercial. "You mean Norbert Tuffy?"

"I think that's his name. He won an Emmy or something years ago. What's he doing these days?"

"Sort of difficult to explain."

After the block of commercials we got a grinning closeup of Mack Naydell. "This next guest's long been one of my favorite people and a damn fine writer. I'm kicking myself it took a near-tragedy to remind me to have him drop in to visit us," he said. "Let's welcome a very talented guy, Macho Sweeze."

They cut to a medium shot to show Macho come striding out to shake hands and sit in an armchair next to the affable host.

"Happy to be here, Mack," Macho said.

"He's got a sexy voice," said my secretary.

"Before we talk about your recent experiences," said Naydell, leaning in the direction of his guest, "I'd like to talk about the Blind Butcher books."

Up in the woods above the theater Fritz Momand made the final adjustments to his rifle. He had Macho in the crosshairs now and was waiting for just the right second to fire. He figured he'd have time for two, maybe three shots. As he waited he listened to them talking.

"Up until recently," Naydell was saying, "no one knew you'd written these great suspense novels, Macho. One of which will soon be a major movie. But now you've come out from behind the Dan X. Spear pen name."

"Yeah, I got tired of hiding my light under a bushel," said Macho, grinning. "Now I am openly admitting that I am the author of the Blind Butcher series."

Fritz's finger tightened on the trigger.

Then up out of the audience leaped Norbert Tuffy. Before anyone could restrain him, he hopped right on the stage and ripped the lapel mike off Macho's checkered jacket.

"That's a lie!" Norbert shouted, and turned, arm raised high and facing the audience. "My name is Norbert Tuffy and I'm the true and only author of the Blind Butcher books!"

Fritz hesitated. He wasn't sure which one, Macho or Norbert, had written the books and had had an affair with his wife.

He decided to play it safe.

He shot both of them.

JUST A GAG

by Tex Hill

Tex Hill is from the Rio Grande border country of south-west Texas and has worked as a movie actor, cowboy, horse trainer, and for fifteen years, as a Texas police officer and deputy sheriff. He has written more than two dozen short stories and magazine articles, although "Just a Gag" is his first published work in the mystery field. He has recently completed a mystery novel, Three Days of Fear. *Mr. Hill now resides in California.*

Some films are easy to work, others are dangerous and demanding. Then there are those that make you ask yourself, how do I get out of this turkey? *Bandits of the Border* was worse than that. It was a disaster from the first day on the set.

I've been a stunt man since the early Sixties, and to me and my creditors a buck is a buck. I've never turned down any gags except for a few that were so unsafe and unpredictable that not even the great Bill James would have tried them. This picture was just a routine western-adventure flick with the usual gags—horse falls, saddle falls, fistfights—nothing out of the ordinary. But the scale was still union, so I took the contract.

Wonder Studios had never produced anything worthy of much artistic notice. In fact, there's an old joke around Hollywood that goes "If it's a good picture, it's a real Wonder!" This one was done in their normal quickie style, with the fading screen legend, Buck Baker, as the star. In the old days, Buck had been the number-one box office draw with the sagebrush and six-gun fans. Now, as the saying goes, he couldn't get arrested in Hollywood. *Bandits of the Border* was his last gasp as a film hero.

I'd worked with some of the best in the business and had seen the ego problems, professional jealousies, and personal dislikes of all of them. Buck was the complete opposite of most of today's stars, quiet and mannerly,

144

an old pro at the movie game. He was on the set the first morning I arrived and he impressed me with his firm handshake and his air of bored indifference to his status as the star of the film.

We were introduced by the assistant director, a stylish young eager-beaver type, Jay Miller. I told Buck how pleased I was to work with him and how much I'd enjoyed his earlier pictures.

"Thanks," he said in that soft rich baritone. "I've always tried to give my fans what they wanted to see." He appraised me for a long moment and added, "I've heard good things about you too. They say you're one of the best riders in the business."

"I like horses," I said.

"Good. I used to do all my own stuff, but—" he patted his slight paunch with his sun-browned hand "—the years seem to be catching up with me."

I smiled. "You look in pretty good shape to me." I meant it. He did look good for a man his age. He was as slim and trim as his publicity photos made him appear—a few pounds heavier, perhaps, but still solid.

"Yeah, well. Just make me look good and we'll get along," he said.

I returned his easy grin and watched as he strode back to his chair in the shade of his assigned trailer. Then turning to the A.D. I said, "Anything I should know about working with Mr. Baker?"

Jay smiled and shrugged. "Just stay with his style in the action scenes and don't let him see you mistreat his horse."

"No problem there," I told him. "I really do like horses."

"Fine." He shrugged again. "C'mon, I'll show you the trailer we rented for you. Get your gear put away and then come on over to that silver trailer. The big shots are all over there drinking coffee and going over the storyboard."

As soon as I had my pads stored and my suitcases in the bedroom, I lit a cigarette and walked over to meet the producer and director. The May sun was starting to heat things up. It really felt good on my back. Lifting the latch, I opened the door and stepped inside the air-conditioned office trailer.

The four men who sat around the table looked up at my entrance with a hint of annoyance. Then the big fat man in the terrycloth jumpsuit stood up and held out his hand. "Welcome aboard, Steve." He motioned toward the others. "This is Steve Holt, our stunt coordinator. Fred Akers, your director, and Craig Gates, our co-star."

I shook hands with each of them in turn. The director was a thin nervous man with an air of authority. I didn't know him but I knew *of* him, and his work was above average—a surprise, considering the studio producing this picture.

Craig Gates I knew. He was another surprise, one of the fastest-rising young stars in the film world, a heartthrob in the truest sense of the word. He was also a first-class pain in the neck. Some of my friends had worked on a few of his films, and considered him an arrogant, coke-sniffing egomaniac. He looked the part. I got a sinking feeling in my gut.

The fourth man had not been included in the introductions, so I nodded to him. He smiled, showing a mouthful of teeth that reminded me of Bruce, the mechanical shark. "H. R. Boghan," he said coldly. "I'm Mr. Gates' manager." He made no move to accept the hand I offered so I stuck the hand into my hip pocket and leaned against the wall. My old friend Gordon Victor, the producer, sat down and in his jovial tone told me to get a cup of coffee and find a chair. After I did both he said, "Here's a copy of the script, Steve. Nothing you can't handle."

While they went back to their discussion I sipped my coffee and scanned the rivet-bound pages. It was simple stuff, just like I'd figured. Lots of hard riding and brawling, a couple of thirty-foot falls. A regular Buck Baker special. I finished and sat back in polite silence.

The conversation had been heating up and I listened to the anger with misgivings. Now, don't misunderstand me—all pictures have problems of one kind or another. There are always arguments about the script or costuming or something, but this was different— there was a personal viciousness in some of Craig Gates' remarks.

"I don't give a damn," America's newest male sex symbol was shouting, his plastic-handsome features twisted with rage, "I'm not playing second fiddle to some old washed-up cowboy!"

"Now, calm down, Craig," Vic replied, his voice low, the effort to remain calm himself an obvious strain. "I can't rewrite the whole script. Buck's already agreed to share the billing with you on an equal basis and the contracts are all signed. The studio expects you to live up to your commitment." He fixed the agent with a hard stare. "Boghan understood the terms, so if there's a problem it's between you and him. Filming begins in the morning and you'll be on the set, ready to work, or we'll have to—"

"Don't threaten me!" Gates said imperiously.

"No one's threatening anybody. I'm just reminding you we have a legal contract," the producer replied levelly, "the terms of which are enforceable in any court."

At this turn of events, Boghan showed his first sign of emotion. He coughed and laid a restraining hand on his young client's shoulder. "I'm sure this can be worked out to everyone's satisfaction. But first I think, Craig, you and I should talk things over in private." He stood and began to urge Gates toward the door. "There will be no problems, Mr. Victor. We'll honor our end of the contract. Completely."

The door closed behind them and Vic sighed heavily. Akers, the director, broke his pencil in half and threw the pieces against the wall. I buried my nose in my coffee and said nothing. I was sure Craig Gates would honor the contract, but there would be problems. I could smell them coming.

I went over the script again then, avoiding anything that was none of a stunt man's business. Vic and Akers approved my suggestions, gave me a rundown of tomorrow's schedule, and went into a worried huddle as I let myself out into the sunny brightness of the Arizona morning.

When my stunt men arrived later in the day, I went over the action with them, treated them to dinner at a steakhouse down the highway, and then drove back to the location to turn in early. Most of the trailers were dark and silent, but a single light showed in Buck Baker's window. He had always prided himself on knowing his lines, and it was clear that he did it by studying them while others were in town partying. He was the last of his kind, a holdover from the days when a star owed his fans the best he could give them.

The day started out smoothly enough. The first shot was set up within an hour. Most of the horses were a bit frisky, giving my boys a chance to show off their skill as they took the edge off them. I got Buck's big snow-white stallion out of the pen and saddled him myself.

Just as I was prepared to mount up, Baker took the reins from me and climbed aboard, giving me a smile. "Thanks, Steve," he said, "but I'm not that old." With a firm seat and an easy grace, he put the stud through his paces. I watched with genuine admiration. Buck was nearing sixty, but no one could have told it the way he handled that animal. It was easy to see why he'd been called The Greatest Cowboy in the World.

Most of the shots being dialogue, there wasn't much for my crew to do that morning. After lunch we mounted up for a stagecoach chase and Buck was visibly pleased with the way I doubled him in the transfer leap from his horse to the top of the wildly careening coach. I was taking a breather when he approached.

"Steve," he said, "that was really something. I could see myself twenty years ago, watching you do that."

"Hell, Buck," I answered modestly, "you invented the gag. I just copied your style from *Ranger Legion*."

He smiled a bit sadly. "Yeah—back in 1943." His big shoulders seemed to droop just a little as he walked away.

Since everyone knew that Craig Gates resented having to share star credit with Buck, their first scene together was witnessed with great interest by the entire cast and crew. It was plain to see that tension existed, but the scene came off well and Akers was impressed by the performances. He asked for a retake for safety's sake and Gates complied without a fuss. Baker gave his usual professional attention to the direction and was very good.

I had about decided that things were going along as smoothly as on any other shoot when it happened.

It was the last setup of the day and I was getting out of the costume that was a copy of the one Buck would be wearing all through the film when there was a sudden commotion from the direction of the set.

Betty, the makeup girl, was holding her face and crying. Craig Gates was yelling at her and threatening to slap her again. I started toward them and put myself in the middle of the argument. "Take it easy, Mr. Gates," I warned.

"This is none of your concern!" he snapped.

"See you later, Betty," I told her.

The blow came in fast. My reflexes saved me from the full force of it, but I still went down hard. I felt the hot blood rising in my face and I got up fast, my fists clenched and ready.

"Don't do it, Steve."

The calm, quiet voice broke my rage, and I took a deep breath to relax. "I'm cool—thanks, Mr. Akers," I said, giving the actor a grim look. The director's intervention had helped save my career and Craig Gates' million-dollar face—this time.

The rest of the week, I kept out of Gates' way, only speaking to him when I had to. He continued to ride Betty about every little thing. His pancake was either too heavy or too light, his eyes weren't lined dark enough—he went on and on until she became a quivering wreck. Take it from me, that set became the most unpleasant location I or anyone else had ever been contracted on. Buck Baker was too professional to say so, but you could see that he was becoming more and more disgusted with his arrogant co-star.

As we moved into the second week of shooting, most of the heavy stuntwork began. We were really earning our money now and there was little time for anything else. I had almost forgotten about Gates.

The shot called for Gates' character to gallop up to the edge of a fifty-foot cliff and then leap his mount off into the river below. I was doubling Buck, so Chet Jackson put on the costume for Gates' stunt gag. Gates was trying to tell Chet how to do his job and was being ignored for the most part.

Before I could prevent it, Buck's stallion, Snowking, reached out and nudged Gates with his nose. Either the push was harder than it looked or Gates was off balance because the blond actor went down on his face in the biggest pile of manure I'd ever seen.

Sputtering with fury, Gates leaped up amidst the gales of laughter and, cursing savagely, kicked the big white stallion in the belly. The startled horse squealed with pain and began to buck wildly. I held onto the reins desperately and tried to get him under control. When I finally managed to stop him a shout of warning caused me to turn.

Gates had picked up a section of dolly track and was walking toward the snorting horse with murder in his eyes. But before he reached him Buck Baker pulled back a gloved hand, spun Gates around, and in classic cowboy style smashed a right cross into the younger man's face. Dropping the piece of track, Gates cursed and threw a punch of his own. Buck ducked under it and with a one-two combination laid the other man out cold on the ground. Looking around somewhat self-consciously, Buck straightened his Stetson and said softly, "No son of a bitch hits my horse." He took the reins from me and walked off with the animal, looking a little younger somehow.

The next two days were happy ones. Craig Gates refused to leave his trailer. His manager raised a stink, but Buck was still too big a star to tangle with—he just listened in silence, then told Boghan to go soak his head.

When his bruises were sufficiently healed to allow him to show his face in public once more, Gates returned to work, very quiet and subdued. Maybe he had learned something, I thought. The first scene the two stars played together went very smoothly.

As the filming approached the final days, the only sign that there was still a problem was in Gates' attempts to upstage the older actor. Baker fended them off with the ease of many years of practice and experience and often made the other man look foolish without appearing to do so.

Then one night I awoke suddenly from a sound sleep,

not quite sure what had disturbed me. I lay still for a second, then got up and walked to the door of my trailer in my underwear. The night breeze was cool as I stepped outside. There was a moan from the direction of the horse pens. I went over and peered into the corral.

In the middle of the area, the big white body of Snowking lay on its side, the animal's head stretched out, the nostrils wide and flaring in agony. I ran back to the trailer, pulled on a pair of pants, and raced to the office trailer to call into town for a vet.

In the chilly pre-dawn grayness I stood with the others, watching silently as the great horse gave up and died. Dr. Gonzales stood up and shook his head.

"I did my best," he said. "I'm sorry."

A loud sob broke the stillness and I nearly cried myself as Buck Baker began to weep, openly and without shame. Those two went back quite a few years together, and Snowking had been a fine horse. I knew how a man could form an attachment to an animal like that, but for Buck it was more than that—it was the death of the last link to his years of glory.

Vic went to Buck, slipped an arm around his shoulders and said, "I'm really sorry, Buck. He was up in years though—it was bound to happen someday."

Buck nodded. "I know. I'm just a sentimental old fool, crying over a horse—"

Dr. Gonzales, who was packing his instruments, said, "That horse died from foundering. It's my guess he got into enough sweetfeed to kill him."

We all looked up quickly. Buck's face turned hard and cold. All eyes swiveled to the wrangler, Tex Jenkins. The young cowboy looked around with a shocked expression and held up his hands. "Wait a minute!" he said. "Don't blame me! I fed all these animals their normal amount and then put the sack back in the storage bin."

"You're sure?" Vic asked.

"Yes, sir. I wouldn't forget something like that!"

Without a word, Buck turned and walked toward the bin, all of us trailing behind in silence. Opening the door, he reached inside and pulled out an empty grain sack. "One hundred pounds of grain," he said in a deadly tone of voice. "The punk might as well have fed him arsenic."

We all knew who he was talking about. In a group, we followed him to Gates' trailer. Whatever happened next was going to be richly deserved and not one of us would dream of lifting a finger to prevent it. We watched as Buck banged on the door until it was opened.

Gates stood blinking at the surrounding circle of serious faces.

"Why?" Buck asked him.

"What?"

"Why didn't you just shoot him?"

"Baker, have you gone nuts? What the hell are you raving about?"

His face scarlet, Buck grabbed Gates around the neck and began to shake him violently. "My horse, damn you! You fed my horse enough grain to kill an elephant!"

Prying himself loose, Gates staggered back and drew in a ragged breath. "What are you talking about? I just gave him a good feed!" He looked around at the rest of us in panic. "I was sorry about kicking him that day. I just wanted to make up with him."

"You dirty—" Buck lunged at the young actor. They struggled for a minute, then the older man choked, gasped, clutched his chest, and fell heavily to the ground.

A stroke, the attendants told Vic as they loaded Buck into the ambulance. The red lights flashed across our faces as we surrounded the vehicle. The doors slammed and we parted to let it race for the hospital, siren wailing. Buck Baker would probably live, the medics had said, but how much damage the stroke had done they couldn't be certain.

Craig Gates stood weakly against the wall of his trailer, his pale face turned to us.

"For the love of God, fellas," he stammered, "I never meant for anything like this to happen, I swear it!"

Gordon Victor walked up and snapped his pudgy fingers. "Gates, you are the lowest form of life I've ever laid eyes on! You're through in the movie business, I promise you that!" Turning on his heel, he stalked off, and one by one the rest broke apart and drifted away,

leaving me staring at the crestfallen actor as the pink-
ness of the rising sun washed across the landscape.

"Steve!" Gates looked at me with shocked awareness.
"You've got to believe me! I didn't mean it—I just wanted
to—"

"Don't say it, Gates. I don't want to hear about how
you wanted to make friends with Snowking."

"All right!" he shouted. "So I didn't! I admit it—I
wanted to make the damned horse sick. I figured to
give him such a bellyache he'd get sick. But it was just
a gag, a prank that backfired, that's all—just a gag!"

"Nobody's laughing," I told him, then turned my back
and went to get some coffee.

In Hollywood, business is business and the dollar is
almighty. Vic called a production meeting that morning
and told us that since there were only two scenes left
to film the picture would be finished with me doubling
for the stricken star. It was action stuff, so there would
be no problem with dialogue or facial shots.

I dressed in Buck's costume and took my place on
the balcony of the saloon set. A few minutes later a
pale and remorseful Gates appeared. He mounted the
stairs and joined me. I gave him a flat stare but kept
my mouth shut.

When the cameras were set and the lighting was
correct, Akers gave us the signal. I asked Gates in a
neutral tone if he understood the gag. We were to struggle at the railing, trade a couple of punches, then go
over the breakaway railing and fall onto the prop table
below. He nodded and I cued Akers we were ready.

It was a pretty easy stunt as gags go—just a fall of
fifteen feet onto a table that was rigged to fold at the
correct angle to allow us to break our fall and roll off
onto the floor. Gates could've asked for a stunt man,
but he was too ashamed, I guess. Anyway, I would be
on the bottom, so most of the impact would be on me.

Everything went like clockwork. The fight was as
hard and realistic-looking as we could make it. The
railing gave way just at the right time, and down we
went. But stunt work is mostly a matter of timing and
split-second coordination. Sure, training and experience are big factors too, but when the gag is going down

you have to be on time, or accidents can occur. You'd be surprised how easy it is to be permanently crippled or even killed if your timing is thrown off enough to drop you on your neck from fifteen feet in the air.

No, sir, a stunt gag isn't funny if it goes wrong. A man can get killed, even a big star. I began to shift my weight just enough, seeing the look of horror on Gates' face with a certain amount of justified pride at the speed of my trained reflexes.

THE SPY WHO STAYED UP ALL NIGHT

by Edward D. Hoch

The literary output of Edward D. Hoch is amazing. His short stories appear regularly in Ellery Queen's Mystery Magazine *and* Alfred Hitchcock's Mystery Magazine, *and number over four hundred. They are published under his own name as well as under several aliases. Many of them center around series characters such as Captain Leopold, Simon Ark, Jeffery Rand, and Nick Velvet. In 1967 his story about Captain Leopold, "The Oblong Room," won the Edgar award from the Mystery Writers of America for best short story.*

Rand was at his desk in the little downstairs office that Leila had decorated for him when she came to the door to tell him he was wanted on the phone.

"Not London, I hope." He'd had a few months free of Hastings' calls for help, and he was deep into the memoirs he'd been promising to write ever since his retirement.

"It is London, but not what you think. It's Cap Curtiss."

"Who?"

"You know, Cap Curtiss, the American chap with the all-night radio show."

They'd caught snatches of it once or twice, generally on the car radio while driving home from a late party or a gathering at Leila's university. The show had never penetrated very deeply into Rand's consciousness, though he was aware it had a large following among insomniacs.

"Whatever can *he* want?" Rand grumbled, going to answer the call.

Cap Curtiss on the telephone was very much like Cap Curtiss on all-night radio. Though he'd tried to adopt some British mannerisms his voice sounded more like an American sideshow barker than a staid English broadcaster for BBC Radio.

"Mr. Rand, Cap Curtiss here. Perhaps you've heard my show on the wireless? *All Night Long With Cap Curtiss and Friends*? I generally have three guests in the studio and we kick around a variety of subjects from midnight till five in the morning. I'd love to have you as a guest next Friday night if you could make it."

"Oh, I'm afraid—"

"Before you decline let me tell you what I have in mind. My other two guests are Roland Nees, who wrote that massive book on codes and ciphers, and Judith Fry, who cracked the German codes during world War Two."

"Of course I'm familiar with both names," Rand said.

"The public is always interested in codes and spies and inside stories of wartime espionage. Judith Fry has never written her memoirs, and I believe she has a great deal to tell."

"The Official Secrets Act—"

"Oh, come now, Rand! We won't be getting into anything current. The war was a lifetime away. My God, Judith Fry is nearly eighty years old!"

"I've always wanted to meet the woman," Rand admitted. "She's something of a legend in the business."

"Then you will come! Good, good!"

"I didn't say—"

"Here's the format of the show. We chat back and forth for the first two and a half hours. Then we take a half-hour break at 2:30 and I have some Chinese food sent in. We're back on the air at three and we take phone calls from listeners for the last two hours."

"Look, this isn't really my—"

"We're at Broadcast House in London. Can you be there a half hour early next Friday? At 11:30?"

Rand surrendered. "I suppose so."

"I'll look for you then. Bye-bye!"

He was still standing by the telephone when Leila came into the room. "What was all that about?"

"I'm going to be on the radio," he said. "All night long."

Cap Curtiss came bounding along the corridor and intercepted Rand at the reception desk, giving him a

vigorous handshake and leading him back to the studio.
"Miss Fry is here already and I expect Nees to show up
any minute. Say, you're a young chap to be retired from
intelligence work. I expected someone older."

"I retired while I could still enjoy it," Rand said. "But
I'm fifty-four now, so I'm not all that young anymore.
I always wanted to retire when I was fifty and that's
what I did."

"That's good," Curtiss said. "Save it for on the air."
He led Rand through a door and into a small studio
where an elderly woman sat knitting at a kidney-shaped
table. She brightened and smiled pleasantly as they
entered. "Oh, you must be Mr. Rand. I've heard a great
deal about you."

"Not nearly as much as I've heard about you," he
insisted. "In my early days with Concealed Communications hardly a day passed without someone quoting
Judith Fry."

He could see that pleased her. "It's good to be remembered by your colleagues. Though I told Mr. Curtiss here that I doubt the public even knows my name."

"We'll remedy that tonight," he assured her. Then,
glancing out the thick soundproof window to the corridor, he said, "There's Roland Nees now. Pardon me."

Rand seated himself next to Judith Fry. Her white
hair was carefully in place and her fingers moved quickly
over the knitting. "You're very good at that."

"I find it helps my arthritis," she said. "At my age
one has to keep the body active or it simply rusts away."

Cap Curtiss reentered the studio with a somber-look-
ing man in a black turtleneck sweater. Rand recognized
him at once from the jacket photograph on the back of
The Cryptographers' Encyclopedia. "This is Roland
Nees," Curtiss said. "I believe you know Miss Fry already, and here's Jeffery Rand."

"A pleasure to meet you," Nees said, not really
sounding as if he meant it. "I wanted to interview you
for my book but you were out of the country at the time.
In Russia, I believe."

"No matter, it was a fine job." Rand was feeling generous. "I'm sure it's become the bible down at Double-
C."

Cap Curtiss glanced at the clock. "Just five minutes

to air time. We'd better all get seated. Talk into the microphone, but don't touch it and don't tap on it with your pencils." There were pencils and pads at each of their places. "I'll introduce you all at the beginning of the show, and then again at the start of each hour for those listeners who have tuned in late."

A youngish man with sandy hair entered from the control room. "All set, Cap?"

"This is my producer, Glen Bridge." He introduced them all. "Glen's the brains behind this program. I told him how successful all-night talk shows were back in the States and he helped launch them over here."

Glen Bridge smiled. "People berate me for Americanizing the country, but I just tell them they don't have to listen if they don't like it."

Cap waved to another man in the control room—a balding fellow with a potbelly. "The other chap's our engineer, Eddie White. He keeps us on the air—or cuts us off if the language gets too rough. So watch your step!" He chuckled and added, "Though I guess you three aren't likely to give us any grief. Last week I had some punk rockers on and Eddie was working overtime bleeping out words."

"Is the broadcast delayed?" Rand asked.

"Just seven seconds. They wouldn't let us do it otherwise."

"Air time," Bridge said. "Cut the chatter, Cap."

Rand watched the red second hand move around the big studio wall clock. Then Eddie signaled from the control room and Cap Curtiss opened the show.

"Good evening, ladies and gentlemen. From the heart of London this is *All Night Long With Cap Curtiss and Friends*. I'm Cap Curtiss and I think we've got a really fascinating show for all you late-nighters. Three experts on codes and ciphers are with me in the studio tonight, and we're going to have a lively time chatting about their cloak-and-dagger days. We'll be on the air with our guests until 2:30, and then after our usual half-hour break for recorded symphonette music, we'll be back on the air to take calls from our listeners.

"And now to introduce our guests. First and foremost is Miss Judith Fry, a legendary name in the annals of cryptography. Judith Fry began her career working with the Americans during the final days of Prohibition there, helping to crack the codes used by rum-runners. She also aided the Canadian government in breaking a complicated code used by opium smugglers in the late 1930s, before returning to England at the outbreak of the Second World War. Some historians have called her war work the most important single factor in the breaking of Hitler's codes and the duplication of the complex German coding machine known as Enigma. Judith, it's a pleasure to have you here tonight."

She smiled and said a few words in reply before Curtiss moved on to the next guest. "Roland Nees is the author of a massive thousand-page study titled *The Cryptographers' Encyclopedia*. What started out as a hobby for Mr. Nees has grown into a full-scale occupation—the study of codes and ciphers and their place in world history.

"And finally as our third guest we have Jeffery Rand, former director of Britain's Department of Concealed Communications. Mr. Rand joined British Intelligence in the late 1940s as a young code clerk in the famous Calendar Network. He rose through the ranks to head up Double-C by the mid-1960s, a position he held for more than ten years until his retirement at the age of fifty. I understand Mr. Rand still performs occasional services for the British government on request. Is that correct?"

"They've called me back a few times," Rand admitted. "It's not unusual for intelligence agencies to rehire former employees on a contract basis. America's Central Intelligence Agency does it a great deal."

Cap Curtiss settled back. With the introductions out of the way he asked the most obvious question. "How has espionage changed—how have codes and ciphers changed—since the 1930s and '40s when Judith was active?"

"It's all machines now," the woman responded, still keeping busy with her knitting. "I wouldn't know the first thing about the computers they now use."

Roland Nees cleared his throat. "Of course the computers are, in a sense, merely an outgrowth of the onetime pads that came into use during the last war." His voice droned on, much like a slightly boring college professor's, Rand decided. He wondered if Leila, a professor herself, had the same thought at home where she was listening.

Rand was surprised at how quickly the time passed. It was one o'clock before he knew it, and Curtiss was repeating the introductions for the second hour. Perhaps Leila was asleep by now, though she'd promised to stay awake for all of it. Rand had set his tape machine to record the show and she had to change tapes for him every ninety minutes.

"... must be one cipher you were never able to crack," Cap Curtiss was saying, as the hour rolled around to 1:30. "How about it, Mr. Rand? What was your toughest one?"

"I can say in all modesty that I was never completely stumped," Rand said. "Of course I had the help of a fine group of dedicated co-workers."

"I don't remember being stumped either," Judith Fry said, "although those Canadian opium smugglers came close."

"How do you relax from such a grueling task?"

"I read Samuel Johnson's Dictionary," she replied with a little laugh. "And I knit. I love them both."

Shortly after 2:00 A.M. Curtiss suggested there were no further applications to be made of codes and ciphers in today's world. "I disagree," Nees said. "Back in the States companies are using a variety of coded video signals in pay-television systems. There are people in America trying to break these codes and unscramble the image so they can sell illegal equipment to non-subscribers."

Judith Fry nodded. "A man approached me just last month with such an offer. Imagine—a seventy-nine-year-old woman getting involved with electronic gadgets!"

"It shows that people still remember your skills," Curtiss said.

"It must have been someone who read about you in Roland's book," Rand suggested. "That was a remarkable chapter he devoted to you."

"But cable television is beyond my comprehension!" she insisted.

"What sort of offer was it? Something illegal?"

"I don't remember the details," she replied, suddenly turning vague. "But I turned it down, of course. I'm too old for that."

Rand had taken the precaution of napping for a few hours that afternoon, but he was beginning to feel tired by the time 2:30 rolled around. Curtiss urged his listeners to stay tuned and get their questions ready, then settled back with a sigh as the microphone light went out and the engineer signaled they were off the air. "Now," he said, "that wasn't so bad, was it?"

"Where's this food you promised us?" Judith Fry asked. "If I have to stay up all night, at least you can feed me."

Cap Curtiss chuckled. "You know, you're a lively woman for your age. I can understand people wanting to put you back to work. I'd hire you myself if I had any decoding to be done. Frankly, I was a bit hesitant about having you on an all-night show, but Glen assured me you could do it."

The producer had just come in, leading a pair of oriental men bearing cartons of food in paper bags. "Oh, sure," he confirmed, joining in the conversation. "I met Judith last month at a concert and poetry reading where I played the piano. I knew she'd be perfect for the show."

Everyone helped themselves to the cartons of Chinese food and Rand was relieved to see he wasn't expected to eat it with chopsticks. Eddie White came out of the control room to join them.

"The symphonette on?" Bridge asked him.

Eddie nodded. "That'll put our audience to sleep quickly enough. You'd get more questions with a livelier musical interlude."

"You want to play Top 40 like Capital radio? We get enough calls," Bridge said, munching on an eggroll.

The food tasted good to Rand that night. He sat next to Judith Fry as they ate, chatting about their decoding experiences. "I hope people still try to hire me when I'm your age," he said.

She brushed a wisp of gray hair from her eyes, like a girl on a date with a boy she wanted to impress. He remembered some of the pictures from Nees' book and knew she'd been quite attractive in her younger days. "I keep going," she said. "I keep my hand in."

"We all should do that."

"There's a difference, though. You're married, aren't you?"

"Yes," he admitted.

"I never was. Sometimes I regret it, but not often. It allowed me to concentrate my attention on the problems at hand. With a husband and a family I'd have been an entirely different person. I'd have led a different life."

"I can understand that, but—"

"It's almost three," Cap announced. "Finish up your food, please."

Judith Fry carefully closed her cartons. "Mine tasted *awful*," she confided to Rand.

Glen Bridge placed new cups of water at everyone's elbow and Eddie White gathered up the half-finished cartons of food. Cap finished his coffee and cleared his throat. Then they were back on the air.

The first caller was a man with a thick foreign accent. "I want to direct my question to Roland Nees," he said.

"Yes?"

"What is your opinion of the Shakespearean ciphers which seem to prove that the plays of Shakespeare were really written by Sir Francis Bacon?"

"The Shakespearean ciphers were discounted long ago," Nees said, using his most authoritative voice. "One can find possible ciphers in the daily newspaper if one looks hard enough and has that sort of mind."

Rand thought Judith Fry was looking suddenly tired. She took a sip of water but it didn't seem to help much. A caller came on with a question for her but when Curtiss turned to her for a reply her face was sagging badly. "Are you all right?" Rand asked.

"I . . . food poisoned . . ."

"What?"

"Electronics . . . he said not to talk . . ."

Rand looked up at Curtiss. "She's ill."

Curtiss signaled the control room and said quickly into the microphone. "We'll return shortly. In the meantime we invite you to listen to a recorded interlude of symphonette music." The red light on his desk went off, indicating the microphones were dead. "What's the matter with her? Is she having a stroke?"

Rand bent forward and sniffed her breath. "I think she's been poisoned."

"Poisoned? On my show?"

Glen Bridge ran in from the control room. "What is it, Cap? Should I call an ambulance?"

Rand straightened up. "You can call one but it won't do any good. She's dead."

The detective in charge, Sergeant Kennerson, confirmed Rand's suspicions. "I'd say she died of cyanide poisoning, but we'll need the autopsy to be certain. Where's this Chinese food you were all eating?"

Eddie White looked nonplused. "I threw the cartons down the incinerator, just like I do every night. The cleaning people raise hob if they're still around in the morning."

Kennerson was younger than Rand, but he seemed to settle on him as the most likely one to question. "I understand you're in British Intelligence, sir?"

"I used to be. I'm retired now."

"Maybe you can give me the best account of what happened."

Rand tried, relating some of the on-air conversation and describing the break for food at 2:30. Kennerson turned his attention to Curtiss. "These two Chinese who delivered the food—are they the same people every night?"

"I suppose so. I don't really pay that much attention. They all look a bit alike, don't you know?"

Glen Bridge sighed. "They were the same men, Sergeant. From the Golden Dragon down the street. They're in here five nights a week, always the same two men."

Cap Curtiss was pacing the floor. "Damn it, somebody at the restaurant slipping cyanide into the food! Someone who was listening to the show! But why?"

"They were afraid of what she might say," Nees suggested. Of all of them he seemed to be taking her death most calmly.

"No," Rand said. "They weren't afraid of her. Obviously only one carton of food was poisoned or we'd all be dead now. But how could the killer know she'd get it? They were passed out quite at random. In fact, we all chose our own."

Curtiss smacked his forehead. "They were after *me!* Someone was trying to kill me!"

"Calm down," Bridge said. "That's not too likely. There are six of us here who ate the food. The killer had only one chance in six of getting any single person."

"Maybe it was an accident," the engineer, Eddie, suggested.

"She didn't think it was an accident when she was dying," Rand pointed out. "She gasped something about electronics, about him telling her not to talk. She thought the food had been poisoned because of that."

"I'll want to hear a tape of the program," Sergeant Kennerson decided. "Meanwhile her next of kin should be notified."

"She has a younger sister, I believe," Roland Nees said. "They were living together when I interviewed her, and I assume the sister is still alive."

"We have the address," Bridge said.

Rand managed to get free long enough to phone Leila at home. "What happened?" she demanded. "They're still playing that awful music on the station."

"Judith Fry died. The police are here."

"Oh, no! It wasn't—?"

"I'm afraid so. You might as well go to bed. I may not be home for a while."

The sergeant was waiting for Rand in the hall. "I've been on the telephone myself, sir, to a gentleman named Hastings."

"Ah, yes. I used to work for him."

"He says I should cooperate fully with you in the investigation."

"Just what made you telephone Hastings?"

"It seems like a national-security matter to me, sir. From what you've all been telling me, she might have been killed by enemy agents."

"Why would enemy agents murder a seventy-nine-year-old woman who hasn't worked for the government to any great extent since the Second World War?"

"You tell me, sir."

"I'll try to," Rand said.

"Then try this too. The dead woman carried an appointment book in her purse. As you might expect from a woman her age, it isn't too full of engagements—a luncheon here and there, about every other week. That type of thing."

Rand saw what the man was getting at. "But she mentioned a man who approached her just last month with an offer. If we could find that in her appointment book—"

"Oh, it's here all right—on the tenth of last month. But she's written the name in some sort of code."

"What?"

"Look for yourself."

He held out the small leather-bound pocket diary and Rand read the notation in Judith Fry's shaky hand. *Lunch with Gleek. Electronics.*

"Gleek?" Rand repeated.

"Gleek."

Rand turned a few of the weekly pages with his finger until he came upon today's date. *Futile Swarm,* the book read. "It's something, all right. Her own private shorthand system, I suppose."

"Do you go along with the idea the poison was meant for someone else?" the detective asked Rand.

"No."

"If Judith Fry was the intended victim, you know what that means."

Rand nodded. "The poison couldn't have been put in the food at the Chinese restaurant. It had to be done here in the studio."

"By one of you five people."

"Correct." He looked at the appointment book again. "So perhaps *Gleek* refers to one of us. The first three letters are the same as Glen Bridge's name. It has the same double-e as Nees. And of course in a simple substitution cipher the double-e could stand for the double-d in Eddie or the double-s in Curtiss."

"So it could be any of them?"

Rand smiled. "There's even a double-f in my first name."

"Now you're merely playing games."

"Cryptography is game-playing, to a large extent. Why else should this old woman bother to enter appointments in her book in code? Who did she think would ever see it, or care? But her life had been devoted to secret writing and she couldn't break the habit."

"So we're left with Gleek, which could be any of them."

"But only one of them had the motive, Sergeant. If we find the one involved with an electronics scheme that needed Judith Fry's help, we'll have our killer."

"Why would she taunt him like that, mentioning the scheme on the air?"

"She only hinted at it, really. It was more game-playing, I suppose, only this time it cost Judith Fry her life."

Rand left the sergeant and went back into the studio. Curtiss and Bridge were arguing about whether they should come back on the air with an announcement or merely let the music play and explain the whole thing on the next broadcast. Finally Curtiss' view prevailed and he returned to the microphone to make a brief announcement. Rand stood at the kidney-shaped desk watching him, seeing the pads and pencils by each of their places, the coffee cup at Cap's elbow, the paper cups of water by his place and Nees'. He thought it was too bad Judith Fry hadn't lived long enough to write the name of her killer on the pad.

The microphone light went on and Cap Curtiss said, "Good evening again, ladies and gentlemen. I'm very sorry for the curtailed show this evening, but it was unavoidable. One of our guests, Miss Judith Fry, was stricken during the last segment and was in need of urgent medical attention. In view of that, we are bringing you recorded music for the balance of the hour until five o'clock. But we'll be back on Monday with our regular show. Good morning from Cap Curtiss and friends!"

When he was off the air, Curtiss explained, "I didn't mention her death, in case the police haven't yet notified her sister."

Bridge, coming out of the control room, agreed. "I don't think it was necessary now, but there's no harm done. You can tell the whole story on Monday."

Rand wandered into the control room, where Eddie White was playing the symphonette recording. "They can all go back to sleep now," he said. It was just 4:30.

"Do you chaps have much contact with the visual

end?" Rand asked. "Cable television systems and the like?"

"That's not here, that's America," the engineer replied. "Sure, we all look to get into video because that's where the real money is. All of us except Cap, that is. He's content with radio."

Rand glanced through the thick glass window and saw Roland Nees slipping into his coat. He hurried out to intercept the man. "Are you leaving now?"

"I thought I would. I've told the police what little I know."

"How about telling me something before you go? When you interviewed Judith for your book, did she ever mention anything about cryptographic pay-television systems?"

"No, the subject never came up."

"But someone like Judith could be a big help in deciphering such a system?"

"Oh, certainly! Despite her age her wits were very sharp. In fact, if I were an American aiming to break one of the cable-television systems over there, she's exactly the sort of person I'd approach. She would be an ocean away from the scene of the crime, so to speak, and elderly enough so she wouldn't be around long to talk about it."

"Exactly what would they have wanted her to do?"

"Depends on the system. Some years ago Zenith had a system that used five decoder knobs with seven positions each. That's over sixteen thousand possible positions. The company would mail a card with the correct setting to subscribers, and the sets were wired differently so you couldn't use a neighbor's setting on your TV. But by comparing a few past settings a cipher expert could quickly figure the thing out. Other systems use scrambling devices and here too a cipher expert could be a big help."

Rand nodded. "Someone approached her and she turned him down. Tonight on the show she told about it and he was afraid she might tell more during the question period, so he killed her."

"Do you mean one of us?" Nees asked.

"Of course. Haven't you known that all along?"

"Curtiss is an American. He'd have ties to American TV."

"So might Bridge or White. Or you, for that matter. Does the name Gleek mean anything to you?"

He seemed truly puzzled. "Should it?"

"It may have been Judith Fry's name for her killer."

Sergeant Kennerson came along then. "Everybody can go home. We can't hold these people any longer."

Roland Nees headed for the door and Rand said, "It seems odd that the killer would have cyanide available for a spur-of-the-moment murder like this. It's not something people carry around in their pockets."

Nees heard him and paused at the door. "But some people do, Rand. You know that as well as I do. Agents operating in enemy territory often carry cyanide capsules. I understand some IRA terrorists even carry them."

Something flickered in Kennerson's eyes. "Cap Curtiss had an IRA man on the show last year. Got himself in a peck of trouble over it. We've got the man in prison now on a bombing charge."

"Let's go talk to Curtiss," Rand suggested.

Curtiss was sorting his notes in a briefcase and getting ready to leave. He frowned when Kennerson mentioned the IRA interview. "Let's not go through all that again. It was a year ago, for God's sake!"

"Did the man discuss cyanide capsules with you, sir?"

"No, he did not."

Glen Bridge came out of the studio carrying some paper cups and crumpled pieces of paper for the incinerator. "What's the trouble now?" he asked.

"They're dredging up that IRA business again," Curtiss complained.

Bridge shook his head and kept walking. "Sergeant, if you ask my opinion, I think the woman killed herself. She probably—"

"Samuel Johnson," Rand said.

They all looked at him oddly. "What's that?" the detective asked.

"She told us she enjoyed reading Johnson's Dictionary. Don't you see? Gleek and futile and swarm aren't really code words at all. They're words from Samuel Johnson's Dictionary!"

Glen Bridge pulled open the metal door of the incinerator chute. "I don't see what that has to do with anything. Does it tell us who killed her?"

Rand took a deep breath and sprang forward. He collided with Bridge and they both went down, the rubbish scattering across the floor. "Here's your killer," Rand called out to Kennerson. "Get those paper cups! One of them will have traces of cyanide in it!"

Glen Bridge sat handcuffed, refusing to talk, while Rand rummaged through the Broadcast House library until he came up with a copy of Johnson's dictionary. "Here it is!" he declared triumphantly. "Her name, Fry, meant 'swarm' back in Sam Johnson's day, and 'futile' meant 'talkative.' When she wrote 'futile swarm' she simply meant 'talkative Fry,' reminding her she'd be on Cap's talk show tonight."

"And 'gleek' means?" Kennerson asked.

" 'Gleek' in those days meant a musician."

"Musician?" The detective looked puzzled.

"Remember Glen Bridge told us he met Judith Fry at a concert and poetry reading where he played the piano. Her first knowledge of him was as a musician, and that's how she noted it when he asked her to have lunch and discuss his electronic decoding scheme."

"All this from Johnson's Dictionary?" the detective asked.

"I didn't really need the dictionary clue to tell me Bridge was the killer."

The handcuffed producer looked interested for the first time, but it was Cap Curtiss who spoke. "How'd you know the poison was in the water cup and not in the Chinese food?"

"Because cyanide kills almost instantly, within seconds," Rand explained. "That's why spies and terrorists carry it as a suicide capsule. Now think back to this night's events. We had the Chinese food, Judith Fry complained it didn't taste good, the show went back on the air, you re-introduced us as you did each hour, a man with an accent called to ask about Shakespeare, and you were actually answering a second call before she really took ill. I saw her sipping water just before she collapsed. If the poison was cyanide it had to be in the water, not in the food, which she'd finished eating more than ten minutes earlier. And I could rule out the food for another reason. We all chose our own cartons at random and she sat with me while she ate it. No one had an opportunity to poison it without my seeing something suspicious."

"And the water?" Kennerson asked.

"I remember Glen Bridge putting the cups at our places just as the break ended. Later, while Cap was announcing her illness, I noticed there were only two cups on the desk, by Nees' and my places. The cup Judith had used was missing. Bridge took it after she died, of course, so we wouldn't detect the odor of cyanide and realize the truth about the poisoning. He was on his way to casually drop it down the incinerator just now when I grabbed him."

Kennerson was busy making notes. "You want to talk about it?"

"Not without my lawyer," Glen Bridge answered.

"Check his American contacts," Rand suggested. "See if he was tied in with any cable television people over there. I think you'll find he was, and that he killed Judith Fry to keep her from talking about it. The paper cup still smells of bitter almonds and I'm sure you'll find traces of cyanide in it. Talk to this IRA terrorist you have locked up. I'm sure he'll tell you he gave Bridge a suicide capsule when he appeared on the show last year. A fatal souvenir that Bridge probably kept in his desk without ever mentioning it to anyone."

"So she was wrong about the food being poisoned," Kennerson said.

Rand nodded. "It simply disagreed with her. She was tired and her stomach was upset, but it was that one sip of water that killed her."

The sun was rising as Rand drove home through the English countryside. He couldn't remember the last time he'd stayed up all night.

THE KUMQUATS AFFAIR

by Francis M. Nevins, Jr.

*Francis M. Nevins, Jr., is a many-faceted mystery en-
thusiast. In addition to the numerous short stories he
has contributed to* Ellery Queen's Mystery Magazine,
*he has contributed to the mystery genre by writing book
reviews and articles, by editing* The Mystery Writer's
Art *(1970) and* Nightwebs *(1971), and by writing* Royal
Bloodline: Ellery Queen, Author and Detective *(1974),
for which he won an Edgar.*

The first and last time Loren Mensing saw the man
with the boil on his nose was when Loren stepped out
of the self-service elevator on the eighth floor and boil-
nose stepped in. Loren had come to New York City for
the annual meeting of a law professors' organization,
but in midafternoon he'd slipped out of the convention
hotel, subwayed downtown, and trudged through slush-
blanketed streets to the old twelve-story office building
on Park and Nineteenth. As the elevator door whispered open and Loren emerged, boil-nose elbowed past
him into the empty cage and the door slid shut.

"New York manners," Loren muttered, and walked
down the hallway to a fumed-oak door that read TOMMY
HAGEN ENTERPRISES, INC. and beneath that legend the
single word ENTER. A huge movie poster of the quintessential Tommy dominated each wall of the foyer: the
ageless face atop the reed-thin body, the eyes that
seemed to stare at something no one else could see, the
fingers of both hands intertwined like pretzels in the
famous Hagen gesture.

A flame-haired receptionist polished her nails at a
blondwood desk, and a few feet to her left a circular
staircase with wrought-iron railings wound upward to
the next floor. The receptionist took Loren's name and
spoke it into the communicator. Within seconds Joyce
Brook burst into the foyer with arms outspread in delight and enveloped him in a vigorous hug.

"God, Loren, it's been a hundred *years* since you've been in town! Come on, let me show you my domain. I was just about to call a meeting with my people but—wait, damn it, I will have that meeting, Loren, and I want you in it too!"

She turned to the fiery-haired receptionist. "Donna, buzz Beau and Andy and Kathy. Powwow in my office in five minutes. Come on, Loren." She scooped him up by the arm and gave him a breathless guided tour while propelling him along an inner corridor.

"That's Beau's office, Beau Douglas, he takes care of theatrical and TV revivals of Tommy's movies, and this one belongs to Kathy Ellison, she's my assistant manager, you'll like her, and Andy, that's Andy Lauer, he's in charge of licensing Tommy's image on everything from T-shirts to cereal. Andy's office is up at the top of that spiral staircase, you see there used to be a law firm here and they had their library upstairs—and here we are!"

She pointed Loren to a shiny black leather armchair in her own corner office and seated herself behind the double-sized mahogany desk.

Loren and Joyce had met in college fifteen years ago. With her six-foot height and air of aggressive competence and ambition, she had not been attractive to many men, but she and Loren had seen something in each other, although after graduation they'd drifted apart.

"And you're in charge of the whole East Coast operation, marketing Tommy's old movies and his image. Tremendous." Loren folded his heavy overcoat across the arm of his chair. "Lot of money in it?"

"Bundles! You know, he's been dead twenty years now and everyone still goes ape over him. W. C. Fields, the Marx Brothers, and Tommy Hagen. There are all sorts of books about him, people watch his movies over and over, you can use the image to sell anything. They're marketing a Tommy Hagen peanut butter in the spring. There's only one thing wrong." Her room-filling voice dropped to almost a whisper. "And that's why I'm so glad you dropped by. Loren, someone's trying to sabotage Tommy Hagen Enterprises." She bit down hard on her lower lip. "And it's getting scary."

"Tell me," Loren said simply.

She hunched forward, nesting her chin in her fists. "About a month ago little things began going wrong around the office. Files misplaced. Business appointments being canceled over the phone and then later we found out it was an impostor who called and the appointment hadn't been canceled at all. That kind of thing. Then it got nastier."

"What happened?"

She drew back the handle of the upper right drawer of her desk. "A week ago Tuesday I came to work as usual and opened this drawer to get something, and there were a couple of dozen big fat worms crawling over my stationery. Somebody had broken into the office and put them in the desk during the night."

"Literally broken in?" Loren asked. "Did he leave traces? I assume you called the police."

"No, I didn't bother, and there weren't any traces. This is an old building and you can get into any office by using a credit card on the lock. We're tied into an electronic security system now and that kind of thing can't happen here again. But as if all this wasn't enough harassment, now I've got a new kind of mess on my hands. A legal mess."

Before Loren could ask for details there was a knock on the door and he rose as two men and a woman filed in and Joyce introduced him to her associates. Beauregard Douglas was a dapper bantamweight in his early thirties, elegantly attired, with dark hair cut short enough to please a drill sergeant. Tall gawky Andy Lauer had a high forehead, a habit of slouching against walls, and a preference for knit sweaters rather than suit jackets. Kathy Ellison—short, delightfully plump, blonde and cuddly-looking—contrasted startlingly with Joyce, causing Loren to wonder if that was why she'd been hired as Joyce's assistant manager.

When they were settled Joyce popped a cigarette between her lips without lighting it. "As it happens, gang, Loren is a law professor and can probably explain the mess we're in better than I can. Loren, tell us about Section 24 of the Copyright Act."

Loren had taught a copyright class two semesters ago and had an excellent memory. "Well, I'm oversimplifying more than I would in school, but a copyright runs for twenty-eight years and then is renewable for another twenty-eight. The two periods are completely separate entities. If I copyright a story, say, and then I die before the renewal period, Section 24 determines who takes the renewal interest. The author's surviving spouse and children have the highest priority."

"All right, now here's a movie trivia question for you. Who is Obed Middleton?"

Loren shook his head in perplexity. "Never heard of him."

Joyce nodded at Kathy Ellison and her assistant answered the question in a voice as melodious as Chinese wind bells. "Obed Middleton was a hog raiser in Enid, Oklahoma. Around 1930 he had a short story published in a pulp magazine. One of Tommy Hagen's producers happened to read the story and the studio paid three hundred dollars for the movie rights. Then Tommy and the writers twisted the story around and turned it into *Kumquats.*"

"God, what a memory!" Beau Douglas said beneath his breath, and looked at Kathy as if she were a witch. Her performance had given Loren a clearer insight into why she was the assistant manager, but the exact nature of the legal problem still eluded him. He'd seen *Kumquats* a dozen times and knew that it was Tommy Hagen's most famous movie, a permanent comedy classic like the Marx Brothers' *Duck Soup* or Fields' *It's a Gift.*

"Now Tommy had foresight," Joyce picked up the thread of the story. "He bought up his pictures from the studio in the late forties, just before the big TV boom. Then he died in 1955 and his will left everything to the boy he'd adopted. The lawyers set up Tommy Hagen Enterprises, and since then Keith, the son, has made a mint out of licensing Tommy's image on products and renting the movies to TV stations. Until now, that is."

"But where does Section 24—" Loren squeezed his eyes shut in concentration.

"Wait a minute, I think I see."

"Obed Middleton died in 1950," Joyce said. "In 1958 the renewal came due on his story and the widow renewed the copyright, just for sentimental reasons I guess.

Then a few months ago a chiseler named Orval Cupples went to the nursing home in Tulsa where the old woman is dying by inches and paid her two hundred dollars for the movie rights in that story during the renewal period."

"But the author, Obed Middleton, had died before the renewal period began," Loren pointed out. "So the law treats the renewal period as a separate entity, and the deal Obed made with Tommy Hagen's studio should have been negotiated with the widow a long time ago."

Andy Lauer jerked erect from his slouch as if an alarm had gone off in his ear. "You mean to say Tommy Hagen Enterprises never bothered to do that before it licensed all those hundreds of showings of *Kumquats* on TV? And all those showings were infringements of her copyright?"

"And now the widow's rights belong to this Cupples," Loren reminded him.

"I had an appointment with Cupples right here an hour ago," Joyce continued, her tone hinting that she hadn't enjoyed the experience. "Ratty-looking type with an ugly boil on his nose." *Mr. New York Manners,* Loren recalled. "He wants $100,000 plus a cut of all income from future showings of the picture. Otherwise he'll sue us for all those infringements and keep us from ever renting the picture again. And damn it, we'll probably have to pay. *Kumquats* is the keystone of the Hagen movies. We can't rent a block of them to a TV station without that one."

"It would be like an Orson Welles retrospective without *Citizen Kane,*" Kathy Ellison volunteered brightly.

"What are you going to do about Cupples?" Beau demanded.

Joyce answered him without hesitation. "Call Sheldon Rogers, the copyright lawyer, and make an appointment for tomorrow if I can. Then I have to call Keith in L.A. and fill him in." She pointed her unlit cigarette in Loren's direction. "How about coming with me tomorrow?"

Loren pulled a dog-eared convention schedule from his breast pocket. "Nothing exciting tomorrow. Sure, count me in."

*   *   *

On the street, while he was waving for a cab to take him back to the convention hotel, a thought occurred to him. He shoved open the half-rusted door of an empty phone booth and swung up the directory on its dirty chain. The white pages listed *Cupples Orval Talent Agency* with an address in the mid-Forties and a phone number. There was no other listing for that name in the Manhattan directory, which meant either that Cupples lived elsewhere or had an unlisted home phone.

In his hotel room after dinner he called an old acquaintance who had been a fixture in the New York entertainment world for decades. "Yeah, I know who he is. Small-time grifter, calls himself a talent agent, makes his bread booking over-the-hill strippers into cheap clubs in Jersey and Pennsylvania. Why you want to know?"

Loren answered the question with another. "Was he ever a lawyer? Disbarred maybe?"

"No way," his informant said. "I doubt if he ever got through high school."

"Does he have any close associates who are entertainment lawyers?"

"Negative. In fact, the guy doesn't have close associates, period. Or distant associates. He's a real loner and as devious as they come. If you're in a deal with him, my advice is to get out."

Loren expressed thanks and hung up. The longer he thought about what he had learned, the more his puzzlement grew.

"... And so the descendants of the person whose story was the basis of a film have the power to tie up the film fifty years after it was made. Congress didn't realize that would be the result when it passed the Copyright Act in 1909, but the courts have construed Section 24 in that manner. Just recently the city's educational television station lost a similar infringement suit over an old Rudolph Valentino film."

Sheldon Rogers, Esq.—tall, graying, velvet-voiced, his every word and movement a study in cool deliberation—drew a long cigar from its pale-tan tube and touched flame to the tip, puffing deeply as if to refresh himself after his discourse on copyright. Loren looked down at the discarded tube on the lawyer's desk blotter and read the brand name Montecruz. He'd heard connoisseurs call it the finest cigar in the world.

"It's a shame Pop didn't know about Section 24 when he bought his old pictures from the studio. He could have paid off Mrs. Middleton himself." Beneath the deep California tan there was a ruthless look to Keith Hagen that suggested more loudly than words that whoever stood in his way ran a heavy risk.

Loren had taken an instant dislike to Tommy Hagen's adopted son from the moment they had met this morning in Rogers' anteroom. Keith had arrived on the night flight from Los Angeles, but he looked no less dangerous for lack of sleep.

"Good old klutzy Pop, going into hock to buy up his pictures because he was sure they'd make a mint someday, and then he blows the legal red tape."

With every word Keith spoke, Loren felt increasing delight at the fact that Orval Cupples was tying up the young man's income from his father's masterpiece. Beside Loren on the richly upholstered couch, Joyce Brook chewed her lower lip.

Sheldon Rogers broke the uncomfortable silence. "I take it, Mr. Hagen, that you want me to negotiate with Cupples and persuade him to reduce his price to what I would consider his rock-bottom figure, and then close with him?"

"Right now." Keith snapped out the words savagely.

"Let me try his office." The copyright attorney pressed a button on his phone and instructed an unseen secretary to put through the call for him. When his instrument buzzed he lifted it delicately to his ear. "Good morning, may I speak to Mr. Cupples please... Sheldon Rogers, I'm an attorney representing Tommy Hagen Enterprises... He *what?* My God... No, just a business matter."

The lawyer dropped his phone into its plastic nest as if it were white-hot and gazed bleakly at his three visitors. "That was a police officer. Orval Cupples was found dead by his secretary when she came to work this morning. Murdered. They're going to want to know what my business with him was."

"That's privileged. You tell them nothing." Beneath his tan Keith Hagen had turned fishbelly-white.

"You forget," Loren pointed out with a certain perverse satisfaction, "that Mr. Rogers gave the name of Tommy Hagen Enterprises over the phone just now. They don't need him or his privileged information. They can go straight to you and Joyce, and when they do they're going to find out that you had one hundred thousand reasons to kill Cupples. What time did your plane get in this morning?"

"Landed at JFK about 2:45 A.M.," Keith snarled. "Why?"

"You'd better pray Cupples died before then," Loren told him.

They cabbed downtown in chilly silence and trooped into the lobby of the office building on Park and Nineteenth just as an elevator door slid shut and the indicator began to ascend. "Damn new elevators," Joyce remarked. "They're built so they have to go all the way to the top before they come down again." She stamped her feet impatiently in the underheated lobby and the three of them watched the indicator rise to twelve, then crawl downward.

As soon as the cage reached ground level they piled in and Loren punched the button for the eighth floor. They marched into the Hagen Enterprises suite just as a bulky lizard-skinned man in a shapeless gray suit with a topcoat slung over his arm was coming down the spiral staircase. When he saw the newcomers enter he took the last steps two at a time and blocked their path, flipping open a worn leather case.

"Lieutenant Genetelli, Homicide. I've been waiting for you to get back. Are you Joyce Brook?"

Whatever Joyce was about to say caught in her throat and she nodded, her face muscles tense.

"I've been upstairs questioning Lauer, your products man. You were at this lawyer Rogers' office when Rogers called Orval Cupples for an appointment, weren't you?"

"We all were," Loren replied for her. He introduced himself and Keith Hagen followed suit, and the four strode down the inner corridor to Joyce's office.

"I came down from Cupples' shop to find out what I could about Tommy Hagen Enterprises." The lieutenant draped his overcoat across his lap as he sank into a chair. "We found some memoranda about this place in Cupples' private papers. Looks as if he'd bought up some rights you needed and was holding you up for a bunch of money, huh?"

"If you know so much you don't need to ask," Keith snapped.

"Now wait a minute." Loren stepped into the breach. "Maybe we can help more if you'll tell us a bit more. Could you at least let us know when and how Cupples was killed?"

Genetelli rubbed the stubble on his pouchy cheeks. "I don't suppose that's a secret. The medical examiner says he died between 7:00 and 8:00 A.M. His secretary found him on the floor when she got to work at 8:15. His skull was fractured with a big hunk of rock he kept on his office wall. Hawaiian fertility symbol. Looks like a stone rolling pin to me. His memo pad says he had an appointment at 7:30 this morning with a T.H."

"Tommy Hagen!" Joyce gave a little gasp of amazement.

"Pop's been dead for twenty years," Keith grated. "You think he came back from the grave to protect the rights to his movie?"

An almost forgotten scrap of trivia ascended to Loren's consciousness. Hadn't the great comic's full name been Thomas Keith Hagen? Yes, he was sure it had. Then wasn't it quite likely that Tommy had given his own name to his adopted son? If Keith's full name was Thomas Keith Hagen, Jr., then his initials would match those on the memo pad in Cupples' office.

And since Keith's plane had landed at Kennedy Airport more than four hours before the murder, the young hothead had had plenty of opportunity to kill Cupples. Of course the initials on the memo pad could refer to Tommy Hagen Enterprises rather than to any person, or they might mean someone or something unconnected with the Hagen affairs. But at the moment Keith was clearly the prime suspect, and Loren wondered how long it would take Genetelli to recognize that fact.

After fifteen minutes of asking questions and scribbling in a pocket notebook, the lieutenant allowed himself a frosty little smile as the pattern took shape. Another ten minutes and he snapped the notebook shut, thanked the three of them, and left.

As soon as Genetelli was out of the office Keith Hagen sprang to his feet and began to pace the shag carpet uncontrollably. "My God!" he shouted. "The fool thinks I did it!" His voice was a mixture of fury and fear.

Joyce Brook clutched Loren's arm in a grip of desperation. "What's going to happen now?"

"Nothing, for a while," he said. "They don't have enough of a case yet. They'll question all the employees and guests at your hotel, Mr. Hagen, trying to find someone who may have seen you slip out this morning in time to keep a certain 7:30 appointment. They'll check your home phone in L.A., the pay phone at the airport, the phones in your hotel, trying to prove you placed a call to Cupples and made that appointment. If they prove it, you're up to your neck. Did you kill him?"

"No, no, no! I swear I never laid eyes on the man. You're a lawyer, Mensing, you're supposed to be some kind of detective, help me for God's sake, will you?"

Loren turned back to Joyce and without saying anything she nodded. The look of concern on her face was one that Loren knew from years past. Whenever she saw anyone in trouble, no matter how richly deserved the trouble might be, her instinct was to do something about it.

"All right," he said. "Spring semester doesn't begin for ten days. I'll gamble with you. You'll pay my expenses, and you'll write a $5,000 check to the City University Law School Student Aid Fund. Win, lose, or draw, you write those checks. And if I find you're lying to me, Hagen, I go to Genetelli and give him everything I learn. Remember, I'm not your lawyer, I'm not even licensed to practice law in New York, and nothing you tell me is privileged. Now the first thing you do is call Sheldon Rogers back and retain him to take care of your Section 24 problem."

"But doesn't Cupples' murder take care of that?" Joyce wondered.

"Not in the least. The rights he bought from Mrs. Middleton are now part of his estate. Cupples' will governs who takes the rights after his death, or the intestacy law if he didn't leave a will. Rogers will have to find out who the legatees are and strike a deal with them. Probably the surrogate's court will have to approve the deal as long as the estate is in probate. Another thing, get Rogers to hire an Oklahoma detective who can look into Mrs. Middleton's assignment of rights to Cupples. Maybe he can find some legal grounds for overturning the deal in court. Meanwhile I'm going to investigate a few angles here."

"Loren," Joyce said, "you're not licensed as a private detective. Can't you get in hot water for—"

He patted her hand. "Not the way I'm going to do it."

That afternoon he made a long-distance call to his home city. Bubbly-voiced Marcus Jaan Hooft, head of The Hooft Agency, which occasionally did investigative work for him, gave Loren the name of a reliable New York detective.

At ten the next morning, the last day of the year, Loren climbed three flights of stairs in a shabby office building near Columbus Circle and knocked on the pebbled-glass door of *Madison Investigations*. Moses Madison was a small dandyish black man who kept three phones half buried in the clutter of papers on his ancient desk. From the calls that punctuated their discussion Loren gathered that most of Madison's investigative work was on contract to the city's legal-aid and public-defender offices. He seemed to delight in role-playing, talking like a Bedford-Stuyvesant street dude one minute and like a Rhodes scholar the next.

"Your theory is based on an assumption," he pointed out to Loren. "Namely, the Cupples murder is connected with the petty sabotage at Tommy Hagen Enterprises."

Loren shifted in his uncomfortable wooden chair. "With your help I hope to prove that assumption. That's why I want your operatives to comb every place in the metropolitan area that sells live worms. Let's see if we can't establish a sale to one of our suspects."

Madison ticked off their names on callused fingers. "Beau Douglas, Andy Lauer, Kathy Ellison. And you want a background report on each of them plus twenty-

four-hour surveillance. It's going to cost you, Professor.
But I know Tommy Hagen's son can pay my price." The
detective crossed one purple-trousered ankle over the
other on the edge of the venerable desk. "I still think
you should add that receptionist to the list, Donna
whatever her name is."

"Not necessary." Loren shook his head. "She's brand-
new at the office and wasn't working there when the
trouble started, and the girl whose place she took left
to get married and is now living in Denver, so she's out
of it too."

"But of course you do want reports on anyone who
seems to have a close association with any of the three
suspects?"

"With one exception," Loren said. "Me. I'm going to
be cultivating them myself over the next few days."

Madison's lips split in raucous laughter and he
slapped his palms together. "Why, man, you don't think
I'd bill you for a report on *you!*"

"The thought never sullied my mind," Loren said
innocently.

The private detective's response was a mild obscen-
ity, and they grinned at each other in mutual understanding.

"Hey, Prof," Madison asked as Loren was leaving,
"you want a signal to call off my shadow in case you
get lucky, uh, cultivating the Ellison chick?"

Loren spent New Year's Eve with Joyce Brook in her
homey cluttered apartment in an East Village highrise. They sipped eggnog spiked with chocolate liqueur
and called back memories of old times and old loves as
if that could exorcise the unacknowledged loneliness
that each of them sensed in the other.

Late in the afternoon of the first day of 1975 Loren
took a cab through empty slushy streets to the precinct
station. For Lieutenant Genetelli this was not a holiday. Sitting in a scarred chair next to the lieutenant's
gunmetal-gray desk, Loren summarized his work as
deputy legal adviser and occasional detective without
portfolio for his home city's police department. He was
careful not to mention that at the moment he was more
or less working for Genetelli's prime suspect in the Cup-

ples murder. After a few long-distance phone calls the lieutenant was impressed enough to give Loren a status report on the case.

"We can't prove the contact," he growled. "Joyce Brook called Keith Hagen the afternoon before the killing, 3:23 P.M. New York time. That was the first Keith had ever heard of Orval Cupples. If he called Cupples to make that date for 7:30 the next morning, it had to be after 12:23 P.M. Pacific time and it had to be a long-distance call. Cupples' secretary swears the office got no long-distance calls at all that afternoon, at least not before five o'clock when she went home. Cupples stayed late. We know he got the call making the appointment while he was in the office because he made that note on the office memo pad, but so far we can't connect the call to Hagen."

"Any luck finding a witness who saw him leave his hotel around seven the morning of the murder?"

"Not yet," Genetelli grunted. "But we'll find one."

Loren said nothing that might suggest the existence of other suspects. The time for that, he thought, would come later.

Loren's headquarters the next day was Tommy Hagen Enterprises. He spent the morning in Andy Lauer's office at the top of the spiral stairs, belaboring the tall gawky products expert's patience with endless questions about the business of marketing Tommy's image. When Lauer seemed on the point of losing his temper, Loren reminded him that he was merely trying to save Lauer's employer from a murder charge. At twelve sharp, having learned nothing of value, he left by the ninth-floor exit door that served Lauer's office and went out for a coffee-shop lunch.

His target for the early afternoon was Beau Douglas. Making himself at home in Douglas' office along the eighth-floor inner hallway, Loren studied the form contracts that licensed theaters and film societies and television stations to exhibit Tommy Hagen movies, and asked several technical questions about the interpretation of certain clauses which the pedantic little Southerner was unable to answer.

At four o'clock he gave up to allow himself time for

Kathy Ellison, who looked cool and tempting in a pink pants suit. In the hour before closing Loren learned that she had been working at Tommy Hagen Enterprises for eight months, that Joyce personally had hired her as assistant manager, and that both Lauer and Douglas had resented not having been promoted to the higher-paying position themselves.

At five Loren invited Kathy to join him for a cocktail and they sipped Scotch sours in a dimly lit lounge on Sixteenth; but after one drink Kathy excused herself—"Dinner date tonight," she smiled—and slid from the red leather booth. As she left the lounge a middle-aged man in a rumpled gray mackinaw took a last gulp of beer, set his stein on the bar, and headed for the door in her wake as if he'd forgotten an urgent appointment.

Late the next day Loren returned to Columbus Circle and the cluttered office of Moses Madison. The black detective picked out three manila folders from the debris of his desk top and handed them to Loren. A fourth folder he slid neatly between his vest and jacket.

"They ain't as much detail as they should be, but you know how it is, I got a license to keep and Equal Opportunity cats I got to stroke, so I have to hire a certain number of incompetent white help."

Madison grinned with infinite self-delight as Loren dropped into a hard chair and skimmed the files.

Subject: Beauregard Douglas. Georgia born and bred, served two tours with the Marines in Vietnam, lived in a converted brownstone in the Bronx, used hashish on occasion.

Subject: Andrew Lauer. Master's degree in marketing, a girl friend in her third year at N.Y.U. Law School and another who worked in a Greek bellydance joint, expensive tastes in consumer goods and a habit of living beyond his means.

Subject: Kathleen Ellison. Presently having an affair with a married stockbroker, reputation for displaying a violent temper when she'd drunk too much.

In ten minutes of speed reading Loren absorbed enough information about three people's private lives to make him thoroughly disgusted with himself. On the other hand, these reports all but clinched the case, and that, he tried to convince himself, was what counted.

"You finished?" Moses Madison asked. When Loren nodded, the private detective removed the fourth folder from beneath his jacket and waved it tantalizingly just out of Loren's reach.

"This is a report one of my men gave me after he paid a visit to Chester's Bait and Tackle in Boonton, New Jersey. You want to try and dee-duce which one of them bought the worms?"

A grin spread slowly across Loren's face. He took off his glasses, polished them on his coatsleeve, and screwed up his features as if in agony of cerebration. Then he pronounced one of the three names and nonchalantly adjusted his glasses on his nose again.

Madison slapped his palms together in appreciation. "Good shot!" he chuckled. "Give the professor a see-gar."

"Make it a Montecruz," Loren said as he reached for the fourth folder.

That evening he paid a return visit to Genetelli's cubicle at the police station. After talking for more than an hour he finally persuaded the dubious lieutenant to do two things: Genetelli agreed to have the suspect's neighborhood canvassed in search of someone who might have seen the suspect leave early the morning of the murder, and to have a fingerprint man dust the suspect's office at Tommy Hagen Enterprises in search of the fingerprints of Orval Cupples.

By noon the next day both a witness and the prints had been found, and the arrest had been made.

Joyce Brook crushed another barely smoked cigarette into the overflowing tray on her desk. Loren saw that behind her quiet rage she was close to tears. He doubted that she was following his explanation. The truth had hit her too hard.

"My assumption was that the acts of sabotage here were connected with the murder. The 'T.H.' memo on Cupples' desk pad pointed in that direction, of course, but we couldn't consider the memo absolute proof.

"As you described the sabotage to me, it included things like the deliberate misplacing of files and the cancellation of important appointments with fake phone calls. That kind of dirty trick suggested a trickster who had detailed knowledge of your operations and access to your office. In short, *a trickster who worked here.*

"And then Orval Cupples enters the picture, a cheap talent agent with no legal background and no lawyer associates, who just happened to have grasped a subtle point about Section 24 of the Copyright Act and bought the rights which tied up the most valuable Tommy Hagen movie. Assuming that he was working as an agent for our trickster, where did he get his legal knowledge? Answer: in one way or another, from the trickster.

"So our trickster works here, and knows a lot of law or has access to such knowledge. Was it Beau Douglas? Kathy Ellison? Andy Lauer? None of them is a lawyer.

"Almost from the start I had a clue as to which of them it was. Not mathematical proof, but a clue. On my first visit here, when I got out of the elevator at the eighth floor, it happened that Cupples was just leaving after making his demands on you, and bumped into me as he got into the cage I'd just left. Now I didn't realize this until you mentioned it later, but the self-service elevators in this building are a lot newer than the building itself. They're the type that have to go all the way to the top floor before they can come down again.

"What does that mean? It means that when Cupples stepped into that car, he wasn't going down. *He was going up.*

"Does any of our suspects work above the eighth floor of this building? Yes, just one. Andy Lauer, whose office has its own private entrance and exit onto the ninth-floor hallway, which I used when I went out to lunch two days ago. In addition, he has a girl friend in law school, and she happens to have taken a copyright course last spring, as I verified this morning. And, as Madison's report proves, it was Lauer who bought the worms that were dumped into your desk.

"After meeting with you, Cupples must have gone upstairs to report to Lauer. I think he must also have demanded a lot more money than Lauer was paying him to act as front man. Later in the afternoon Lauer called Cupples' office and made that appointment for 7:30 the next morning. They had a fight over the division of the money you were going to pay Cupples, and Lauer killed him. Lauer was living way over his income and needed every cent for himself."

"He didn't do all this just for the money," Joyce said. She seemed calmer now but Loren was afraid it might be the calm before an explosion, because her remark told him that she knew what lay behind the sabotage.

"No, not just for the money," he said, choosing his words judiciously. "He was angry when you—well, when you hired a woman as assistant manager instead of promoting him. I think he hoped to make such a mess here that you'd either quit or be fired. He figured Keith would give him your job, and he also saw the chance to make a nice piece of change on the side out of the Cupples deal. Now he's under arrest, Keith's off the hook on the murder charge, Sheldon Rogers thinks he can prove Cupples made misrepresentations to Mrs. Middleton which will get her assignment to him invalidated in court, and you won't find any more worms crawling over your letterheads." He couldn't look directly into the moistness of her eyes. "Happy endings all around, right? So why are you so glum?"

"Damn all men to hell!" she burst out. "All of them!" And she buried her face in her hands and wept.

When she spoke again it was without raising her eyes to him. "Could you—just do me a favor and let me alone for a while, will you, Loren?"

Loren wanted desperately to say the right words to her but he knew that there were no right words to say. "Sure," he muttered. "See you next time I'm in town." He let himself silently out of the office and took the elevator down eight flights to the slushy street and cabbed back to his hotel to pack his bags and get out of New York. In a week or so, he thought, he'd give her a call.

Author's Note

In 1977, two years after this story first appeared in EQMM, the U.S. Court of Appeals for the Second Circuit reversed the lower court decision in the case involving the old Rudolph Valentino film on which the legal aspects of the story were based. And under the new Copyright Act, which took effect at the beginning of 1978, it is impossible for the public availability of a movie to be frustrated as the corpse in "The Kumquats Affair" tried to do. Any readers who might wish to learn more about the legal problem treated in the story are referred to my article "Rx for Copyright Death," *Washington University Law Quarterly,* Fall 1977.

THE ADVENTURE OF THE
HANGING ACROBAT

by Ellery Queen

"Ellery Queen" was the pseudonym of two Brooklyn-born cousins, Frederic Dannay and Manfred B. Lee. Their contrasting personalities combined to create a detective protagonist who shared the pen name of his creators, thus making him difficult to forget. Their many short stories and novels about the sophisticated New York sleuth made Ellery Queen a household name in mystery fiction. When they teamed up to found Ellery Queen's Mystery Magazine, which began publishing in 1941, they provided a launching pad for the writing careers of many of the finest mystery writers of the second half of the twentieth century.

Long, long ago in the Incubation Period of Man—long before booking agents, five-a-days, theatrical boarding houses, subway circuits, and *Variety*—when Megatherium roamed the trees, when Broadway was going through its First Glacial Period, and when the first vaudeville show was planned by the first lop-eared, low-browed, hairy impresario, it was decreed: "The acrobat shall be first."

Why the acrobat should be first no one ever explained; but that this was a dubious honor every one on the bill—including the acrobat—realized only too well. For it was recognized even then, in the infancy of Show Business, that the first shall be last in the applause of the audience. And all through the ages, in courts and courtyards and feeble theatres, it was the acrobat—whether he was called buffoon, *farceur,* merry-andrew, tumbler, mountebank, Harlequin, or *punchinello*—who was thrown, first among his fellow-mimes, to the lions of entertainment to whet their appetites for the more luscious feasts to come. So that to this day their muscular miracles are performed hard on the overture's last wall-shaking blare, performed with a simple resignation that speaks well for the mildness and resilience of the whole acrobatic tribe.

Hugo Brinkerhof knew nothing of the whimsical background of his profession. All he knew was that his father and mother had been acrobats before him with a traveling show in Germany, that he possessed huge smooth muscles with sap and spring and strength in them, and that nothing gave him more satisfaction than the sight of a glittering trapeze. With his trapeze and his Myra, and the indulgent applause of audiences from Seattle to Okeechobee, he was well content.

Now Hugo was very proud of Myra, a small wiry handsome woman with the agility of a cat and something of the cat's sleepy green eyes. He had met her in the office of Bregman, the booker, and the sluggish heart under his magnificent chest had told him that this was his fate and his woman. It was Myra who had renamed the act "Atlas & Co." when they had married between the third and fourth shows in Indianapolis. It was Myra who had fought tooth and nail for better billing. It was Myra who had conceived and perfected the dazzling pinwheel of their finale. It was Myra's shapely little body and Myra's lithe gyrations on the high trapeze and Myra's sleepy smile that had made Atlas & Co. an "acrobatic divertissement acclaimed from coast to coast," had earned them a pungent paragraph in *Variety,* and had brought them with other topnotchers on the Bregman string to the Big Circuit.

That every one loved his Myra mighty Brinkerhof, the Atlas, knew with a swelling of his chest. Who could resist her? There had been that baritone with the dancing act in Boston, the revue comedian in Newark, the tap dancer in Buffalo, the *adagio* in Washington. Now there were others—Tex Crosby, the Crooning Cowboy (Songs & Patter); the Great Gordi (successor to Houdini); Sailor Sam, the low comic. They had all been on the same bill together now for weeks, and they all loved sleepy-eyed Myra, and big Atlas smiled his indulgent smile and thrilled in his stupid, stolid way to their admiration. For was not his Myra the finest female acrobat in the world and the most lovely creature in creation?

And now Myra was dead.

It was Brinkerhof himself, with a gaunt suffering look about him that mild spring night, who had given the alarm. It was five o'clock in the morning and his Myra had not come home to their theatrical boarding-house room on Forty-seventh Street. He had stayed behind with his wife after the last performance in the Metropole Theatre at Columbus Circle to try out a new trick. They had rehearsed and then he had dressed in haste, leaving her in their joint dressing room. He had had an appointment with Bregman, the booker, to discuss terms of a new contract. He had promised to meet her back at their lodgings. But when he had returned—*ach!* no Myra. He had hurried back to the theatre; it was locked up for the night. And all the long night he had waited....

"Prob'ly out bummin', buddy," the desk lieutenant at the West Forty-seventh Street station had said with a yawn. "Go home and sleep it off."

But Brinkerhof had been vehement, with many gestures. "She never haf this done before. I haf telephoned it the theatre, too, but there iss no answer. Captain, find her, please!"

"These heinies," sighed the lieutenant to a lounging detective. "All right, Baldy, see what you can do. If she's piffed in a joint somewhere, give this big hunk a clout on the jaw."

So Baldy and the pale giant had gone to see what they could do, and they had found the Metropole Theatre locked, as Brinkerhof had said, and it was almost six in the morning and dawn was coming up across the Park and Baldy had dragged Brinkerhof into an all-night restaurant for a mug of coffee. And they had waited around the theatre until seven, when old Perk the stage door man and timer had come in, and he had opened the theatre for them, and they had gone backstage to the dressing-room of Atlas & Co. and found Myra hanging from one of the sprinkler pipes with a dirty old rope, thick as a hawser, around her pretty neck.

And Atlas had sat down like the dumb hunk he was

and put his shaggy head between his hands and stared at the hanging body of his wife with the silent grief of some Norse god crushed to earth.

When Mr. Ellery Queen pushed through the chattering crowd of reporters and detectives backstage and convinced Sergeant Velie through the door of the dressing room that he was indeed who he was, he found his father the Inspector holding court in the stuffy little room before a gang of nervous theatrical people. It was only nine o'clock and Ellery was grumbling through his teeth at the unconscionable inconsiderateness of murderers. But neither the burly Sergeant nor little Inspector Queen was impressed with his grumblings to the point of lending ear; and indeed the grumblings ceased after he had taken one swift look at what still hung from the sprinkler pipe.

Brinkerhof sat red-eyed and huge and collapsed in the chair before his wife's dressing table. "I haf told you everything," he muttered. "We rehearsed the new trick. It was then an appointment with Mr. Bregman. I went." A fat hard-eyed man, Bregman the broker, nodded curtly. "Undt that's all. Who—why—I do not know."

In a bass *sotto voce* Sergeant Velie recited the sparse facts. Ellery took another look at the dead woman. Her stiff muscles of thigh and leg bulged in *rigor mortis* beneath the tough thin silk of her flesh tights. Her green eyes were widely open. And she swayed a little in a faint dance of death. Ellery looked away and at the people.

Baldy the precinct man was there, flushed with his sudden popularity with the newspaper boys. A tall thin man who looked like Gary Cooper rolled a cigarette beside Bregman—Tex Crosby, the cowboy-crooner; and he leaned against the grime-smeared wall and eyed the Great Gordi—in person—with flinty dislike. Gordi had a hawk's beak, a sleek black mustache and long olive fingers and black eyes; and he said nothing. Little Sam, the comedian, had purple pouches under his tired eyes and he looked badly in need of a drink. But Joe Kelly, the house manager, did not, for he smelled like a brew-

ery and kept mumbling something drunken and ob-
scene beneath his breath.

"How long you been married, Brinkerhof?" growled
the Inspector.

"Two years. *Ja.* In Indianapolis that was, *Herr In-
spektor.*"

"Was she ever married before?"

"*Nein.*"

"You?"

"*Nein.*"

"Did she or you have any enemies?"

"*Gott, nein!*"

"Happy, were you?"

"Like two doves we was," muttered Brinkerhof.

Ellery strolled over to the corpse and stared up. Her
ropy-veined wrists were jammed behind her back, bound
with a filthy rouge-stained towel, as were her ankles.
Her feet dangled a yard from the floor. A battered stepladder leaned against one of the walls, folded up; a man
standing upon it, he mused, could easily have reached
the sprinkler pipe, flung the rope over it, and hauled
up the light body.

"The stepladder was found against the wall there?"
he murmured to the Sergeant, who had come up behind
him and was staring with interest at the dead woman.

"Yep. It's always kept out near the switchboard light
panel."

"No suicide, then," said Ellery. "At least that's something."

"Nice figger, ain't she?" said the Sergeant admir-
ingly.

"Velie, you're a ghoul.... This *is* a pretty problem."

The dirty rope seemed to fascinate him. It had been
wound tightly about the woman's throat twice, in par-
allel strands, and concealed her flesh like the iron neck-
lace of a Ubangi woman. A huge knot had been fashioned
beneath her right ear, and another knot held the rope
to the pipe above.

"Where does this rope come from?" he said abruptly.

"From around an old trunk we found backstage, Mr.
Queen. Trunk's been here for years. In the prop room.
Nothin' in it; some trouper left it. Want to see it?"

"I'll take your word for it, Sergeant. Property room,

eh?" He sauntered back to the door to look the people over again.

Brinkerhof was mumbling something about how happy he and Myra had been, and what he would do to the *verdammte Teufel* who had wrung his pretty Myra's neck. His huge hands opened and closed convulsively. "Joost like a flower she was," he said. "Joost like a flower."

"Nuts," snapped Joe Kelly, the house manager, weaving on his feet like a punch-drunk fighter. "She was a floozy, Inspector. You ask *me*," and he leered at Inspector Queen.

"Floo-zie?" said Brinkerhof with difficulty, getting to his feet. "What iss that?"

Sam, the comic, blinked his puffy little eyes rapidly and said in a hoarse voice: "You're crazy, Kelly, crazy. Wha'd'ye want to say that for? He's pickled, Chief."

"Pickled, am I?" screamed Kelly, livid. "Aw right, you as' *him*, then!" and he pointed a wavering finger at the tall thin man. "What is this?" crooned the Inspector, his eyes bright. "Get together, gentlemen. You mean, Kelly, that Mrs. Brinkerhof was playing around with Crosby here?"

Brinkerhof made a sound like a baffled gorilla and lunged forward. His long arms were curved flails and he made for the cowboy's throat with the unswervable fury of an animal. Sergeant Velie grabbed his wrist and twisted it up behind the vast back, and Baldy jumped in and clung to the giant's other arm. He swayed there, struggling and never taking his eyes from the tall thin man, who had not stirred but who had gone very pale.

"Take him away," snapped the Inspector to Sergeant Velie. "Turn him over to a couple of the boys and keep him outside till he calms down." They hustled the hoarsely breathing acrobat out of the room. "Now, Crosby, spill it."

"Nothin' to spill," drawled the cowboy, but his drawl was a little breathless and his eyes were narrowed to wary slits. "I'm Texas an' I don't scare easy, Mister Cop. He's just a squarehead. An' as for that pie-eyed sawback over there"—he stared malevolently at Kelly—"he better learn to keep his trap shut."

"He's been two-timin' the hunk!" screeched Kelly.

"Don't b'lieve him, Chief! That sassy little tramp got what was comin' to her, I tell y'! She's been pullin' the wool over the hunk's eyes all the way from Chi to Beantown!"

"You've said enough," said the Great Gordi quietly. "Can't you see the man's drunk, Inspector, and not responsible? Myra was—companionable. She may have taken a drink or two with Crosby or myself on the sly once or twice—Brinkerhof didn't like her to, so she never drank in front of him—but that's all."

"Just friendly, hey?" murmured the Inspector. "Well, who's lying? If you know anything solid, Kelly, come out with it."

"I know what I know," sneered the manager. "An' when it comes to that, Chief, the Great Gordi could tell you somethin' about the little bum. Ought to be able to! He swiped her from Crosby only a couple o' weeks ago."

"Quiet, both of you," snapped the old gentleman as the Texan and the dark mustached man stirred. "And how could you know that, Kelly?"

The dead woman swayed faintly, dancing her noiseless dance.

"I heard Tex there bawl Gordi out only the other day," said Kelly thickly, "for makin' the snatch. An' I saw Gordi grapplin' with her in the wings on'y yest'day. How's 'at? Reg'lar wrestler, Gordi. Can he clinch!"

Nobody said anything. The tall Texan's fingers whitened as he glared at the drunken man, and Gordi the magician did nothing at all but breathe. Then the door opened and two men came in—Dr. Prouty, Assistant Medical Examiner, and a big shambling man with a seared face.

Everybody relaxed. The Inspector said: "High time, Doc. Don't touch her, though, till Bradford can take a look at that knot up there. Go on, Braddy; on the pipe. Use the ladder."

The shambling man took the stepladder and set it up and climbed beside the dangling body and looked at the knot behind the woman's ear and the knot at the top of the pipe. Dr. Prouty pinched the woman's legs.

Ellery sighed and began to prowl. Nobody paid any

attention to him; they were all pallidly intent upon the two men near the body.

Something disturbed him; he did not know what, could not put his finger precisely upon the root of the disturbance. Perhaps it was a feeling in the air, an aura of tension about the silent dangling woman in tights. But it made him restless. He had the feeling...

He found the loaded revolver in the top drawer of the woman's dressing table—a shiny little pearl-handled .22 with the initials *MB* on the butt. And his eyes narrowed and he glanced at his father, and his father nodded. So he prowled some more. And then he stopped short, his gray eyes suspicious.

On the rickety wooden table in the center of the room lay a long sharp nickel-plated letter opener among a clutter of odds and ends. He picked it up carefully and squinted along its glittering length in the light. But there was no sign of blood.

He put it down and continued to prowl.

And the very next thing he noticed was the cheap battered gas burner on the floor at the other side of the room. Its pipe fitted snugly over a gas outlet in the wall, but the gas tap had been turned off. He felt the little burner; it was stone cold.

So he went to the closet with the oddest feeling of inevitability. And sure enough, just inside the open door of the closet lay a wooden box full of carpenter's tools, with a heavy steel hammer prominently on top. There was a mess of shavings on the floor near the box, and the edge of the closet door was unpainted and virgin fresh from a plane.

His eyes were very sharp now, and deeply concerned. He went quickly to the Inspector's side and murmured: "The revolver. The woman's?"

"Yes."

"Recent acquisition?"

"No. Brinkerhof bought it for her soon after they were married. For protection, he said."

"Poor protection, I should say," shrugged Ellery, glancing at the Headquarters men. The shambling red-faced man had just lumbered off the ladder with an expression of immense surprise. Sergeant Velie, who had returned, was mounting the ladder with a penknife clutched in his big fingers. Dr. Prouty waited expectantly below. The Sergeant began sawing at the rope tied to the sprinkler pipe.

"What's that box of tools doing in the closet?" continued Ellery, without removing his gaze from the dead woman.

"Stage carpenter was in here yesterday fixing the door—it had warped or something. Union rules are strict, so he quit the job unfinished. What of it?"

"Everything," said Ellery, "of it." The Great Gordi was quietly watching his mouth; Ellery seemed not to notice. The little comedian, Sam, was shrunken in a corner, eyes popping at the Sergeant. And the Texan was smoking without enjoyment, not looking at any one or anything. "Simply everything. It's one of the most remarkable things I've ever run across."

The Inspector looked bewildered. "But, El, for cripe's sake—remarkable? I don't see—"

"You should," said Ellery impatiently. "A child should. And yet it's astounding, when you come to think of it. Here's a room with four dandy weapons in it—a loaded revolver, a letter cutter, a gas burner, and a hammer. And yet the murderer deliberately trussed the woman with the towels, deliberately left this room, deliberately crossed the stage to the property room, unwound that rusty old rope from a worthless trunk discarded years ago by some nameless actor, carried the rope and the ladder from beside the switchboard back to this room, used the ladder to sling the rope over the pipe and fasten the knot, and strung the woman up."

"Well, but—"

"Well, but why?" cried Ellery. "Why? Why did the murderer ignore the four simple, easy, handy methods of murder here—shooting, stabbing, asphyxiation, bludgeoning—and go to all that extra trouble to *hang* her?"

Dr. Prouty was kneeling beside the dead woman, whom the Sergeant had deposited with a thump on the dirty floor.

The red-faced man shambled over and said: "It's got me, Inspector."

"What's got you?" snapped Inspector Queen.

"This knot." His thick red fingers held a length of knotted rope. "The one behind her ear is just ordinary; even clumsy for the job of breakin' her neck." He shook his head. "But this one, the one that was tied around the pipe—well, sir, it's got me."

"An unfamiliar knot?" said Ellery slowly, puzzling over its complicated convolutions.

"New to me, Mr. Queen. All the years I been expertin' on knots for the Department I never seen one like that. Ain't a sailor's knot, I can tell you that; and it ain't Western."

"Might be the work of an amateur," muttered the Inspector, pulling the rope through his fingers. "A knot that just happened."

The expert shook his head. "No, sir, I wouldn't say that at all. It's some kind of variation. Not an accident. Whoever tied that knew his knots."

Bradford shambled off and Dr. Prouty looked up from his work. "Hell, I can't do anything here," he snapped. "I'll have to take this body over to the Morgue and work on it there. The boys are waiting outside."

"When'd she kick off, Doc?" demanded the Inspector, frowning.

"About midnight last night. Can't tell closer than that. She died, of course, of suffocation."

"Well, give us a report. Probably nothing, but it never hurts. Thomas, get that doorman in here."

When Dr. Prouty and the Morgue men had gone with the body and Sergeant Velie had hauled in old Perk, the stagedoor man and watchman, the Inspector growled: "What time'd you lock up last night, Mister?"

Old Perk was hoarse with nervousness. "Honest t' Gawd, Inspector, I didn't mean nothin' by it. On'y Mr. Kelly here'd fire me if he knew. I was that sleepy—"

"What's this?" said the Inspector softly.

"Myra told me after the last show last night she an' Atlas were gonna rehearse a new stunt. I didn't wanna wait aroun', y'see," the old man whined, "so seein' as nob'dy else was in the house that late, the cleanin' women gone an' all, I locked up everything but the stage door an' I say to Myra an' Atlas, I says: 'When ye leave, folks,' I says, 'jest slam the stage door.' An' I went home."

"Rats," said the Inspector irritably. "Now we'll never know who could have come in and who didn't. Anybody could have sneaked back without being seen or waited around in hiding until—" He bit his lip. "You men there, where'd you all go after the show last night?"

The three actors started simultaneously. It was the Great Gordi who spoke first, in his soft smooth voice that was now uneasy. "I went directly to my rooming house and to bed."

"Anybody see you come in? You live in the same hole as Brinkerhof?"

The magician shrugged. "No one saw me. Yes, I do."

"You, Texas?"

The cowboy drawled: "I moseyed round to a speak somewhere an' got drunk."

"What speak?"

"Dunno. I was primed. Woke up in my room this mornin' with a head."

"You boys sure are in a tough spot," said the Inspector sarcastically. "Can't even fix good alibis for yourself. Well, how about you, Mr. Comedian?"

The comic said eagerly: "Oh, I can prove where I was, Inspector. I went around to a joint I know an' can get twenny people to swear to it."

"What time?"

"Round midnight."

The Inspector snorted and said: "Beat it. But hang around. I'll be wanting you boys, maybe. Take 'em away, Thomas, before I lose my temper."

Long, long ago—when, it will be recalled, Megatherium roamed the trees—the same lop-eared impresario who said: "The acrobat shall be first," also laid down the dictum that: "The show must go on," and for as little reason. Accidents might happen, the juvenile might run off with the female lion-tamer, the ingénue might be howling drunk, the lady in the fifth row, right, might have chosen the theatre to be the scene of her monthly attack of epilepsy, fire might break out in Dressing Room A, but the show must go on. Not even a rare juicy homicide may annul the sacred dictum. The show must go on despite hell, high water, drunken managers named Kelly, and The Fantastic Affair of the Hanging Acrobat.

So it was not strange that when the Metropole began to fill with its dribble of early patrons there was no sign that a woman had been slain the night before within its gaudy walls and that police and detectives roved its backstage with suspicious, if baffled, eyes.

The murder was just an incident to Show Business. It would rate two columns in *Variety*.

Inspector Richard Queen chafed in the hard seat in the fifteenth row while Ellery sat beside him sunk in thought. Stranger than everything had been Ellery's insistence that they remain to witness the performance. There was a motion picture to sit through—a film which, bitterly, the Inspector pointed out he had seen—a newsreel, an animated cartoon....

It was while "Coming Attractions" were flitting over the screen that Ellery rose and said: "Let's go backstage. There's something—" He did not finish.

They passed behind the dusty boxes on the right and went backstage through the iron door guarded by a uniformed officer. The vast bare reaches of the stage and wings were oppressed with an unusual silence. Manager Kelly, rather the worse for wear, sat on a broken chair near the light panel and gnawed his unsteady fingers. None of the vaudeville actors was in evidence.

"Kelly," said Ellery abruptly, "is there anything like a pair of field glasses in the house?"

The Irishman gaped. "What the hell would you be wantin' *them* for?"

"Please."

Kelly fingered a passing stagehand, who vanished and reappeared shortly with the desired binoculars. The Inspector grunted: "So what?"

Ellery adjusted them to his eyes. "I don't know," he said, shrugging. "It's just a hunch."

There was a burst of music from the pit: the Overture.

"Poet and Peasant," snarled the Inspector. "Don't they ever get anything new?"

But Ellery said nothing. He merely waited, binoculars ready, eyes fixed on the now footlighted stage.

And it was only when the last blare had died away, and grudging splatters of applause came from the orchestra, and the announcement cards read: "Atlas & Co.," that the Inspector lost something of his irritability and even became interested. For when the curtains slithered up there was Atlas himself, bowing and smiling, his immense body impressive in flesh tights; and there beside him stood a tall smiling woman with golden hair and at least one golden tooth which flashed in the footlights. And she too wore flesh tights. For Brinkerhof with the mildness and resilience of all acrobats had insisted on taking his regular turn, and Bregman the booker had sent him another partner, and the two strangers had spent an hour rehearsing their intimate embraces and clutches and swingings and nuzzlings before the first performance. The show must go on.

Atlas and the golden woman went through an intricate series of tumbles and equilibristic maneuvers. The orchestra played brassy music. Trapezes dived stageward. Simple swings. Somersaults in the air. The drummer rolled and smashed his cymbal.

Ellery made no move to use the binoculars. He and the Inspector and Kelly stood in the wings, and none of them said anything, although Kelly was breathing hard like a man who has just come out of deep water for air. A queer little figure materialized beside them; Ellery turned his head slowly. But it was only Sailor Sam, the low comic, rigged out in a naval uniform three sizes too large for his skinny little frame, his face daubed liberally with greasepaint. He kept watching Atlas & Co. without expression.

"Good, ain't he?" he said at last in a small voice.

No one replied. But Ellery turned to the manager and whispered: "Kelly, keep your eyes open for—" and his voice sank so low neither the comedian nor Inspector Queen could hear what he said. Kelly looked puzzled; his bloodshot eyes opened a little wider; but he nodded and swallowed, riveting his gaze upon the whirling figures on the stage.

And when it was all over and the orchestra was executing the usual *crescendo sostenuto* and Atlas was bowing and smiling and the woman was curtseying and showing her gold tooth and the curtain dropped swiftly, Ellery glanced at Kelly. But Kelly shook his head.

The announcement cards changed. "Sailor Sam." There was a burst of fresh fast music, and the little man in the oversize naval uniform grinned three times, as if trying it out, drew a deep breath, and scuttled out upon the stage to sprawl full-length with his gnomish face jutting over the footlights to the accompaniment of surprised laughter from the darkness below.

They watched from the wings, silent.

The comedian had a clever routine. Not only was he a travesty upon all sailormen, but he was a travesty upon all sailormen in their cups. He drooled and staggered and was silent and then chattered suddenly, and he described a mythical voyage and fell all over himself climbing an imaginary mast and fell silent again to go into a pantomime that rocked the house.

The Inspector said grudgingly: "Why, he's as good as Jimmy Barton any day, with that drunk routine of his."

"Just a slob," said Kelly out of the corner of his mouth.

Sailor Sam made his exit by the complicated expedient of swimming off the stage. He stood in the wings, panting, his face streaming perspiration. He ran out for a bow. They thundered for more. He vanished. He reappeared. He vanished again. There was a stubborn look on his pixie face.

"Sam!" hissed Kelly. "F'r cripe's sake, Sam, give 'em 'at encore rope number. F'r cripe's sake, Sam—"

"Rope number?" said Ellery quietly.

The comedian licked his lips. Then his shoulders drooped and he slithered out onto the stage again. There was a shout of laughter and the house quieted at once. Sam scrambled to his feet, weaving and blinking blearily.

"'Hoy there!" he howled suddenly. "Gimme rope!"

A *papier-mâché* cigar three feet long dropped to the stage from the opposite wings. Laughter. "Naw! Rope! Rope!" the little man screamed, dancing up and down.

A blackish rope snaked down from the flies. Miraculously it coiled over his scrawny shoulders. He struggled with it. He scrambled after its tarred ends. He executed fantastic flying leaps. And always the tarred ends eluded him, and constantly he became more and more enmeshed in the black coils as he wrestled with the rope.

The gallery broke down. The man *was* funny; even Kelly's dour face lightened, and the Inspector was frankly grinning. Then it was over and two stagehands darted out of the wings and pulled the comedian off the stage, now a helpless bundle trussed in rope. His face under the paint was chalk white. He extricated himself easily enough from the coils.

"Good boy," chuckled the Inspector. "That was fine!"

Sam muttered something and trudged away to his dressing-room. The black rope lay where it had fallen. Ellery glanced at it once, and then turned his attention back to the stage. The music had changed. A startlingly beautiful tenor voice rang through the theatre. The orchestra was playing softly *Home on the Range*. The curtain rose on Tex Crosby.

The tall thin man was dressed in gaudiest stage-cowboy costume. And yet he wore it with an air of authority. The pearl-butted six-shooters protruding from his holsters did not seem out of place. His big white sombrero shaded a gaunt Western face. His legs were a little bowed. The man was real.

He sang Western songs, told a few funny stories in his soft Texan drawl, and all the while his long-fingered hands were busy with a lariat. He made the lariat live. From the moment the curtain rose upon his lanky figure the lariat was in motion, and it did not subside through the jokes, the patter, even the final song, which was inevitably *The Last Round-Up*.

"Tinhorn Will Rogers," sneered Kelly, blinking his bloodshot eyes.

For the first time Ellery raised the binoculars. When the Texan had taken his last bow Ellery glanced inquiringly at the manager. Kelly shook his head.

The Great Gordi made his entrance in a clap of thunder, a flash of lightning, and a black Satanic cloak, faced with red. There was something impressive about his very charlatanism. His black eyes glittered and his

mustache points quivered above his lips and his beak
jutted like an eagle's; and meanwhile neither his hands
nor his mouth kept still.

The magician had a smooth effortless patter which
kept his audience amused and diverted their attention
from the fluent mysteries of his hands. There was nothing startling in his routine, but it was a polished performance that fascinated. He performed seeming
miracles with cards. His sleight-of-hand with coins and
handkerchiefs was, to the layman, amazing. His evening clothes apparently concealed scores of wonders.

They watched with a mounting tension while he went
through his bag of tricks. For the first time Ellery noticed with a faint start, that Brinkerhof, still in tights,
was crouched in the opposite wings. The big man's eyes
were fixed upon the magician's face. They ignored the
flashing fingers, the swift movements of the black-clad
body. Only the face... In Brinkerhof's eyes was neither
rage nor venom; just watchfulness. What was the matter with the man? Ellery reflected that it was just as
well that Gordi was unconscious of the acrobat's scru-
tiny; those subtle hands might not operate so fluidly.

Despite the tension the magician's act seemed in-
terminable. There were tricks with odd-looking pieces
of apparatus manipulated from backstage by assistants.
The house was with him, completely in his grasp.

"Good show," said the Inspector in a surprised voice.
"This is darned good vaudeville."

"It'll get by," muttered Kelly. There was something
queer on his face. He too was watching intently.

And suddenly something went wrong on the stage.
The orchestra seemed bewildered. Gordi had concluded
a trick, bowed, and stepped into the wings near the
watching men. Not even the curtain was prepared. The
orchestra had swung into another piece. The conduc-
tor's head was jerking from side to side in a panicky,
inquiring manner.

"What's the matter?" demanded the Inspector.

Kelly snarled: "He's left out his last trick. Good hunch,
Mr. Queen.... Hey, ham!" he growled to the magician,
"finish your act, damn you! While they're still clappin'!"

Gordi was very pale. He did not turn; they could see
only his left cheek and the rigidity of his back. Nor did

he reply. Instead, with all the reluctance of a tyro, he slowly stepped back onto the stage. From the other side Brinkerhof watched. And this time Gordi, with a convulsive start, saw him.

"What's coming off here?" said the Inspector softly, as alert as a wren.

Ellery swung the glasses to his eyes.

A trapeze hurtled stageward from the flies—a simple steel bar suspended from two slender strands. A smooth yellow rope, very new in appearance, accompanied it from above, falling to the stage.

The magician worked very, very, painfully slowly. The house was silent. Even the music had stopped.

Gordi grasped the rope and did something with it; his back concealed what he was doing; then he swung about and held up his left hand. Tied with an enormous and complicated knot to his left wrist was the end of the yellow rope. He picked up the other end and leaped a little, securing the trapeze. At the level of his chest he steadied it and turned again so that he concealed what he was doing, and when he swung about once more they saw that the rope's other end was now knotted in the same way about the steel bar of the trapeze. He raised his right hand in signal and the drummer began a long roll.

Instantly the trapeze began to rise, and they saw that the rope was only four feet long. As the bar rose, Gordi's lithe body rose with it, suspended from the bar by the full length of the rope attached to his wrist. The trapeze came to a stop when the magician's feet were two yards from the stage.

Ellery squinted carefully through the powerful lenses. Across the stage Brinkerhof crouched.

Gordi now began to squirm and kick and jump in the air, indicating in pantomime that he was securely tied to the trapeze and that not even the heavy weight of his suspended body could undo the knots; in fact, was tightening them.

"It's a good trick," muttered Kelly. "In a second a special drop'll come down, an' in eight seconds it'll go up again and there he'll be on the stage, with the rope on the floor."

Gordi cried in a muffled voice: "Ready!"

But at the same instant Ellery said to Kelly: *"Quick! Drop the curtain! This instant. Signal those men in the flies, Kelly!"*

Kelly leaped into action. He shouted something unintelligible and after a second of hesitation the main curtain was dropped. The house was dumb with astonishment; they thought it was part of the trick. Gordi began to struggle frantically, reaching up for the trapeze with his free hand.

"Lower that trapeze!" roared Ellery on the cut-off stage now, waving his arms at the staring men above. "Lower it! *Gordi, don't move!*"

The trapeze came down with a thud. Gordi sprawled on the stage, his mouth working. Ellery leaped upon him, an open blade in hand. He cut quickly, savagely, at the rope. It parted, its torn end dangling from the trapeze.

"You may get up now," said Ellery, panting a little. "It's the knot I wanted to see, Signor Gordi."

They crowded around Ellery and the fallen man, who seemed incapable of rising. He sat on the stage, his mouth still working, naked fear in his eyes. Brinkerhof was there, his muscular biceps rigid. Crosby, Sailor Sam, Sergeant Velie, Kelly, Bregman...

The Inspector stared at the knot on the trapeze. Then he slowly took from his pocket a short length of the dirty old rope which had hanged Myra Brinkerhof. The knot was there. He placed it beside the knot on the trapeze.

They were identical.

"Well, Gordi," said the Inspector wearily. "I guess it's all up with you. Get up, man. I'm holding you for murder, and anything you say—"

Without a sound Brinkerhof, the mighty Atlas, sprang upon the man on the floor, big hands on Gordi's throat. It took the combined efforts of the Texan, Sergeant Velie, and Manager Kelly to tear the acrobat off.

Gordi gasped, holding his throat: "I didn't do it, I tell you! I'm innocent! Yes, we had—we lived together. I loved her. But why should I kill her? I didn't do it. For God's sake—"

"*Schwein,*" growled Atlas, his chest heaving.

Sergeant Velie tugged at Gordi's collar. "Come on, come on there...."

Ellery drawled: "Very pretty. My apologies, Mr. Gordi. Of course you didn't do it."

A shocked silence fell. From behind the heavy curtain voices—loud voices—came. The feature picture had been flashed on the screen.

"Didn't—do—it?" muttered Brinkerhof.

"But the knots, El," began the Inspector in a bewildered voice.

"Precisely. The knots." In defiance of fire regulations Ellery lit a cigarette and puffed thoughtfully. "The hanging of Myra Brinkerhof has bothered me from the beginning. Why was she *hanged*? In preference to one of four other methods of committing murder which were simpler, more expedient, easier of accomplishment, and offered no extra work, as hanging did? The point is that if the murderer chose the hard way, the complicated way, the roundabout way of killing her, then he chose that way *deliberately*."

Gordi was staring with his mouth open. Kelly was ashen pale.

"But why," murmured Ellery, "did he choose hanging deliberately? Obviously, because hanging offered the murderer some peculiar advantage not offered by any of the other four methods. Well, what advantage could hanging conceivably offer that shooting, stabbing, gassing, or hammering to death could not? To put it another way, what is characteristic of hanging that is not characteristic of shooting and the rest? Only one thing. *The use of a rope*."

"Well, but I still don't see—" frowned the Inspector.

"Oh, it's clear enough, dad. There's something about the rope that made the murderer use it in preference to the other methods. But what's the outstanding significance of this particular rope—the rope used to hang Myra Brinkerhof? *Its knot*—its peculiar knot, so peculiar that not even the Department's expert could identify it. In other words, the use of that knot was like the leaving of a fingerprint. Whose knot is it? Gordi's, the magician's—and, I suspect, his exclusively."

"I can't understand it," cried Gordi. "Nobody knew

my knot. It's one I developed myself—" Then he bit his lip and fell silent.

"Exactly the point. I realize that stage magicians have developed knotmaking to a remarkable degree. Wasn't it Houdini who—?"

"The Davenport brothers, too," muttered the magician. "My knot is a variation on one of their creations."

"Quite so," drawled Ellery. "So I say, had Mr. Gordi wanted to kill Myra Brinkerhof, would he have deliberately chosen *the single method that incriminated him,* and him alone? Certainly not if he were reasonably intelligent. Did he tie his distinctive knot, then, from sheer habit, subconsciously? Conceivable, but then why had he chosen hanging in the first place, when those four easier methods were nearer to his hand?" Ellery slapped the magician's back. "So, I say—our apologies, Gordi. The answer is very patently that you're being framed by some one who deliberately chose the hanging-plus-knot method to implicate you in a crime you're innocent of."

"But he says nobody else knew his confounded knot," growled the Inspector. "If what you say is true, El, somebody must have learned it on the sly."

"Very plausible," murmured Ellery. "Any suggestions, *Signor?"*

The magician got slowly to his feet, brushing his dress suit off. Brinkerhof gaped stupidly at him, at Ellery.

"I don't know," said Gordi, very pale. "I thought no one knew. Not even my technical assistants. But then we've all been traveling on the same bill for weeks. I suppose if some one wanted to..."

"I see," said Ellery thoughtfully. "So there's a dead end, eh?"

"Dead beginning," snapped his father. "And thanks, my son, for the assistance. *You're* a help!"

"I tell you very frankly," said Ellery the next day in his father's office, *"I* don't know what it's all about. The only thing I'm sure of is Gordi's innocence. The murderer knew very well that somebody would notice the unusual knot Gordi uses in his rope-escape illusion. As for motive—"

"Listen," snarled the Inspector, thoroughly out of

temper, "I can see through glass the same way you can. They all had motive. Crosby kicked over by the dame, Gordi...Did you know that this little comedian was sniffin' around Myra's skirts the last couple of weeks? Trying his darnedest to make her. And Kelly's had monkey business with her, too, on a former appearance at the Metropole."

"Don't doubt it," said Ellery sombrely. "The call of the flesh. She was an alluring little trick, at that. Real old Boccaccio melodrama, with the stupid husband playing cuckold—"

The door opened and Dr. Prouty, Assistant Medical Examiner, stumped in looking annoyed. He dropped into a chair and clumped his feet on the Inspector's desk. "Guess what?" he said.

"I'm a rotten guesser," said the old gentleman sourly.

"Little surprise for you gentlemen. For me, too. The woman wasn't hanged."

"What!" cried the Queens, together.

"Fact. She was dead when she was swung up." Dr. Prouty squinted at his ragged cigar.

"Well, I'll be eternally damned," said Ellery softly. He sprang from his chair and shook the physician's shoulder. "Prouty, for heaven's sake, don't look so smug! What killed her? Gun, gas, knife, poison—"

"Fingers."

"Fingers?"

Dr. Prouty shrugged. "No question about it. When I took that dirty hemp off her lovely neck I found the distinct marks of fingers on the skin. It was a tight rope, and all that, but there were the marks, gentlemen. She was choked to death by a man's hands and then strung up—why, *I* don't know."

"Well," said Ellery. "Well," he said again, and straightened. "*Very* interesting. I begin to scent the proverbial rodent. Tell us more, good leech."

"Certainly is queer," muttered the Inspector, sucking his mustache.

"Something even queerer," drawled Dr. Prouty. "You boys have seen choked stiffs plenty. What's the characteristic of the fingermarks?"

Ellery was watching him intently. "Characteristic?" He frowned. "Don't know what you mean—Oh!" His gray eyes glittered. "Don't tell me.... The usual marks point upward, thumbs toward the chin."

"Smart lad. Well, these marks don't. They all point *downward*."

Ellery stared for a long moment. Then he seized Dr. Prouty's limp hand and shook it violently. "Eureka! Prouty, old sock, you're the answer to a logician's prayer! Dad, come on!"

"What is this?" scowled the Inspector. "You're too fast for me. Come where?"

"To the Metropole. Urgent affairs. If my watch is honest," Ellery said quickly, "we're just in time to witness another performance. And I'll show you why our friend the murderer not only didn't shoot, stab, asphyxiate, or hammer little Myra into Kingdom Come, but didn't hang her either!"

Ellery's watch, however, was dishonest. When they reached the Metropole it was noon, and the feature picture was still showing. They hurried backstage in search of Kelly.

"Kelly or this old man they call Perk, the caretaker," Ellery murmured, hurrying his father down the dark side aisle. "Just one question..."

A patrolman let them through. They found backstage deserted except for Brinkerhof and his new partner, who were stolidly rehearsing what was apparently a new trick. The trapeze was down and the big man was hanging from it by his powerful legs, a rubber bit in his mouth. Below him, twirling like a top, spun the tall blonde, the other end of the bit in her mouth.

Kelly appeared from somewhere and Ellery said: "Oh, Kelly. Are all the others in?"

Kelly was drunk again. He wobbled and said vaguely: "Oh, sure. Sure."

"Gather the clans in Myra's dressing room. We've still a little time. Question's unnecessary, dad. I should have known without—"

The Inspector threw up his hands.

Kelly scratched his chin and staggered off. "Hey, Atlash," he called wearily. "Stop Atlash-ing an' come on." He swayed off toward the dressing rooms.

"But, El," groaned the Inspector, "I don't understand—"

"It's perfectly childish in its simplicity," said Ellery, "now that I've seen what I suspected was the case. Come along, sire; don't crab the act."

When they were assembled in the dead woman's cubbyhole Ellery leaned against the dressing table, looked at the sprinkler pipe, and said: "One of you might as well own up...you see, I know who killed the little—er—lady."

"You know that?" said Brinkerhof hoarsely. "Who is—" He stopped and glared at the others, his stupid eyes roving.

But no one else said anything.

Ellery sighed. "Very well, then, you force me to wax eloquent, even reminiscent. Yesterday I posed the question: Why should Myra Brinkerhof have been hanged in preference to one of four handier methods? And I said, in demonstrating Mr. Gordi's innocence, that the reason was that hanging permitted the use of a rope and consequently of Gordi's identifiable knot." He brandished his forefinger. "But I forgot an additional possibility. If you find a woman with a rope around her neck who has died of strangulation, you assume it was the rope that strangled her. I completely overlooked the fact that hanging, in permitting use of a rope, also accomplishes the important objective of *concealing the neck*. But why should Myra's neck have been concealed? By a rope? Because a rope is not the only way of strangling a victim, because a victim can be *choked* to death by fingers, because choking to death leaves marks on the neck, and because the choker didn't want the police to know there *were* fingermarks on Myra's neck. He thought that the tight strands of the rope would not only conceal the fingermarks but would obliterate them as well—sheer ignorance, of course, since in death such marks are ineradicable. But that is what he thought, and that *primarily* is why he chose hanging for Myra when she was already dead. The leaving of Gordi's knot to implicate him was only a secondary reason for the selection of rope."

"But, El," cried the inspector, "that's nutty. Suppose

he did choke the woman to death. I can't see that he'd be incriminating himself by leaving fingermarks on her neck. You can't match fingermarks—"

"Quite true," drawled Ellery, "but you *can* observe that fingermarks are on the neck *the wrong way*. For these point, not upward, but downward."

And still no one said anything, and there was silence for a space in the room with the heavily breathing men.

"For you see, gentlemen," continued Ellery sharply, "when Myra was choked she was choked *upside down*. But how is this possible? Only if one of two conditions existed. Either at the time she was choked she was hanging head down above her murderer, or—"

Brinkerhof said stupidly: "*Ja*. I did it. *Ja*. I did it." He said it over and over, like a phonograph with its needle grooved.

A woman's voice from the amplifier said: "But I love you, darling, love you, love you, love you..."

Brinkerhof's eyes flamed and he took a short step toward the Great Gordi. "Yesterday I say to Myra: 'Myra, tonight we rehearse the new trick.' After the second show I see Myra undt that *schweinhund* kissing undt kissing behind the scenery. I hear them talk. They haf been fooling me. I plan. I will kill her. When we rehearse. So I kill her." He buried his face in his hands and began to sob without sound. It was horrible; and Gordi seemed transfixed with its horror.

And Brinkerhof muttered: "Then I see the marks on her throat. They are upside down. I know that iss bad. So I take the rope undt I cover up the marks. Then I hang her, with the *schwein's* knot, that she had once told me he had shown to her—"

He stopped. Gordi said hoarsely, "Good God. I didn't remember—"

"Take him away," said the Inspector in a small dry voice to the policeman at the door.

"It was all so clear," explained Ellery a little later, over coffee. "Either the woman was hanging head down above her murderer, or her murderer was hanging head down above the woman. One squeeze of those powerful paws..." He shivered. "It had to be an acrobat, you see.

And when I remembered that Brinkerhof himself had said they had been rehearsing a new trick—" He stopped and smoked thoughtfully.

"Poor guy," muttered the Inspector. "He's not a bad sort, just dumb. Well, she got what was coming to her."

"Dear, dear," drawled Ellery. "Philosophy, Inspector? I'm really not interested in the moral aspects of crime. I'm more annoyed at this case than anything."

"Annoyed?" said the Inspector with a sniff. "You look mighty smug to me."

"Do I? But I really am. I'm annoyed at the shocking unimaginativeness of our newspaper friends."

"Well, well," said the Inspector with a sigh of resignation. "I'll bite. What's the gag?"

Ellery grinned. "Not one of the reporters who covered this case saw the perfectly obvious headline. You see, they forgot that one of the cast is named—of all things, dear God!—Gordi."

"Headline?" frowned the Inspector.

"Oh, lord. How could they have escaped casting me in the rôle of Alexander and calling this The Affair of the Gordian Knot?"

TEN PERCENT OF MURDER

by Henry Slesar

*The work of Henry Slesar has reached both the ears and
the eyes of the American public. His 100 teleplays for*
Alfred Hitchcock Presents *and his 39 plays for the CBS*
Radio Mystery Theatre *are topped by the nine years he
spent as head writer for the television serial,* The Edge
of Night. *His many science fiction and mystery stories
are clever, and his work has been compared to that of
O. Henry. Slesar won the Mystery Writers of America's
Edgar Allan Poe award in 1960 and 1977 and an Emmy
in 1974.*

You know what makes me laugh? Those glossy photographs that line my office walls, with all the sleek,
bright-eyed faces of my clients, grinning at me over
handwritten inscriptions that read: *To Matt, with deep
fondness and gratitude.* Boy, what a gallery of phonies!
When they make their personal appearances at my desk,
all the toothpaste smiles are replaced by frowns, and
they show about as much fondness and gratitude as a
snake being clobbered with a stick. But that's what I
get for being a theatrical agent, a ten per center. I
walked into the business with my eyes wide open.

The worst of the lot was Hildegarde Hayes, but that
was to be expected, too. Hildy was my bread-and-butter
client; more than half my income was dependent upon
the plays she starred in, the TV guest shots she made,
her infrequent movies. Hildy was my Big Name, and
if she wanted to scowl and scream and thump my desk,
that was all right with Matt Lafferty. Me, I'm understanding. Me, I'm the original wooden Indian.

But when Hildy got me on the phone that Wednesday
afternoon, I have to admit that my mahogany compo-
sure started to crack. Talk about hysteria!—she made
the snake pit sound like a rest home. I had four people
in my office from NBC, and we were at the have-a-
cigar-and-let's-talk-contract stage, and I was in no mood

to play nursemaid to a temperamental star. But Hildy raved on, and after a while I got the idea. Either I headed for her apartment, and fast, or my Big Name would be on somebody else's client list. I made my apologies as best as I could, grabbed my hat, and taxied to Hildy's duplex on Central Park South.

Jimmy, the apartment house doorman, and Pete, the elevator jockey, gave me respectful salutes and knowing grins. Both these worthies knew the purpose of my visit because it was always the same. Hildy tossed her prima-donna tantrums about once every two weeks, and the reasons varied from a drunken fight with her husband—a TV western star named Kevin Culver—to frantic concern over her poodle's upset stomach. I didn't know what to expect this time when I punched the doorbell and Hildy let me in.

She was calm now—like a dormant volcano. She was wearing a feathery housecoat, and her make-up was clotted in pink patches on her face. Some critic once said that Hildy had hair like golden wheat. Now it looked more like shredded wheat. But what really riveted my attention was Hildy's eyes. There wasn't even a spark in what were usually twin furnaces.

"What's the matter now?" I said. "Poochie got the pip again?"

"Don't joke," she said hoarsely. "For God's sake, no jokes, Matt."

I threw my hat on the sofa and sat down. "All right, let's hear it. I broke up a crucial meeting for this, so better make it good."

She didn't answer. She went to the window and stared at the light drizzle outside like Sadie Thompson. I figured it was an act, and was all set to say so, when Hildy turned around. I knew she wasn't *that* good an actress, so the ghastly expression she was wearing made me sit up straight.

"Something awful's happened," she whispered. "I killed Kevin."

"You did *what?*"

"I killed him. With that little gun he bought for me last Christmas. About half an hour ago."

"Now cut it out," I said, wanting to believe it was a

gag and knowing even then that she was serious. "This is no time to play games, Hildy."

She walked to the bedroom door and opened it. She didn't go inside, just stood there with her hand on the knob.

"He's in there, on the floor. Oh my God, I can't believe it's true!"

I whipped out of the chair and brushed past her to the bedroom. At first I didn't see anything but the mile-wide bed and plush furnishings. Then I saw a pair of shiny shoes near the end table, and Kevin Culver's feet were still in them. He was stretched out like one of his own victims in the western TV show, and there wasn't any blood visible. The bullet had entered the back of his head and killed him instantly. I stood up, saw myself in the vanity mirror, and almost shrieked; then I returned quietly to the living room.

Hildy had a tumblerful of whiskey in her hand. I grabbed it from her, swallowed half, and handed back the rest. She finished it while I sat down and rubbed my eyes.

"Now do you believe me?" she said, with a weird note of triumph.

"I believe you. But *why*, for God's sake?"

"I don't know what came over me. I knew about that Sudderth woman for a long time; I didn't think I really cared—"

"Wilma Sudderth?"

"Oh, don't act so innocent—you know Kevin was carrying on with her. I've known about it for two months, but I didn't think it was any more serious than a bad cold. But then Kevin came home around four and started to pack a bag; he was going up to that ritzy mountain lodge of hers—"

I groaned, and tried to fight off visions of poverty. I didn't feel any great sorrow in the world's loss of Kevin Culver, or even in the arrest of Hildegarde Hayes. All I could foresee was the end of my livelihood.

I said, "But why *shoot* him? Was he worth it?"

Hildy looked thoughtful. "Now that I look back, I guess not. But I wasn't thinking. I reached for a tissue in the drawer of the night table when I saw the gun. It felt so dramatic pointing it at him, and the next thing

I knew—" She slammed her whiskey glass to the table. "You've got to help me out of this, Matt."

"What?"

"You've got to find me a way out. I'm not a *murderer*, for heaven's sake. You know that."

"Technically, Hildy—"

"Oh, don't be difficult! You manage everything else for me, don't you? Well, I want you to manage this."

She was sounding like the old Hildy again.

"Now, look," I said, "this isn't part of an agent's service—"

"You've got a lot at stake, Matt, and don't tell me different. Without me your little agency isn't worth getting up in the morning for."

It was true, of course.

"Well, what do you expect me to do? Take the rap for you?"

"There must be *something* you can do!" Her voice went from a screech to a scream. "Get rid of him! Drop him in an alley or something. Make the police think he killed himself—"

"That would be ducky. Only how does a suicide shoot himself in the back of the head? The least you could have done was make it look better—"

"I wasn't *thinking* at the time, don't you understand?"

"You sure weren't, baby."

But I was thinking now, and the more I thought, the blacker the situation looked. It was funny how a beautiful career could be blotted out by one split second of passion and stupidity—my career, I mean, the hell with Hildy's. And if I wanted to save the pieces, I had to come up with some fancy thinking.

"All right," I said, getting to my feet. "I'll try and work something out. Best thing for you to do is get dressed and get out of here. But go some place where I can reach you in a hurry."

She looked at me like a puppy dog, fond and grateful at last. "You're wonderful, Matt."

"We'll see how wonderful."

She headed for the bedroom, yipped when she remembered the body was still there, then became quiet. I did some painful cerebration and picked up the telephone. I dialed the number of a New York newspaper and prayed that Larry Cole would be available. Luckily, he was.

"Hello, Larry? This is Matt Lafferty."

The columnist didn't exactly cheer.

"Listen, Larry, I got some hot poop for you, but I don't want you to sit on it all week. Column all closed up for tomorrow's paper?"

"Hard to say," Cole answered. "What's the story?"

"It's about Hildy's husband, Kevin. Now for God's sake, don't tell Hildy where you got the information or she'll kill me. But Hildy's asked him for a divorce, and the poor slob's all broken up."

"No kidding?"

"Yeah. You know how nuts Kevin is about Hildy— he'd climb the Alps for her. He even threatened to kill himself if she walked out on him—"

"When did this happen?"

"Today, right before my eyes. I'm with Kevin now, trying to console him. But he's drinking pretty heavy—"

"Well, I dunno, Matt. Seems to me I got an item about Culver already—"

"But it's a great story! TV star threatens to kill himself when actress wife gives him the air. Hell, I'm not trying to write it for you, Larry, you know that. Oh-oh—"

"What's the matter?"

"Kevin's coming out of the bedroom. I thought he'd passed out. You want me to call you back, or is that enough?"

"I'll see about it, Matt—"

"Sure," I said, detecting interest in his casual response. Then I hung up.

Hildy came out of the bedroom a couple of minutes later, having performed a miracle with a girdle, a comb, and a box of paints. She went to the door and said, "I'll be at Toots'. I hope it goes okay, Matt."

"You and me both."

When she was gone I went into the bedroom and took another look at Hildy's handiwork. I got myself a face cloth and wiped away the blood on Kevin's neck.

In the closet I found Kevin's wide-brimmed hat and

stuck it on his head. Then I hoisted him up with his arms around my shoulders and dragged him toward the doorway. He wasn't a big man, despite the fact that he looks nine feet two on television, but I found out what they mean by dead weight. I was puffing and wheezing by the time I had him across the living room carpet and out the front door.

I propped him against the wall, hoping he would remain stable. But as I walked to the elevator, he started to slide to the floor of the hallway. I was scared, but I had to take the chance. I punched the elevator button, then scrambled back to pick up the body.

I had him back in position by the time Pete, the elevator man, slid open the door and blinked at us.

"Now come on, Kevin," I said to the corpse. "You don't *really* want to go out again—"

"Need any help?" Pete grinned.

"It's okay, Pete. Mr. Culver's been celebrating, but we've had our fun for the day. How about it, Kev? Come on inside and I'll make us some coffee..."

"Boy!" Pete whistled. "He's really out like a light, huh, Mr. Lafferty?"

"Killed a whole quart," I said confidingly. "Now he wants to go out and paint the town—"

"He'll never make it," Pete laughed.

"I guess not," I laughed back. "Come on, Kev, let's get that coffee..."

I steered him back to the apartment door and pushed it open. "Sorry to bother you, Pete," I said.

"That's okay, Mr. Lafferty."

The elevator door slid shut.

I was so exhausted at this point that I let Kevin's body drop to the carpet in an ungainly heap. Then I sat down, winded, and lit a cigarette, figuring out the next move. This was hard work.

Finally I got up and went to the window. The apartment was on the seventeenth floor of the twenty-story building and the windows faced the street. It was a long, long way to some mighty hard pavement. There wouldn't be very much for a suspicious eye to see once Kevin Culver ended that vertical trip.

I raised the double-hung window as far as I could, then dragged the body to the ledge. It took all the strength I could muster to lift him into position, to make his limp body sit on the ledge in precarious balance without toppling over prematurely. It was gruesome labor, let me tell you, but I finally got him there.

Then I left the apartment and went to the elevator.

"How's Mr. Culver?" Pete asked, hungry for some elevator small talk besides the weather.

"Okay, I guess," I frowned. "He's feeling pretty blue, though. Talking real crazy—"

"Gosh," Pete said, round-eyed.

On the lobby floor I strolled out under the front canopy and took a cigarette from my pocket. Then I went through an act of patting pockets and looking for a match before approaching Jimmy the doorman.

"Thanks," I said, when he lit me. "Getting cooler, don't you think?"

"Yeah, I guess so," Jimmy said amiably.

I walked out a few steps, away from the awning, and looked upward at the apartment building, trying hard to be nonchalant.

"Hope Kev's all right," I said. "You ever watch him on TV, Jimmy?"

"Naw, I don't get the chance, Mr. Lafferty. My wife, she likes them quiz programs."

"That's too bad. *Hey!*"

I didn't give the line much of a reading, but I'm an agent, not an actor.

"What's wrong, Mr. Lafferty?"

"Am I seeing things?"

I kept staring up, and the doorman joined me, shading his eyes against the light with his hand.

"What is it?"

"I don't know. Looks like a man out on the ledge—"

"My God, you're right!"

"What floor is that? Twenty, nineteen, eighteen— oh, my God!"

"That guy must be nuts!"

"It's Kevin!" I shouted. "It's Kevin's floor!"

"What'll we do?" Jimmy started to quake so hard his epaulets shook.

"Better call the police! I'll go upstairs and see if I can stop him—"

"Yeah, yeah," the doorman said, and started in four directions at once. Finally he took off for the phone in the lobby, and I went straight to the elevator. Pete looked baffled at my return, but I didn't say anything, not wanting him to follow me during the rest of my routine.

I got off on the seventeenth and rushed for the apartment door. I went through it like a fullback hitting the line, and kept on going until I reached the window. It didn't take much of a shove to send Kevin's body flying into space.

Then I gave out with the loudest yell you ever heard. It was so convincing that I scared myself.

Pete came running. I covered my eyes with one hand and pointed to the open window with the other, speechless. He ran to the ledge and looked down.

"Poor Mr. Culver," he whispered.

Well, I was proud of myself. I was proud of the way Jimmy and Pete told their stories to the police. I was proud of the heartbroken act Hildy put on, and the free-flowing tears she produced. It was her greatest performance.

I almost chuckled when I heard Pete, the elevator man, describe his version of the episode. He swore that Kevin had rung for the elevator a few minutes before his suicide, and had been arguing with me drunkenly. As for the doorman, he gave a dramatic account of how Kevin was up there on the window ledge, waving his arms and yelling. Instead of suspicion, all Hildy and I got was sympathy, and there wasn't any mention of the word autopsy.

The cops let me go home around midnight, and I stopped at the corner newsstand and bought the morning edition of the tabloid where Larry Cole's column appeared.

I waited until I got upstairs to open it.

As soon as I scanned it, I realized that Cole had decided against including it. But that wasn't the worst part. The worst was the item he *did* use.

Kevin Culver, star of the TV western Fast on the Draw, *has been squiring food-store heiress Wilma*

*Sudderth to the local niteries. Friends say he's ready
to call it quits with his wife, actress Hildegarde
Hayes...*

I went icy reading it. The story was exactly the opposite of the one I had planted! If the police saw it, they'd start asking questions, start wondering why a man ready to leave his wife for an heiress would commit suicide...

Well, I guess you know what happened after that. The cops saw the column, all right, and called Larry Cole down for questioning. He made them curious enough to order an autopsy and they found the bullet in Kevin's head. It was a cinch to match it up with the neat little revolver in Hildy's night table. She was convicted of second-degree murder and got twenty years. I was convicted as an accomplice after the fact, and with good behavior, got off with two. Wouldn't you know it would be ten percent?

CREDIT TO SHAKESPEARE

by Julian Symons

Julian Symons is a well-known poet, mystery reviewer, and writer of crime novels. Several of his novels have won awards: Bloody Murder *(1972) received a special award from the Mystery Writers of America,* The Color of Murder *(1957) was judged best of the year by the British Crime Writers' Association (CWA) and* The Progress of a Crime *(1960) was a CWA runner-up. It also received the Mystery Writers of America's Edgar for best novel.*

"It won't do," said acidulous dramatic critic Edgar Burin, to private detective Francis Quarles. "The fact is that this young producer's too clever by half. You can't play about with a masterpiece like *Hamlet*."

Burin wrinkled his thin nose in distaste as the curtain rose on Act Five.

This *Hamlet* first night was notable because the production was by a young man still in his twenties named Jack Golding, who had already obtained a reputation for eccentric but ingenious work. It was also notable because of the casting. Golding had chosen for his Hamlet a star of light comedy named Giles Shoreham. His Laertes, John Farrimond, had been given his part on the strength of Golding's intuition, since Farrimond had played only one walk-on part in the West End.

Olivia Marston as the Queen and Roger Peters as the King were acknowledged Shakespearean actors, but their choice was remarkable in another sense. For the name of Olivia Marston, an impressive personality on the stage and a notorious one off it, had been linked by well-informed gossip with those of Peters, Farrimond, and even with Jack Golding himself.

Those were the rumors. What was certain was that Olivia, a tall handsome woman in her forties, had been married a few weeks ago to Giles Shoreham who was fifteen years her junior.

This agreeably scandalous background was known to most of the first-night audience, who watched eagerly for signs of tension among the leading players. So far, however, they had been disappointed of anything more exciting than a tendency on the part of Giles Shoreham to fluff his lines.

By Act Five the audience had settled to the view that this was, after all, only another performance of *Hamlet,* marked by abrupt changes of mood from scene to scene, and by the producer's insistence of stressing the relationship between Hamlet and the Queen.

So the curtain rose on Act Five. Golding had taken unusual liberties with the text, and Burin sucked in his breath with disapproval at the omission of the Second Gravedigger at the beginning of this scene. Giles Shoreham, slight and elegant, was playing now with eloquence and increased confidence.

Then came the funeral procession for Ophelia and Hamlet's struggle with Laertes in Ophelia's grave. Here one or two members of the audience sat forward, thinking they discovered an unusual air of reality as Shoreham and Farrimond struggled together, while Roger Peters, as the King, restrained them and Olivia Marston looked on.

Shoreham, Quarles thought, had gained impressiveness as the play went on. With Osric he was now splendidly ironical, and in the opening of the duel scene he seemed to dominate the stage for all his slightness of stature compared with Farrimond's height and breadth of shoulder.

This scene was played faster than usual, and Quarles vaguely noted cuts in the speeches before the duel began. There was Laertes choosing his poisoned foil; there was the poisoned cup brought in and placed on a side table. Then foils were flashing, Hamlet achieved a hit, took the cup to drink and put it down without doing so, with the speech, "I'll play this bout first; set it by a while."

Then another hit, and the Queen came over to wipe Hamlet's brow, picked up the cup, and drank. Laertes wounded Hamlet with his poisoned foil, and Hamlet snatched it from him and wounded Laertes. The Queen, with a cry, sank down as she was returning to the throne, and at once there was a bustle around her.

Osric and two attendants ran to her. The King moved upstage in her direction.

"How does the Queen?" Hamlet asked, and the King made the appropriate reply. "She swoons to see them bleed."

There was a pause.

Should not the Queen reply?

Quarles searched his memory while Burin grunted impatiently by his side.

Hamlet repeated, "How does the Queen?" and knelt down by her side.

The pause this time was longer.

Then Hamlet looked up, and on his face was an unforgettable expression of mingled anguish and irresolution. His lips moved, but he seemed unable to speak. When the words came they seemed almost ludicrous after the Shakespearean speech they had heard.

"A doctor," he cried. "Is there a doctor in the house?"

The other players looked at him in consternation. The curtain came down with a rush. Five minutes later, Roger Peters appeared before it and told the anxious audience that Miss Marston had met with a serious accident.

When Burin and Quarles came onto the stage, the players were standing together in small, silent groups. Only Giles Shoreham sat apart in his red court suit, head in hands.

A man bending over Olivia Marston straightened up and greeted Quarles, who recognized him as the well-known pathologist, Sir Charles Palquist.

"She's dead," Palquist said, and his face was grave. "She took cyanide, and there's no doubt she drank it from that cup. Somebody knocked the cup over and it's empty now, but the smell is still plain enough."

"Now I wonder who did that?" Quarles said. But his meditation on that point was checked by the arrival of his old friend, brisk, grizzled Inspector Leeds.

The Inspector had a wonderful capacity for marshaling facts. Like a dog snapping at the heels of so many sheep, he now extracted a story from each of the actors on the stage, while Quarles stood by and listened.

When the Inspector had finished, this was the result. The cup from which Olivia Marston had taken her fatal drink was filled with red wine and water. The cup had been standing ready in the wings for some time, and it would have been quite easy for anybody on the stage—or, indeed, anybody in the whole company—to drop poison into it unobserved.

As for what had happened on the stage, the duel scene had been played absolutely to the script up to the point where Peters, as the King, said, "She swoons to see them bleed." The Queen should then have replied to him, and her failure to do so was the reason for the very obvious pause that had occurred.

Shoreham, as Hamlet, then improvised by repeating his question, "How does the Queen?" and went on his knees to look at her, thinking that she felt unwell. But when he saw her face, half turned to the floor, suffused and contorted, he knew that something was seriously wrong. Shoreham was then faced with a terrible problem.

Clasping his hands nervously, white-faced, Shoreham said to the Inspector, "I could have got up and gone on as though nothing had happened—after all, in the play the Queen was dead—and within ten minutes the play would have been over. That way we should have completed the performance." Shoreham's large eyes looked pleadingly round at the other members of the cast. "But I couldn't do it. I couldn't leave her lying there—I just couldn't."

"Since the poor lady was dead, it didn't make any difference," said the Inspector in his nutmeg-grater voice. "Now, this lady became Mrs. Shoreham a few weeks ago, I believe? And she was, I imagine, a pretty wealthy woman?"

Giles Shoreham's head jerked up. "Do you mean to insinuate—?"

"I'm not insinuating, sir—I'm merely stating a fact."

Quarles coughed. "I think, Inspector, that there may be other motives at work here."

He took the Inspector aside and told him of the rumors that linked the names of Farrimond, Peters, and

Golding with Olivia Marston. The Inspector's face lengthened as he listened.

"But that means any of the four might have had reason to kill her."

"If they felt passionately enough about her—yes. Which would you pick?"

The Inspector's glance passed from Farrimond, big and sulky, to the assured, dignified, gray-haired Peters and on to the young producer Jack Golding, who looked odd in his lounge suit and thick horn-rimmed spectacles among this collection of Elizabethans. "I'm hanged if I know."

"May I ask a few questions?" The Inspector assented. Quarles stepped forward. "A small point perhaps, gentlemen, but one I should like to clear up. The cup was found on its side with the liquid spilled out of it. Who knocked it over?"

There was silence.

With something threatening behind his urbanity Quarles said, "Very well. Let us have individual denials. Mr. Shoreham?"

Shoreham shook his head.

"Mr Farrimond?"

"Didn't touch a thing."

"Mr. Peters?"

"No."

"Any of you other gentlemen who were on the stage? Or did anyone see it done?" There were murmurs of denial. "Most interesting. Miss Marston replaced the cup on the table and then some unknown agency knocked it on its side."

The Inspector was becoming impatient. "Can't see what you're getting at, Quarles. Do you mean she didn't drink out of it?"

Quarles shook his head. "Oh, no, she drank from it, poor woman. Mr. Shoreham, did you know that you had some rivals for your wife's affections? And did she ever hint that any one of them was particularly angry when she decided to marry you?"

A wintry suggestion of a smile crossed Shoreham's pale face. "She once said she'd treated everybody badly except me and that one of these days she'd get into trouble. I thought she was joking."

"Mr. Golding." The producer started. "I'm not a Shakespearean scholar, but I seem to have noticed more cuts in this *Hamlet* than are usually made."

"No," said Golding. The thickness of his spectacles effectively masked his expression. *"Hamlet* is very rarely played in full. I haven't made more cuts than usual, I've simply made different ones."

"In this particular scene, for instance," Quarles went on, "you've cut the passage early—where the King drinks and sends somebody across to Hamlet with the cup."

"That's right. It seems to me an unnecessary complication."

"What about the rest of the scene? Any cuts in that?"

"None at all. After what you saw we adhere to the standard printed version."

Quarles bent his whole great body forward and said emphatically, "Doesn't that suggest something to you, Mr. Golding? Remember that the cup was knocked over and emptied. Do you understand?"

On Golding's face there was suddenly amazed comprehension.

The Inspector had been listening with increasing irritation. "What's all this got to do with the murder? Why the devil was that cup emptied?"

"Because the murderer thought he would have to drink from it. Remember what happens after the Queen dies, crying that her drink was poisoned. Laertes tells Hamlet that he has been the victim of treachery. Hamlet stabs the King. And what happens *then,* Mr. Peters?"

Roger Peters, truly kingly in his robes, was smiling. "Hamlet puts the poisoned cup to the King's mouth and forces him to drink."

"Correct. In fact, Shoreham stopped the play before that point was reached. But the murderer couldn't be sure that Shoreham's instinct as an actor wouldn't impel him to go on and say nothing. And then what would have happened? The King would also have had to drink from the poisoned cup. You couldn't risk that, could you, Mr. Peters?"

Peters' hand was at his mouth. "No. You are a clever man, Mr. Quarles."

"So there was only one person who would have had any motive for knocking over that cup."

"Only one person. But you are a little late, Mr. Quarles. I had two capsules. I swallowed the second a few seconds ago. I don't think, anyway, that I would have wanted to live without Olivia."

Peters' body seemed to crumple suddenly. Farrimond caught him as he fell.

"Well," said Burin, the dramatic critic, afterward, "you had no evidence, Quarles, but that was a pretty piece of deduction."

"I was merely the interpreter," Quarles said mockmodestly. "The credit for spinning the plot and then unraveling it goes to someone much more famous."

"Who's that?"

"William Shakespeare."

DEATH AT THE OPERA

by Michael Underwood

"Michael Underwood" (John M. Evelyn) is a retired British barrister who worked as a member of the Department of Public Prosecutions in London from 1946 to 1976, finishing his career as an Under-Secretary. Not surprisingly, his thirty crime and mystery novels usually take place in courtrooms and/or involve the law in a major way. His first twelve books feature Inspector (later Superintendent) Simon Manton and begin with Murder on Trial *(1954). With the exception of two novels which star Martin Ainsworth, all of his subsequent works have been discrete books without series characters, all solid, entertaining mysteries—particularly* Murder with Malice *(1977) and* Victim of Circumstance *(1980). Mr. Underwood has certainly made good use of his vocation, and his books are models of the "legal caper" genre.*

Whenever I have occasion to dip into *Who's Who,* I usually look first to see what the contributor has listed under "Recreations." This can often tell one more about the person than all the lines taken up with his accomplishments. It invariably paid me dividends when I was still an estate agent and dealing with important clients. It always helped if I was able to talk to the person concerned about gardening or theater or sailing or whatever the subject might be. The fact that my own knowledge of it might be minimal mattered far less than that I showed an interest.

Of course, sometimes the failure to mention a particular hobby could prove even more revealing. I recall selling a property for a High Court judge on one occasion. He was a stiff, unbending man without any noticeable sense of humor. "Walking" and "reading" were listed as his unexceptionable recreations. It was only when I visited his house I learned quite by chance that he would pass his winter evenings doing embroidery.

His obvious desire to keep this fact secret lowered him still further in my estimation.

But all this is really by the way. What I had been going to say was that, had I ever been invited to contribute an entry to that prestigious volume, I would have headed my list of recreations with "Opera, especially Wagner."

I have a passion for Wagner that has taken me to performances in places as far apart as Moscow and San Francisco, Vienna and Buenos Aires. In fact, since I retired five years ago, most of my traveling has been devoted to his cause, with an annual statutory visit to Bayreuth, the shrine for all Wagnerians.

I ought perhaps to say that my passion is unshared by most of my friends who regard it as an aberration in an otherwise reasonably normal person.

But however strong the lure of Wagner, attendance at his operas can bring hazards of their own. For example, you can find yourself sitting next to someone who fidgets or coughs, or be faced in the foyer by a notice regretting the indisposition of one of the leading singers. These things can, of course, happen at performances of other operas, but with less disastrous effect. And even if you manage to escape these particular hazards, others still lurk, for no composer loaded his singers and musicians, not to mention his producers and stagehands, with such superhuman difficulties. Even when the singing and orchestral playing are sublime, disaster can still strike. The dragon in *Siegfried* can get inextricably caught up in a piece of scenery, the hero's sword can break in two just after it has been invincibly forged, and majestic Valhalla can develop an incurable wobble like a jelly on a vibrating surface. The list is almost inexhaustible.

And recently I was involved in a nightmarish drama that not even a practiced Wagnerian has ever envisaged. Death on the stage is one thing, but sudden death in the auditorium is something different altogether, particularly when, to use the police colloquialism, foul play is suspected.

When a few years ago the well-known philanthropist, Sir Julius Meiler, announced that he was proposing to build an opera house in the park of his Oxfordshire home and devote it primarily to an annual festival of Wagner operas, there was great enthusiasm among us devotees. Sir Julius went quietly ahead with his plans. Since he could no longer travel to Wagner, he would realize an ambition and bring the composer's work to his own doorstep. He employed top men at heaven knows what expense and from his drawing-room window he was able to sit and watch the edifice slowly rise up a quarter of a mile across the parkland.

Even if he never entertained any doubts about the ultimate success of the project, there were many, like myself, who saw it all ending with the old boy's death or in hideous bankruptcy. But neither of these events occurred and six months before the first performances were due to be given, the box office opened.

Needless to say, Sir Julius had himself decided which operas were to be performed and long before the final bricks were laid, conductors, singers, and producers had been engaged for the first season. There were to be two cycles of *The Ring* and three performances each of *Parsifal* and *Tristan and Isolde*.

Though, as I say, I had been skeptical about the outcome of the project, I had made up my mind that, if it did come off, I would be there, come hell or high water. Fortunately I had a contact in the box-office manager, who was a friend of a friend.

I can still remember my excitement the day my tickets arrived. They were for the second cycle of *The Ring* and for performances of the other two operas. Not even the horror of subsequent events has dimmed my recollection of that sunny June morning when our cheerful postman delivered the self-addressed envelope that had accompanied my application.

There were still three months to go before that fateful performance of *Die Walküre* on Tuesday, the 22nd of September.

For the non-Wagnerian, I ought to explain that *The Ring* (full title: *Der Ring des Nibelungen*) consists of four operas amounting to about twenty hours of music, if you include the intervals. Wagner believed in giving his fans their money's worth and some of his "acts" are

as long as whole operas by other composers. So far as
The Ring is concerned, *Das Rheingold,* which is the
first, is the shortest. It lasts just under two and a half
hours and is performed without an interval. From this
you will gather that stamina is almost as important as
love of the music. If you're given to fidgets, you'd better
stay at home and listen to recordings.

I had been over to Bargewick Park, Sir Julius Meiler's place, a couple of times before the festival opened—
once to a large and noisy party to which I was invited
by my friend, the box-office manager, and once for a
privately conducted tour of the opera house itself which
I had found much more interesting. It wasn't an elegant
building to look at, but the acoustics were said to rival
those at Bayreuth. Sir Julius had insisted that everything should be subordinated to the acoustics, hence
the somewhat functional interior. The seats might be
on the hard side, but they were guaranteed not to ab-
sorb any of the sound.

I greeted Monday, the 21st of September, with a sense
of great exhilaration. It was almost beyond the dream
of any Wagnerian that the operas were about to be
performed with internationally famous singers in a
brand-new theater almost on his own doorstep. Bargewick Park was, in fact, twelve miles from where I lived.
The Gods could not have been more beneficent.

Das Rheingold was scheduled to start at half-past
seven and I arrived a good hour before that. The car
park was already quite full and I made my way to the
long bar which ran the length of one side of the building
and bought myself a glass of champagne. What else on
such an occasion! Almost everyone was in evening dress
and the air of expectation was enormous. Wagnerians
had flocked from all points of the compass to attend the
opening performance.

After a second glass of champagne to put the seal on
my mood, I decided to go and claim my seat. I had
studied the plan in advance and knew exactly where it
was—one from the end of the twelfth row of the stalls.

An elderly man and his arrogant-looking younger
companion were already occupying the two seats to the
right of mine. They tucked their legs in with a poorly
concealed lack of grace to let me pass, for which I mur-

mured my thanks. Seeing that there were still fifteen minutes to go before the curtain rose, their attitude seemed rather churlish. Wagner may bring us together, but, as I've discovered before, he doesn't necessarily make us love each other.

The seat on my left, which was against the wall, was still empty and I wondered who was to be my neighbor on that side.

A sudden outburst of applause greeted the arrival of Sir Julius Meiler who was wheeled in his chair into a specially prepared space in the center of the circle.

The house lights were dimming when I became aware of upheaval at the end of our row as a middle-aged woman pushed her way along to the empty seat on my left.

She was obviously hot and bothered and almost fell headlong over the feet of the two men next to me. I stood up to let her pass more easily and then held her seat down for her. She murmured profuse thanks and sank back with an audible sigh of relief as those incredible opening chords rose from the orchestra pit, signifying our immediate transportation to the bottom of the Rhine.

It was not long, however, before I became aware of suppressed coughing on my left and I shot her a quick glance to indicate my awareness. Then at the very moment when Alberich the dwarf seized the Rhinemaiden's gold, she began rummaging in her handbag. Recognizing the symptoms all too well, I realized that in her rush to arrive on time she had left her cough lozenges at home.

She held a tissue to her mouth and tried to clear her throat in silence, which, as everyone knows, is quite impossible. Hastily I reached into my pocket for the throat pastilles I always carry on visits to the opera. I seldom require them myself and am motivated entirely by self-protection. I passed her the whole tin and she communicated her gratitude by patting my hand.

They obviously did the trick for there were no further disturbances and the performance reached its majestic end with the Gods making their entry into a satisfyingly solid-looking Valhalla.

"Wonderful, wonderful," she murmured to me several times in the course of the curtain calls which continued for fifteen minutes.

Eventually the house lights came up and we both sat back in our seats temporarily exhausted while the two men on my other side thrust their way out as if they had a last train to catch.

"You enjoyed the performance?" I said to her after the curtain had come down for the last time.

"Enormously. Surely you did, too?"

"Very much. Though wasn't it Ernest Newman who said one'll have to wait till one reaches heaven for the perfect performance of Wagner?"

"If the rest of the cycle is as good as that, it'll be an unnecessary wait as far as I'm concerned," she said.

I laughed. "I'll reserve judgment until we've heard more."

She reached down for her program which had fallen to the floor and gave a hitch to her shawl which had slipped from one shoulder. "I do hope I didn't disturb you with my chokes. You saved my life with your cough sweets. I was sure I had some in my bag, but I must have forgotten them in the rush of leaving home. I kept on being held up and thought I was never going to get here. I think I'd have lain down and died if they hadn't let me in."

"You certainly ran it rather close," I remarked. "Don't forget that tomorrow's performance starts at six."

"My husband'll be at home to see I set off in good time. He was out at a meeting this evening or I'd never have been late. He's one of those punctual people who has never missed a train in his life. I shan't dare tell him I forgot to bring my cough lozenges." With a laugh she added, "He regards them as a minimum requirement for sitting through Wagner. But then he's hopelessly unmusical. We have a pact. He lets me come to the opera and I let him go off catching butterflies."

"He's an entomologist?"

"He's written a book on the subject," she said with a touch of pride.

As we walked together toward the car park, she told me a bit more about herself. She lived in North Oxford and her husband, who had been a supply officer in the navy, now worked in the bursar's office of one of the colleges.

I estimated her age as being around sixty. She had a pleasant round face and, I suspected, a perennial weight problem.

We reached the car park and were about to part company when she let out an exclamation.

"I've never given you back your cough sweets." She fumbled with her handbag and promptly dropped it.

"Keep them," I said, retrieving her bag. "You may need them tomorrow. And, anyway, I've got more at home."

With that I bade her good night and went in search of my car.

The next evening I arrived at Bargewick Park soon after five o'clock and once more fortified myself with two glasses of excellent champagne before going to my seat.

I was both surprised and gratified to find Mrs. Sharpe already in her place—she had told me her name was Helen Sharpe before we parted company the previous evening.

"See!" she said with a note of triumph. "I'm not the scatty female you obviously thought I was."

"No problems getting here this evening then?" I said with a smile.

"My husband pushed me out of the house far sooner than was necessary and I've even brought my own cough sweets this time." She gave me a rueful look. "But I've just discovered that I've left yours at home. I'm terribly sorry. They were in my other handbag."

"Don't worry. I've brought a further supply."

"What a couple of philanthropists you and Sir Julius are! One provides the music, the other the cough sweets," she said with a merry laugh.

Shortly afterward the two men on my right took their seats without so much as a nod or glance in my direction and a few minutes later the cellos were whipping up the storm music that forms the prelude of the opera.

Act I of *Die Walküre* is one of my favorite parts of the whole *Ring*. It lasts over an hour, but, for me, there is never one flagging second. And when the roles of Siegmund and Sieglinde are sung as gloriously as they were that evening, I quickly become immersed in the music and oblivious of everything else around me. Mrs. Sharpe could have been coughing her head off and I don't believe I'd have noticed.

I turned to her as soon as the curtain came down and was surprised to see her leaning against the wall on her other side in apparent sleep.

It was only when the lights came up and people began to leave the auditorium that I turned back to her.

With horror I realized it wasn't sleep that had overcome her, but death.

I must say that the authorities at Bargewick Park were as efficient at removing bodies from the auditorium as they were at putting on an opera. In no time at all Mrs. Sharpe's remains were carried out with the minimum of fuss.

I went off to the bar and had a large brandy to help me recover from the shock of my discovery. When we returned for Act II, I realized I was more distracted by the empty seat on my left than I had been by the poor woman's coughing the previous evening. My discomfort was compounded by the man on my right who seemed deliberately to turn his shoulder on me. For the first time I glanced round at the occupants of the two seats immediately behind. They were a middle-aged couple and the woman gave me a nervous smile before quickly looking elsewhere.

I have seldom enjoyed anything less than I did those two remaining acts. When the performance was finally over, I decided I ought to go back and make myself known to someone in authority. It had only occurred to me toward the end that they might still be trying to identify Mrs. Sharpe. I could at least help with that.

Accordingly, I hung back until the theater was almost empty. Even so, I received a number of curious stares and it suddenly dawned on me that people had taken her to be my wife or, at least, my companion for the evening and were now regarding me as some sort of callous monster.

I had just reached the foyer when a man stepped forward.

"Excuse me, sir, but may I have a word with you for a moment?"

"Of course. Is it about Mrs. Sharpe?"

He didn't reply, but led the way to a door marked "Private." It was a small office and there was a man inside whom I recognized as the house manager. His photograph appeared in the souvenir program.

"I believe you're Mr. Mason, sir?" the first man said.

"Yes. Charles Mason." For a second I couldn't think how he knew my name, but then I realized he had obviously found out by checking my seat number against my application form.

"I'm Detective Chief Inspector Jackley," he said. "I gather you knew Mrs. Sharpe?"

"No, I'm afraid not."

He frowned. "But you mentioned her name when I first spoke to you, sir."

"We'd exchanged names when we left together after last night's performance."

"You'd not met her previously?"

"I'd never seen her before in my life."

"I see," he said, in a tone which clearly implied that he was reserving judgment on every word I uttered.

"If you look at my written application for tickets," I said slyly, "you'll see that I'm on my own. I imagine Mrs. Sharpe's will show the same. She told me that her husband wasn't at all musical and never accompanied her on these occasions."

"I see," Jackley said again in the same faintly disconcerting tone. "Well, I think that's all for the moment, Mr. Mason. Can we reach you, if necessary, at the address given on your ticket application form?"

"Yes, that's my home."

"Good, then I needn't detain you further."

I got to the door and paused. "Did she have a sudden heart attack or something?" I asked.

"We shan't know the cause of death until after the autopsy," Jackley said, giving me a funny look.

It was only when I was driving home that it occurred to me to wonder what on earth a Detective Chief Inspector would be doing investigating a case of heart attack.

I spent the next day pottering about the garden trying to take my mind off what had happened, entirely without success. Normally I would have been eagerly looking forward to *Siegfried* the following night and to the final opera of the cycle, when the whole monumental undertaking reaches its musical and dramatic climax. It was no use telling myself that there couldn't be a better way of dying, because I kept on remembering Detective Chief Inspector Jackley's intrusion on the scene.

About half-past five I went indoors and had a wash. I had just settled down to watch the early evening news on television when a car drew up outside and two men got out. One of them I recognized immediately as Jackley. For a few seconds they stared up at the roof as if searching for some structural fault. Then they advanced up the path. I waited until they had rung the bell before going to open the door.

"Good evening, Mr. Mason," Jackley said. "I wonder if my colleague and I might come in and have a word with you? Incidentally, this is Detective Sergeant Denham."

I let the way into the living room.

"Nice home you have," Jackley remarked, glancing about him. "But then it would be surprising if a retired estate agent couldn't pick himself a plum." He gave me a small smile.

My ex-profession had certainly *not* appeared on my application form for opera tickets, so it was obvious that the police had been doing some homework on me. Moreover, they were ready to let me know the fact. I decided to hold my tongue and oblige them to state their business, which Jackley wasn't long in doing.

"I understand you supplied Mrs. Sharpe with some cough lozenges," he said with a mildly quizzical expression.

"Not last night. It was during the performance the previous evening."

"That agrees with what Mr. Fox and Mr. Driver have told us."

"And who might they be?"

"They occupied the two seats on your right. They saw you pass Mrs. Sharpe your tin of cough lozenges."

"Oh, did they!" I exclaimed in a nettled tone.

"You sound put out," Jackley said equably. "I thought you Wagner worshippers were all chums together."

"There was nothing chummy about those two as far as I was concerned."

"But you're not denying you handed Mrs. Sharpe your lozenges?"

"Of course not. Why should I deny it? And, anyway, so what?"

"Ah, so what, you ask. Well, the answer to that, Mr. Mason, is it appears Mrs. Sharpe didn't die a natural death, but was poisoned. Murdered by a dose of potassium cyanide. Now, that's a poison that acts very rapidly and so the irresistible inference is that she must have ingested it during the actual course of the performance. That's where your cough lozenges become relevant."

"Oh, my God, that's terrible!" I said, feeling as if the Chief Inspector had given my room a sudden violent spin. "But it certainly couldn't have been anything to do with the ones I gave her. She left them at home yesterday and brought her own."

"What makes you say that, Mr. Mason?"

"She told me so. Apologized for not returning mine. Said she'd left them in her other bag, the one she'd been carrying the previous evening."

For a moment Jackley looked nonplused. "She told you that?"

"Yes."

"When?"

"When we met at our seats yesterday evening."

"I can't understand why she should have said that," he remarked in a tone of clear disbelief, "because it wasn't true." He reached into his pocket and pulled out a tin which was enclosed in a cellophane envelope. "Is this the tin you gave her?"

"Yes, that's the sort I buy. Buckland's."

"We found this tin in her handbag when we were called to Bargewick Park last night. There was also a packet of Coff-Stop lozenges in the bag. Can you explain why she should have lied to you, Mr. Mason?"

"I can only repeat what she said to me."

"Doesn't it strike you as very odd?"

"I don't know enough about the lady to answer that," I said warily.

"And you still say that you had never met her before?"

"Never."

"You don't live far apart."

"Nor do I from a hundred and twenty thousand other people in this area, but I assure you I don't know them all."

"That's the best you can say?"

"It's all I can say."

"Do you have a further supply of Buckland's lozenges?"

"Yes."

"Any objection to handing them over?"

"None."

"If you tell Sergeant Denham where they are, he can fetch them."

"I'll fetch them myself," I replied frostily.

"You don't trust the police?" Jackley said with an air of faint amusement.

"It doesn't seem that they trust me."

"I assure you I'm doing no more than duty requires, Mr. Mason. At this stage of an inquiry it's questions, questions all the way."

"And I've given you truthful answers."

"Every answer has to be tested. You say that yours are truthful, but I have to be sure."

"You can be."

"But can I?" He fixed me with an intent look. "It doesn't exactly tally with what Mrs. Sharpe told her husband when she arrived home the night before last." The room seemed to take another violent spin as Jackley went on. "According to Mr. Sharpe, you had considerably upset his wife. You behaved so strangely that she began to wonder if you mightn't be a mental patient. And she became even more apprehensive when you forced your cough lozenges on her."

"What absolute rubbish! I don't believe for one moment that she ever said anything of the sort. I've never been a mental patient in my life and there was nothing remotely strange about my behavior. You can ask the couple who were sitting behind us."

"The fact still remains, Mr. Mason, that she did have your tin of Buckland's lozenges in her handbag last night. Are you quite sure she told you she'd left them at home?"

"Absolutely."

"Ah, well!" he said with a sigh. "If you'll just let us have your remaining supply, we'll be on our way. I'll doubtless be in touch with you again."

After their departure I poured myself a large Scotch and sat down to try and sort out my thoughts. To say that I was in a state of shock was a pathetic understatement. I felt as if my whole world had become unpivoted.

The immediate decision which faced me was whether or not to attend the performance of *Siegfried* the next evening. If I didn't go, it would be quickly assumed that I was in some way connected with Mrs. Sharpe's death. If I did turn up, I was going to be the cynosure of furtive glances and whispered comment, the effect of which not even the power of Wagner's music was likely to erase.

Moreover, I kept on recalling that part of the plot involves a character named Mime trying to induce Siegfried to drink a potion of poison. At least, they didn't have cough lozenges in that mythical era; nevertheless it was hardly conducive to an evening for forgetting one's troubles.

In the event, I did go and found the experience every bit as grim as I had expected. My attendance at *Götterdämmerung* two nights later was not quite as bad, though it was still testing enough. On each occasion I sat staring at the stage with fixed concentration, remaining in my seat during the intervals. Mrs. Sharpe's seat was unoccupied at both performances and Messrs. Fox and Driver regarded me with even greater disdain than previously.

What should have been exhilarating occasions had turned into a ghastly ordeal.

A week passed before I heard anything further. I scanned the local paper each day, but news of the case was soon reduced to a small item on an inside page to the effect that police inquiries were still continuing into the "mystery of the opera-goer's death." Earlier Mr.

Sharpe was reported as saying there must be a mad poisoner at large who was prepared to strike indiscriminately as nobody could have had the slightest motive for murdering his wife. I took this to be an arrow shot deliberately in my direction.

I had a great urge to call Detective Chief Inspector Jackley, but refrained from doing so as I feared he might misconstrue my interest in his inquiries. I tried to telephone my friend in the box office at Bargewick Park. Three times, in fact. But once he was at a meeting and the other two times I was told he was out, so that, in my slightly paranoid state, I immediately assumed that he was trying to avoid me.

All in all, it was the most nerve-wracking and miserable week of my life. By the end I had almost become a recluse, finding it even an ordeal to be with friends.

I was just sitting down to a lonely cold lunch one day toward the end of the following week when the telephone rang.

"Mr. Mason? Detective Chief Inspector Jackley here. Are you going to be home this afternoon?"

"As far as I know," I said, trying to sound unconcerned and knowing very well that I would be at home.

"Good, I'll drop by about four o'clock."

His tone had told me nothing and I spent the next three hours in wild speculation about the reason for his visit.

He arrived alone and accepted the offer of a cup of tea, both of which I took to be hopeful signs.

"I think we've got the case just about sewn up," he said, as I handed him his tea. He gave me a wry smile. "As far as I was concerned there were only two suspects from the very outset. The husband and you. And the husband was always the more likely. The problem was to establish a motive."

"And you've been able to do that?"

"Yes."

"What was it?"

"Oh, the usual. Another woman. A much younger person."

"Was she involved too?"

He nodded. "She's a research chemist at one of the laboratories. It was she who doctored the fatal cough lozenge. All he then had to do was put it among the others and wait for his wife to consume it. I gather she sucked them all the time, so he wasn't going to have to wait very long. The only uncertainty was when and where, and he made various contingency plans to meet each situation. For instance, if she had died at home he would have immediately destroyed the packet from which the poisoned lozenge came."

"He certainly lost no time in setting me up as the fall guy," I remarked ruefully.

Jackley nodded. "When she returned home that first evening and told him how you'd offered her your lozenges, he quickly saw his opportunity for diverting suspicion. He not only made sure she took her own the next evening, but reduced the number in the packet so that she was bound to reach the fatal one in the course of the performance. Then, unbeknown to her, he put your tin of Buckland's lozenges at the bottom of her bag where it was bound to be discovered later."

"He's told you all this?"

Jackley smiled. "Once we picked up the bit of gossip about his association with the girl, we were able to apply pressure in the right place." He let out a sigh. "Murderers of his class often fail to foresee how they will react after the event. They envisage themselves as made of steel and discover too late that they're frightened jelly babies."

"Fortunately for you," I remarked drily.

"Oh, we have to apply the correct chemistry as well. I believe catalyst is the word. That's us." He finished his tea and rose. "Anyway, I thought you'd be interested to hear the outcome."

"I'm much more than interested. I'm heartily relieved."

He laughed. "I'm afraid we shall need you as a witness at the trial."

"When will that be?"

"Some time next spring I would think."

"I'm going away in April for about ten days."

"Not Wagner again?"

I nodded. "In Vienna."

He shook his head in mock despair. "Some folk never learn, do they?"